"Sawyer!" Fiona called out.

This time he turned toward her. After giving the coil of rope to another man, he loped down the short distance and relieved her of the blankets.

"Take my arm," he said.

The security of his strength washed over her. He would help her. He would ensure her niece was safe.

"Must help…" she began, but could get no further before gasping for breath.

They managed the last few yards to the top of the dune. There Sawyer released her and returned the blankets to her care.

She caught his arm. "You need to rescue them."

He shook his head. "Don't know if we can with those waves."

"You must. You must." She hung on him with desperation. "My niece. She's only seven. She could be on that ship."

His expression, highlighted in the eerie light of the lighthouse, twisted with concern. "I'll do what I can."

A small-town girl, **Christine Johnson** has lived in every corner of Michigan's Lower Peninsula. She enjoys creating stories that bring history to life while exploring the characters' spiritual journeys. Though Michigan is still her home base, she and her seafaring husband also spend time exploring the Florida Keys and other fascinating locations. You can contact her through her website at christineelizabethjohnson.com.

Books by Christine Johnson

Love Inspired Historical

Boom Town Brides

Mail Order Mix-Up
Mail Order Mommy
Mail Order Sweetheart

The Dressmaker's Daughters

Groom by Design
Suitor by Design
Love by Design

Visit the Author Profile page at Harlequin.com for more titles.

CHRISTINE JOHNSON

Mail Order Sweetheart

HARLEQUIN® LOVE INSPIRED® HISTORICAL

Recycling programs for this product may not exist in your area.

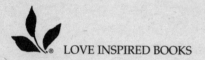

LOVE INSPIRED BOOKS

ISBN-13: 978-0-373-42528-0

Mail Order Sweetheart

Copyright © 2017 by Christine Elizabeth Johnson

www.Harlequin.com

Printed in U.S.A.

And ye shall know the truth,
and the truth shall make you free.
—*John* 8:32

Chapter One

Singapore, Michigan
March 1871

Sawyer Evans stared at what his friends had written. The piece of stationery gleamed white against the oak store counter, but the words leaped off the page.

He shoved the paper across the counter. "I'm not ready for this."

"Neither was I," Roland Decker said with a grin, "but it was the best thing that ever happened. I've never been happier."

His bride of nearly three months curled under Roland's arm and gave him the sort of look that Sawyer dreamed of getting just once—especially from a particular redhead—but placing an advertisement for a wife was not the answer. This idea of theirs would only bring trouble.

"If I remember right," he pointed out, "the advertisement that brought Pearl and the other ladies west was supposed to give your brother a wife, not you."

Roland shrugged. "He did get a wife, and he's just as happy as I am."

Pearl, Roland's wife, nodded emphatically. "Now that you're manager at the sawmill, you can settle down."

"Not yet." Sawyer dreamed of opening his own business, not running someone else's. Marriage would only drain his savings. Even a frugal wife brought added expenses, and the only woman who'd interested him was definitely not frugal.

"Garrett would tell you it's an advantage," Roland said.

Sawyer lifted an eyebrow. "Your brother stayed a widower for two years while he managed the mill. He has children. I don't. Thus, no need for a wife."

Pearl grinned. "Not even a certain redhead?"

Fiona O'Keefe. From the moment Sawyer met her last August, the beautiful woman with the fiery hair and temper had piqued his curiosity. She, on the other hand, barely noticed his existence except when she needed an accompanist for her concerts. She had graced the stages and cafés in New York City with her clear soprano voice, yet came to the lumber town of Singapore in answer to the advertisement that gave Garrett a wife. It made no sense. She could have married easily in New York. Why travel hundreds of miles to a lumber town in search of a husband? He'd watched and listened, but in seven months he still hadn't discovered why she'd come here. Or why she was so desperate to marry.

Sawyer shook his head. "Fiona has set her cap on that ne'er-do-well Blakeney."

The timber speculator had come to town in January, purportedly looking for a location for a new sawmill, but Sawyer had seen enough manipulators before to recognize Blakeney as one of that breed. Unfortunately, Fiona only noticed the man's fancy clothes and lofty intentions. From nearly the moment Blakeney arrived on Singapore's docks, she'd hung on his arm. Sawyer had tried to warn her and got a tongue-lashing for his trouble.

"Then you need to show her what she's missing." Pearl jotted something on the paper and pushed it back toward him. "Fight fire with fire, I say. These tweaks should capture her attention."

Sawyer read the opening line and shook his head. "Up and coming industrial magnate?" Little did Pearl know how close to the truth she'd come. Sawyer wanted nothing to do with that old life, where he was known as Paul Evanston, heir to the Belmont & Evanston Railway. In Singapore he earned an honest wage by the sweat of his brow. It felt good. He slept well at night, knowing he'd done his best to help others, not bleed them dry like Father did. He wanted no part of his father's manipulation and unethical dealings. "All I do is work the saws in the mill."

"You're now mill manager," Roland said, "which is one step closer to becoming a captain of industry."

"A lot of steps away."

"Who knows where this could lead?" Pearl said. "Mr. Stockton might think so highly of your skills that he asks you to oversee operations along this entire side of the state."

"Far-fetched at best." Stockton seldom visited, least of all promoted. "If anyone catches his attention, it'd be you, Roland."

His friend grinned. "You never know. Mr. Stockton has an eye for men with potential."

Sawyer squirmed. He didn't want to gain the lumber baron's attention. Stockton could well know Father and bring the man back into Sawyer's life. "I intend to earn any promotion through hard work."

"No one said you wouldn't." Pearl looked to her husband for confirmation. "I believe in you. We both believe in you."

"Fiona doesn't." He tore up the sheet of paper. "This will only bring trouble. Or don't you remember that the advertisement for your brother attracted too many women? This would do the same."

"Not if it only goes in the local newspaper." Pearl tapped a finger on the counter with each statement, as if she were instructing him the way she taught the schoolchildren. "The *Singapore Sentinel* circulates only in the immediate area. Few would see it. There aren't many women of marriageable age here."

"That's not the point. I don't want to marry. Not now, anyway. And when I am ready, I don't need any help finding a wife." Sawyer had to put a stop to this ridiculous matchmaking effort.

"You might change your mind if Fiona shows interest." Pearl was already piecing the paper together. "Or would you be interested in Louise?"

Sawyer snatched a handful of scraps from Pearl. "You know I have no interest in Mrs. Smythe." The petite widow was quiet and bookish, not at all his type. He preferred Fiona's high spirits.

Pearl brushed aside the remaining scraps of paper and pulled out a clean sheet of paper. "You wouldn't have to meet anyone since the advertisement instructs interested parties to write in care of the mercantile. Give it a try. What do you have to lose? You just might gain Fiona's attention." She began to write.

"And make her forget Blakeney," Roland added.

"Enough!" Sawyer raised his hands. "I appreciate what you're trying to do, but it's not the right time."

The mercantile's doorbell jingled. Seconds later,

Jimmy, the lad who helped out the Deckers, appeared at the counter.

"He's gone." Jimmy managed between gulps of air.

"Who's gone?" Pearl asked.

"Him." Jimmy waved in the air. "Mr. Blakeney."

"Gone?" Sawyer stared at the boy. "You must be mistaken. He was going to take Fiona to the choir concert in Saugatuck. They probably left early."

"No, sir." Jimmy shook his head. "I was over to Saugatuck delivering that cloth Mrs. Wardman ordered and I seen him ridin' out of town like his horse got spooked. So I went and asked the livery boy where he was off to, and he said Mr. Blakeney paid up his bill at the hotel and was headed upriver to Allegan."

"Paid up his hotel bill?" Sawyer echoed. He looked at Roland and Pearl, who had equally astonished looks on their faces. "If he paid up, then that means just one thing."

"He's gone," Pearl and Roland said at the same time.

"And he's not coming back."

"Someone has to tell Fiona," Pearl said, her gaze fixed on Sawyer.

"Oh, no." Sawyer backed away. "This sort of thing is better coming from a woman."

"It's better coming from someone who can console her and perhaps step into the missing man's place," Pearl pointed out.

More matchmaking. Nothing Sawyer had said made a bit of difference. He liked Fiona, but taking Blakeney's place might suggest he was interested in more than friendship.

"The time's not right."

Pearl set a stack of papers on the counter. "Roland and I have to work tonight. She needs to hear this from a friend. You could ease her disappointment by taking her to the concert."

Sawyer knew defeat when he saw it. He threw up his hands and headed for the boardinghouse.

In the privacy of her room, Fiona O'Keefe reread the stunning letter. She wanted to talk some sense into her next-youngest sister, Lillibeth, but there was no time to send a return letter. Singapore didn't have a telegraph office, which left Fiona without any means to respond.

She shoved the letter in the envelope and rubbed her aching temples. What was she going to do? Lillibeth had done the unthinkable, and somehow Fiona would have to pick up the pieces.

"Not now," she groaned.

Two months of effort were about to come to fruition. Mr. Carson Blakeney, who'd come to Singapore to find a good location for his new sawmill, was ready to propose. She could sense it. He just needed that last little push. Her niece couldn't show up now, not until she broached the subject with Carson.

Time had run out. Little Mary Clare could arrive any day now. Lillibeth hadn't been clear about that part, so Fiona had to be ready. Tonight she would secure a marriage proposal from Mr. Blakeney. If not...

Well, there were no other options. She tucked the missive into the bureau drawer and slammed it shut. The sound reverberated through the boardinghouse. That was that. The time for gentle persuasion was over. Tonight she would employ direct pressure and pray the man didn't dart away like a frightened rabbit.

What was Lillibeth thinking? A child of seven should not travel across the country without the accompaniment of a known and trusted adult. The thought of that poor motherless child alone and frightened tugged on her heartstrings. When Mary Clare's mother and Fiona's older sister Maeve died, Fiona promised to care for Maeve's only child. She was doing her best to marry respectably so she could do just that. It meant leaving Mary Clare in Lillibeth's care temporarily, but Fiona sent every dollar she could back to New York. Granted, that hadn't been much lately, but Lillibeth shouldn't have run short unless she was spending that money elsewhere.

Fiona pulled the letter out of the drawer and unfolded it. Oh, yes. Lillibeth complained of hardship at home. Fiona's purse was nearly empty. She hadn't any extra to send until the concerts began again at the hotel. But she'd sent plenty over the last year. A little care could make that stretch over these lean months, but apparently once the flow of money had dwindled, Lillibeth—or more likely that worthless husband of hers—had decided to send poor Mary Clare to her.

There's this group a orphans headin' west, Lillibeth had written, *an the matron said she'll take real good care a Mary Clare.*

Orphans! The poor girl must think she'd been abandoned. Why couldn't Lillibeth wait? Though Fiona's efforts to find a husband in New York had ended in scandal, she was doing her best here.

Last August, Fiona had arrived in Singapore in answer to an advertisement for a bride. Unfortunately, two other women also arrived with the same intent. In January, the groom, Garrett Decker, married one of them. When Carson arrived later that month, Fiona shifted her efforts to him.

Now it was late March. The snow had melted. The ice on the river had broken up, and the sawmill had roared to life when the first logs floated downstream. She had one last chance, and she had to seize it. Tonight.

The door to her room opened a crack.

"Are you busy?" Louise Smythe peered through the opening.

The short, mousy woman—and competitor for a husband—had recently moved back to the boarding-house after losing her position as companion to the ailing Mrs. Elder.

"Not any longer." Fiona tucked the letter into the bureau drawer beneath her unmentionables. Louise wouldn't read it. Fiona had tested her when she first arrived. Louise hadn't touched the note that Fiona placed in the bureau while Louise was watching.

"I didn't want to disturb you," the widow said, still from behind the door.

"It's your room too." Fiona pinned a bright red curl in place. Men loved hair piled high atop a woman's head with curls cascading to the shoulders, and Carson was no exception. She had been blessed with thick, naturally curling locks in a hue that drew attention. "You can come in whenever you wish."

Louise must have had to tiptoe around the Elders' house. Either that or she was simply too meek to barge into her own room. When Captain Elder shuttered his house and took his wife to Chicago for better medical treatment, Louise had lost her position. Though the kindly couple offered to let her stay in the house, Louise had refused, saying she didn't want to live alone. Fiona had offered to share her room. Louise thought her generous, but the lack of paying concerts over the winter had depleted Fiona's funds.

Louise opened the door a little wider. "I wouldn't have bothered you, but you have a caller."

"Carson!" The time had arrived. Fiona straightened the skirts of her green silk gown and then plucked a lavish necklace from her small jewelry box. She placed the sparkling diamond and emerald jewels—all glass—around her neck and then admired the effect in the mirror.

"What do you think?"

Louise stepped into the room for a closer look but then hesitated. "It's...ostentatious."

"Osten-what?"

Louise's gaze darted to the door. "Uh, like something the very wealthy might wear."

"Precisely." Fiona returned her attention to the mirror. "Hopefully, it's enough."

"Enough?"

"To secure an offer." Fiona adjusted the lace edging on her gown.

"Um, Mr. Blakeney isn't the one calling for you."

"What? Who then? I'm expecting Carson. He's escorting me to Saugatuck for the choir's performance of Handel's *Messiah*."

"That might be the case," Louise said slowly, "but Mr. Evans is the one paying a call at the moment."

Fiona bit back irritation. She did not have time to waste on Sawyer Evans. He was a fine accompanist and an uncommonly attractive man, but his prospects were dim to say the least. She hadn't worked so hard to sing on the New York stage only to throw her future away on a sawmill worker. She must marry for Mary Clare's sake, but not to just anyone. Her future husband must hold a position of authority. A tidy nest egg would help too. Carson fit her criteria perfectly.

"Tell Sawyer I'll talk to him later. He probably wants to discuss future concerts." If tonight went as planned, she need not sing ever again. A wave of disappointment swept over her. Singing had been her life for as long as she could remember. As a child, she'd sung to escape the gnawing hunger. As a young woman, she'd seen a beautiful singer arrive at a theater and decided that nothing would stop her from doing exactly the same. She could never have imagined the cost of that decision.

"I don't think that's it." Louise twisted and knotted a length of ribbon that she probably used as a bookmark, considering her insatiable appetite for books. "He said he has something to tell you. Something important. He doesn't look happy."

Fiona stared at her roommate. Had Mary Clare arrived already? "He didn't give you any idea what that was?"

"No." Louise edged toward the door. "Just that he wouldn't leave until he spoke to you."

What a bother! If she didn't get rid of Sawyer soon, Carson could arrive and think the worst. "Very well. Tell him I'll be down in a moment."

Louise cleared her throat. "He likes you, you know."

The statement raised an unexpected flutter in her stomach. Fiona pushed it aside. After all, any woman liked to hear a man found her attractive or interesting. That's all it was. She couldn't possibly *feel* anything for Sawyer Evans. For Louise's sake, she shrugged and continued her toilette.

"Mr. Evans is not the sort of man who likes fancy clothes," Louise continued. "He's an honest, straightforward sort."

Fiona secretly admitted she found that aspect of Sawyer pleasing. Too many men in New York had lied and manipulated her in an attempt to get what they wanted. Carson wasn't anything like that. He was always very straightforward about his aims and his background.

The combination of wealth and openness was perfect. To gain his favor, she had to put her very best forward.

Fiona set down her brush. "Men adore a beautiful woman. Why, in New York, I was the talk of the theater circuit." Though that talk had turned vicious toward the end.

"I'm sure you were," Louise mumbled, "but this isn't New York. People…well, they value different things."

"What are you trying to say?"

"Well…that different bait catches different kinds of fish."

"I'm not going fishing with anyone," Fiona pointed out, though she knew perfectly well what Louise was getting at. What the woman didn't understand was that Carson *did* love the fancy gowns. That was the man Fiona needed to catch. "Carson and I are going to a concert."

"Um, yes. At a church."

"Are you saying I shouldn't wear my best gown in church?"

Louise flushed. "I just thought…well, never mind. Do as you please. I'll tell Mr. Evans that you'll be downstairs shortly." She hurried from the room.

Fiona listened to Louise's footsteps clatter down the staircase as she surveyed her appearance again. Perhaps a feather would look good in her hair. She eyed the white plume from both the left side and the right. Too much. Osten—whatever that word was. She tucked a comb into her bag and shut the clasp. Before leaving, she took one last glance in the mirror. Too pale. She pinched her cheeks for more color. Yes, that would do nicely. She looked fine, hopefully fine enough to push Carson Blakeney toward a proposal.

Her finger needed a ring—now.

* * *

Sawyer paced the boardinghouse drawing room. Though Mrs. Smythe was perched on the edge of the sofa, he couldn't think of anything but how to tell Fiona the bad news. Not that *he* considered the news bad, mind you. Fiona deserved better than Blakeney.

"Do have a seat," Mrs. Smythe insisted. "Fiona will be down shortly. You know how much appearance matters to her."

Did he. He also knew her fiery temper, and the news he had to deliver was sure to set off that storm. He completed another circuit around the room.

"I have a question," Mrs. Smythe interjected into his thoughts, "purely a matter of scientific inquiry."

That caught his attention. "Scientific?" He'd never expected to hear that word come out of any woman's mouth, least of all from Louise Smythe.

The petite woman's chin lifted. "An experiment, shall we say?"

"Can't say I like the sound of that."

"Oh, it's not trying. I simply wished to inquire about your thoughts on a particular topic."

"What topic?" He had the suspicion he was stepping somewhere he shouldn't go.

"A topic of which you are particularly well versed."

"Oh?" This definitely sounded like trouble, but he couldn't imagine what she thought was his area of expertise. Sawing logs, sure, but no woman had any interest in that. Mrs. Smythe couldn't possibly know about his past. Or did she? He steeled himself.

She cast her gaze down. "Which would you say a man prefers—a practically dressed woman or one in all her finery?"

At first Sawyer breathed out in relief. Then he figured there must be a trap in her question, but he wasn't sure what it was. Unless she was fishing for compliments. He had to tread carefully.

He cleared his throat. "I, uh, appreciate both. At the right time."

She lifted her face, which wore a frown. "That doesn't answer the question. If all extenuating circumstances are the same, which would you prefer?"

First she threw a word at him that the Sawyer Evans he'd carefully crafted wouldn't understand. Then she insisted on an answer. Fine. He'd give her the one she wanted.

"You look good, Mrs. Smythe."

A sigh of disgust escaped her lips just as Fiona glided into the room. Relief flooded over him until he recalled what he must tell the beautiful redhead.

"Sawyer, I'm surprised to see you." Fiona always made a grand entrance, and today was no exception. Her right arm floated through the air as if scooping the entire world into her domain. Her hair, her gown, that gaudy necklace, everything about her was designed to make a stunning impression. But her talent impressed him more than all of that put together.

"Fiona." He crossed the room, took her extended hand, just like before their concerts, and kissed it. "You look lovely this afternoon."

Out of the corner of his eye, he saw Louise roll her eyes and heard her snort of disgust. So, the widow was jealous. The idea made him grin. It had been a long time since women competed for his attention. Before the war, he'd drawn his share of female interest even though Father and Mother had long planned for him to marry Julia Spencer. When he courted her, Father had congratulated him on following the plan. Then he learned what sort of man his father truly was, and the world shifted abruptly. He enlisted. Julia abandoned him and married another man. His father opposed him in every way. It was war at home as well as on the front.

"Louise said you had an important message for me." Fiona's voice pulled him out of his thoughts. "Has a ship arrived?"

"A ship? Why would you care about a ship's arrival?"

She seemed to relax. "Then none has docked?"

"Right. No ships." He glanced at Louise, who was still perched on the edge of the sofa, at least pretending to read a book. He didn't want to break the important news with anyone else present, so he rattled on about the other news of importance. "Stockton wants the schooner finished as soon as possible, so Garrett asked me to take over his duties at the mill."

He puffed up a bit at the confidence the sawmill manager had shown in his abilities. Sawyer hadn't been raised for hard labor. Father always said that was reserved for the lower classes. But Sawyer liked the good, honest feel of aching muscles and a job well done.

"That's why you insisted on speaking to me? Because you've been promoted?" Fiona didn't look the slightest bit impressed.

He should have known. "I thought you might be happy for me."

"Of course I am." Her lips curved into a smile, but her eyes darted toward Louise with the obvious intent of sending the widow scurrying.

Louise gathered her book and rose. "Please excuse me. Mrs. Calloway must need help in the kitchen." She left the room.

"There." Fiona breathed out. "I thought she would never leave."

Sawyer hadn't been mistaken. Fiona definitely had more than the usual sense of purpose this afternoon.

She strolled toward the parlor entrance. When he didn't follow, she returned and threaded her arm around his. "Now tell me the real reason you called on me today."

Sawyer swallowed. This wasn't going to be easy, and he didn't relish that she was standing so close when he delivered the news.

"Well?" she demanded.

He cleared his throat and said a quick prayer that he didn't botch this. "Uh, word about Mr. Blakeney arrived at the store."

"Word." Any hint of merriment drained from her voice.

"Uh. Yes."

"And they sent you to tell me." She let go of his arm.

He nodded, his throat as dry as sawdust.

"It's not good news, is it?"

Sawyer blew out his breath. Best to get it out. "He's gone. He headed upriver to Allegan."

He couldn't miss the dots of color on her cheeks.

"Carson left," she said bluntly.

"I'm afraid so."

"When will he return?"

"Uh, he didn't leave word about that. He just paid his hotel bill and left."

It took a moment for understanding to settle in. Then her eyelids blinked rapidly. Oh no, she was going to cry. She never cried. That was one thing Sawyer loved about Fiona. She was a strong woman not prone to fits of emotion.

"Well, then. That's that." But there was bitterness in her voice. "I should have known."

Sawyer wished he could find the right words. Blakeney was all wrong for her. Fiona needed a strong man who could match her energy and wits. Blakeney was one of those slippery types who made promises he never kept. It had taken all of Sawyer's will to hold his tongue around them.

"You deserve better," he said.

She gave him a sharp look. "Who? You?" Her hands braced her hips. "Why should a woman set her sights on a man who hasn't two pennies to rub together?"

Chapter Two

Fiona was left empty-handed with her niece due to arrive any day. She couldn't raise the girl in a boardinghouse. Without a reliable income, she couldn't raise Mary Clare at all. Though she fumed at Blakeney's cowardice, she did so in the privacy of her room. By evening, she was able to set aside her anger and work on a solution.

She spread out every newspaper she could find on the dining-room table. Chicago. Holland. Grand Rapids. Even one very old paper from New York that must have been brought in by a lumberjack stopping on his way upriver to the camps. Even though it was almost three months old, she couldn't discount any possibility.

"What are you doing?" Louise ducked in, book in hand.

"What I should have done long ago." Fiona shot the widow a forceful glance. "Something we both should have done. Find a husband."

"Oh." Louise dropped her book on the table.

"Pride and Prejudice?" Fiona had heard of that novel. "I would have thought you'd read that one by now."

"Several times. It's one of my favorites. Elizabeth

misjudges Darcy so." Louise sighed. "And yet it all works out in the end. Love conquers all."

Fiona raised her eyebrows at Louise's romantic wistfulness. The quiet widow apparently still harbored hope for a loving marriage. She had shown no interest in Garrett Decker, the man looking for a bride, but had swooned over Garrett's younger brother, Roland. They all had, but Roland had settled on the schoolteacher, Pearl, putting an end to their hopes. When the Decker brothers married Pearl Lawson and Amanda Porter in January, the most eligible bachelors in Singapore were taken.

Only lumberjacks and mill workers were left until Carson Blakeney made an appearance. He'd seemed the perfect gentleman with his fine manners and expensive suits, but he'd turned out to be a coward. Once again, the area offered only unsuitable bachelors. Sawyer Evans was intriguing. She'd never met anyone with more natural musical ability, but he couldn't—and wouldn't—provide the sort of future she had in mind for Mary Clare. That was proved by his shocked expression when she flatly suggested it. Then he'd gone and spit out some nonsense about it having to be the right time. Yet another coward!

"Love might win out in storybooks, but real life isn't nearly as tidy," Fiona pointed out. "Now that the Decker brothers are married and Carson left town, there isn't a decent prospect in the area."

"Mr. Blakeney left town?"

"Isn't that what I just said? He apparently had business to attend to elsewhere." Fiona pretended to search the newspaper, though it was not opened to the advertisements.

"I'm terribly sorry."

Louise truly was. Fiona wasn't accustomed to sympathy. Most women held her at arm's length, as if she wasn't good enough to associate with them.

"Well, what's done is done," Fiona asserted, "and there's nothing that will change it."

"Thus the newspapers."

"Thus the newspapers."

"Mr. Evans likes you," Louise stated.

"Humph." The memory of Sawyer's stammered response still hurt. She'd practically asked him to marry her. "Well, I'm not interested in *him*."

"Oh." Louise sank into the chair beside her. "He's doing well. Amanda said he's now the manager at the sawmill."

"That's what he told me."

"And you're still not interested? Garrett Decker was mill manager when he advertised for a wife."

"He didn't advertise," Fiona pointed out. "His children—with the help of Mrs. Calloway—placed the notice in the newspaper. Speaking of which, I intend to locate another prospect at once." She scanned the first column. No personal advertisements.

"Because the hotel hasn't reopened yet?"

"That's part of it." The occasional concerts at the boardinghouse this winter reduced the cost of her room and board but didn't give her money to send home. When the hotel closed in January, they'd all been shocked, but Mrs. VanderLeuven told Fiona that she couldn't make ends meet in the winter once the lumberjacks left for the camps. "It will reopen soon." It had to.

"I hope so."

Fiona looked to Louise. The widow had been out of work all winter also. That's why they were now sharing a room—which would soon include Mary Clare. Three wouldn't do, not with one being a child. Another room would be required, preferably for Louise. "Did you plan to seek employment there?"

Louise lowered her gaze. "It was a possibility."

"You could also remarry. That was your plan when you came to Singapore."

Louise shook her head. "It was the only option at the time. Now?" She sighed. "I still hope for a loving husband who follows the Lord. I can only marry a man of strong faith."

Fiona mulled that over. She had once felt the same, but circumstances had destroyed that hope. No man of faith who heard the vile and unfounded rumors about her in the New York newspapers would ever accept her for a wife.

"I hope you find him." But the issue of Mary Clare's pending arrival weighed on Fiona. Neither she nor Louise could wait for a husband to drop in her lap.

"It's just a dream." Louise's eyes misted, and Fiona wondered what had happened in the widow's marriage to leave her so reluctant to reenter the institution. Direct inquiry had gotten Fiona nowhere, so she stated the obvious.

"Then you must find employment. You might tutor students, I suppose."

Louise brightened. "I would like that."

"Talk to Pearl. She'll know which students need extra help—and which parents can afford to pay for it."

"Thank you." Louise leaned close and lowered her voice. "You don't need to resort to marrying a man you've never met. You could give vocal lessons."

Fiona laughed. "Have you noticed the type of families in the area? Farmers. Mill workers. Lumberjacks. None of these place a high value on musical prowess, not enough to pay for lessons. No, my course is set. I must marry."

"Why not go back to New York?"

No doubt that was the question all the women had wanted to ask her since they first arrived in August, but only quiet little Louise Smythe had actually done it. Maybe that woman had more gumption than Fiona had credited to her.

"There is only heartache in New York." Fiona wasn't ready to reveal more. The men there had courted her either for show or for their own purposes, never with marriage in mind. Fortunately, she always discovered the truth before it was too late, but rumors still threatened. By active involvement with her church and charity, she'd managed to stop most of them. Until last spring. Mr. Winslow Evanston wooed her with gifts and charm that blinded her for a time. When she discovered his lies and refused to become his mistress, he vilified her in the newspapers. Never again would she trust a man without a ring on her finger. "I doubt I'll ever go back."

"Me either."

Fiona really looked at Louise. Her features were nondescript, but she had a strong chin and surprising inner fortitude. "Your husband died in the war, right?"

Louise looked away. "Yes."

Heartache. Fiona could recognize that from miles away. And it wasn't just because he'd died. No, that marriage hadn't been a happy one. It couldn't have been, or the family would have taken her in.

"Well, then. We both need a *good* husband." Fiona ran her finger down the second column. "Here's one—'Handsome man seeks pretty, vivacious wife. Must cook.'"

"That fits you but not me."

"You can cook."

"Not as well as you. The bread and rolls you make melt in my mouth." Louise shook her head. "I don't fit one single criteria. Besides, I'd rather not marry a handsome man."

"Why on earth not?"

"They tend to think too highly of themselves."

Fiona snorted out a laugh. "Honey, they all do, and I can guarantee you'll never find an advertiser that admits he's homely."

"Maybe I won't turn to an advertisement." Once again Louise had squared her shoulders and set her jaw. "Maybe God will send the right man here."

"To Singapore? You've seen the kind of men who come here. Rough lumberjacks and mill workers. There's not a one who cares about book learning. I doubt many of them can read. You'll never find a gentleman here."

Louise looked crestfallen.

Fiona regretted her rash words. "Then again, you never know. Anything could happen."

"It is possible. Roland and Garrett Decker are gentlemen."

"Married gentlemen."

"Yes, but not when we first arrived. Another might step off the next ship. I must hope for it." Louise trembled as she picked up her book. "I believe I'll go to the parlor and read. Best wishes on your search." She rose.

The windows rattled, drawing both ladies' attention. They'd heard it often enough since arriving. First the wind. Then the rain or snow. But this was particularly vicious, considering the calm earlier that day.

Louise left for the parlor, and Fiona tackled the advertisements again. She circled the one she'd read to

Louise, even though the part she hadn't read aloud wasn't nearly as promising. 'Willing to work hard to build a new life.' That sounded like a homesteader. Fiona wasn't opposed to hard work, but she couldn't bring Mary Clare into that sort of life, not when the girl displayed such vocal talent.

She crossed that one off and resumed the hunt.

Sawyer noted the increased wind when he left the boardinghouse kitchen after getting an early supper. He trudged to the mercantile, still irritated over Fiona's jab. She clearly didn't think him worthy of her, but she knew nothing about him. He would have defended himself if she'd stayed in the room. Then again, what could he say? He couldn't admit his past. He'd broken all contact with his manipulative, philandering father. Even though he ached for his mother, Sawyer would never return home. He wrote his mother and prayed for her, but he wouldn't risk encountering Father. Without that parentage, he could never impress Fiona. She wanted a man with money. He didn't want a woman to love him for his father's money. He wanted a woman to love *him*. But not yet. That's why he had to talk to Roland.

The wind tore at his open coat and bit into his neck. He hopped up the steps to the mercantile and pushed open the door. The bell rang. He looked around. The place was empty except for Pearl Decker, who stood behind the sales counter.

"Good afternoon, Mr. Evans. May I help you?"

Pearl had come to Singapore as the new schoolteacher, but it didn't take long for Roland Decker, the mercantile manager, to fall for her. The big fire last November that leveled the schoolhouse had sealed things between them. He proposed. She accepted. And in January, when the itinerant preacher came around, they married.

Sawyer stepped a little farther inside and looked toward the back. No one was gathered around the stove. No one was shopping. "Where's Roland?"

"He headed up to the lighthouse. Word arrived that there's a ship headed for trouble. Mr. Blackthorn lit the light early, trying to warn them off. Naturally, every able-bodied man went to have a look."

"You don't say. Maybe I ought to go too. But first I need to ask you something."

"Oh?"

His palms sweated. Why did he get nervous around women? It had been that way ever since his fiancée, Julia, rejected him.

He cleared his throat. "That, uh, advertisement we were joking about earlier this afternoon… I, uh, wondered if I could have it?" The few scraps of paper in his pocket didn't contain any of the words.

Pearl blinked. "Oh! Of course."

She moved the ledger, then looked under the counter. Then she disappeared from view.

Sawyer moved to the counter and peered over. She was on her hands and knees.

"What are you doing, Mrs. Decker?"

She looked up, her faced flushed. "I don't know where it went."

"It? There were just scraps." He pulled the few he had from his pocket.

"Well, uh, not exactly." She stood, squared her shoulders and looked him in the eye. "I owe you an apology, it seems. I rewrote the advertisement, hoping to persuade you, but now it's gone."

Sawyer got a sick feeling in the pit of his stomach. "Gone where?"

She swallowed. "There's only one place it could have gone. It must have gotten mixed up with the advertisements for the store that I gave to Mr. Hennigan earlier."

"What?" Sawyer gulped as his mind spun with possibilities. "Are you saying that it will be printed?" But he knew the answer. The presses would already be whirring at this hour. By morning, all of Singapore would think he was in the market for a wife.

"I'm so sorry," Pearl said again. "Perhaps nothing will come of it."

"I hope so." Scowling, he tipped a finger to his hat and hustled back out into the wind, where he could concentrate on something much easier to handle. The biting cold was real. That advertisement wasn't. He'd just ignore it. It didn't give his name, after all. Maybe the whole thing would blow over in a few days.

A mournful whistle drew his attention toward Lake Michigan. What was a misplaced advertisement compared to a ship in trouble? One or two vessels had lost propulsion since he arrived in Singapore. Most got into port safely, but some had grounded on the shifting sandbars. With the southwesterly gale blowing in and the sandbars that formed over winter, a ship could easily find itself aground.

He squinted at the lighthouse and made out the light. The sun must be near the horizon by now, but heavy clouds obscured it. Soon enough it would get dark. Hopefully the ship would reach the river mouth before then.

The lighthouse was perched atop the big dune that separated Singapore from the shores of Lake Michigan. Since the first lighthouse had been undercut and toppled into the river, this one was built farther from the water, and the dune had been reinforced with slabs of limestone to stop the seas from eroding the sands beneath it.

The town was nestled between the growing lakeshore dunes and older ones that had once been covered with trees. These days, any gale filled the streets with sand. It even worked its way into the buildings and had to be swept out and shoveled away constantly.

He hurried up the dune. Roland Decker and a handful of men were gathered near the lighthouse, peering at the lake. Already the waves were crashing onshore. Six to eight footers, he'd judge, and they would only build. A passenger steamer rolled in the trough maybe a quarter mile offshore. No smoke trickled from the stack.

"Engines must be down," Sawyer noted to the group, which included mill workers Edwards and Tuggman plus Ernie Calloway from the boardinghouse and Roland's brother, Garrett. The lighthouse keeper, Blackthorn, must be up in the tower, but two of his boys had gathered with the men.

"That's what we figure," Roland confirmed. "Mr. Blackthorn says there's a sandbar about a hundred yards from shore, directly in their path. If they ground, the waves will tear them apart, and that water's too cold for anyone to survive."

Sawyer whistled. "Better hope they get their engines going." How many people were aboard? It looked like the ship that had brought Fiona to town. The thought of women and children going down made him ill. "Have they put up any sail?" He couldn't see if the ship had masts, not without looking through the glass.

"Don't think they got any," Edwards muttered.

Sawyer clenched his hands, visions of Fiona flailing in stiff seas flashing through his mind. "They need something to generate enough power so they can steer toward the river mouth."

"That's something we can pray for," Roland said. "Let's do it."

Sawyer hesitated. Like most, he tossed up the occasional plea, but the barbarities of war had dimmed his belief that God answered every prayer. This was crucial, though, so after Roland led the prayer, Sawyer answered amen.

God often worked through men, so he pointed out, "We need to be ready to rescue them."

The keeper appeared at his elbow. "Too dangerous. We can't go risking people's lives when there's not much chance we could reach 'em."

Sawyer couldn't accept that. "What boats are available?"

Roland shrugged. "We could launch a rowboat."

Even the strongest men couldn't row into that sea. "We need sail or steam. Anything around?"

"My mackinaw boat," Blackthorn offered.

Sawyer was familiar with the small sailing craft. "That's got an awfully shallow draft. It'll struggle to make any headway in these waves."

They all knew it.

"We need a deep-draft sailboat or, better yet, a steam tug," Sawyer pointed out. "Can we get the *Donnie Belle* down from upriver?"

"She must be all the way up to Allegan by now," Edwards said. "She left here Monday and don't come back this way for another week."

Sawyer frowned. Singapore didn't have a steam tug. Neither did Saugatuck, not one that was running this time of year. Without a tug, the people on that steamer didn't stand a chance.

Chapter Three

"There's a passenger ship in trouble," Mrs. Calloway announced to Fiona as she hurried through the dining room on her way to the kitchen. "We're going to need every bed in the place made up and every spare blanket brought over to the lighthouse."

A passenger ship! Fiona's heart leaped into her throat. Mary Clare. What if her niece was on that ship? She pushed aside the newspapers, husband-hunting forgotten, and raced to the entry hall. In a second, she donned her cloak.

"Where are you going?" the boardinghouse proprietress asked.

"I have to do something to help." Fiona couldn't bring herself to mention the fear that was building in her chest. A seven-year-old girl. A sinking ship. Icy water. What if?

"You can help right here. We need to carry blankets to the lighthouse."

The lighthouse would do. From there she could see what was happening and learn what would be done. If the passengers were brought ashore, she could then bring Mary Clare here and warm her up.

"What about the rooms?" Fiona headed for the staircase without removing her cloak. "We'll need to warm the beds and have something hot for them to drink."

"All taken care of, dear. Louise has already begun preparing the rooms, and Pearl and Amanda are on their way. Come with me to the linen closet, and we'll grab the extra blankets."

Fiona took a deep breath. There wasn't anything she could do right now. Mrs. Calloway had said the ship was in trouble, not that it had sunk. "The ship is still afloat, then?"

"Aye, bobbing like a cork, I understand."

Fiona breathed out a shaky sigh of relief. "Is it a large ship?" Maybe if it was very small, Mary Clare wouldn't be aboard. Lillibeth had said something about a group of orphans.

"From what I hear, it's like the one you came in on."

Oh, dear. There had been scores of passengers on the *Milwaukee*. If rescued, where would they go? Mary Clare could join her, but the rest? "We'll never have room for everyone."

"We'll squeeze them in. Some can sleep in the parlor or on the dining-room chairs."

As Fiona followed Mrs. Calloway upstairs, she recalled all too clearly the crowded conditions when she was growing up. Parents, two grandmothers, seven siblings—one with a husband—and a baby all squeezed into the tiny tenement apartment. She and three sisters and the grandmothers shared a single bed—three facing one direction and three the other. She'd been kicked in the back and shoulders numerous times, but the boys had it tougher. They'd line up the wooden chairs for beds—three chairs per bed. Ma and Pa gave up their bedroom to her oldest sister's family, while they slept atop the kitchen table.

Mrs. Calloway was suggesting the same sort of discomfort, except this would be temporary. Fiona hadn't known relief until she began getting paid to sing and moved to a boardinghouse room of her own. It had felt like the height of luxury, and she would never go back.

At the linen shelves, Mrs. Calloway grabbed a stack of blankets and handed them to Fiona. "Is that too much, dear?"

"I can carry more." Fiona had always been strong. As a girl, she'd prided herself on the ability to lift more than boys her age. Contrary to common belief, she did not shirk manual labor.

Mrs. Calloway added a few. "No more, or you won't be able to see in front of you. Come now, let's get these downstairs and then head over to the lighthouse."

After Mrs. Calloway donned her outerwear, they trudged through town. The wind howled off the lake, filling the streets with sand and whipping those particles through the air so they stung every inch of exposed skin. Fiona lowered her head against the wind. Thankfully she'd thought to pull the hood of her cloak over her head, or her hair would be filled with grit.

The drifts of sand made progress through town difficult, but fear for Mary Clare drove Fiona on. Climbing the dune taxed her limits. She gasped for breath and had to pause several times while Mrs. Calloway plodded on, apparently oblivious to the exertion. Maybe Fiona wasn't as strong as she'd thought. The years on the stage had apparently taken their toll.

She pressed onward.

At the top of the dune, the lighthouse flashed a signal in a repeating pattern, but her attention landed on the men standing near the lighthouse entrance. One form was unmistakable. Sawyer. Relief flooded her. She'd never known a stronger man. He could do anything. He would save Mary Clare.

"Sawyer!" The wind shoved her cry back at her.

He would never hear. She must wait until she reached him.

Mrs. Calloway had gained the top of the dune and was talking to an older man bundled in oilskins. Fiona didn't recognize him. Then again, it was dark except for the flashes of light from the tower above. Sawyer joined them, and the older man handed him what looked like a large coil of rope.

Fiona pressed for the summit. Her pulse pounded as a foot slid backward in the soft sand. The lake roared, and the stinging grit got worse with each step. Unlike Louise, she had never climbed the dunes or gone to the lakeshore. From sailing into the harbor, she recalled that the lighthouse sat high on the dune that separated Singapore from the lake, but she could not recall if there was much of a beach on the other side.

"Sawyer!" she called out.

This time he turned toward her. After giving the coil of rope to another man, he loped down the short distance and relieved her of the blankets.

"Take my arm," he said.

The security of his strength washed over her. He would help her. He would ensure Mary Clare was safe.

"Must help," she began, but could get no further before gasping for breath.

They managed the last few yards to the top of the dune, near the man clad in oilskins and Mrs. Calloway. There Sawyer released her and returned the blankets to her care.

"There you are," the boardinghouse proprietress said to Fiona. She didn't display the slightest shortness of breath. "We ought to put the blankets indoors in case of rain."

The man in the oilskins pointed to the keeper's house. "Jane's inside."

He must be the lighthouse keeper, for Jane was the lightkeeper's wife. Though Mrs. Calloway turned to go to the lighthouse, Fiona had to make sure Sawyer knew about Mary Clare. He had stepped away to talk to the rest of the men.

She nudged his arm. "You need to rescue them."

He shook his head. "Don't know if we can with those waves."

"You must." She fought desperation. "My niece. She's only seven. She could be on that ship."

His expression, highlighted in the eerie light of the lighthouse, twisted with concern. "We'll do what we can."

But she could see the doubt in his eyes before he rejoined the men. Poor Mary Clare! Fiona knew no fear when she could take charge, but this was beyond her control. *Lord, please save little Mary Clare.*

She looked toward the water but couldn't see anything. The beam from the lighthouse didn't illuminate the landscape directly below. It pierced the sky above them, a beacon to the ship. Beyond and below the dune, she glimpsed occasional dots of light bob up and then disappear. The beam from the light briefly revealed the tossing tempest.

How could anyone survive those seas?

Mrs. Calloway nudged Fiona with her shoulder, directing her toward the keeper's quarters. "Come."

Fiona couldn't drag her gaze from the unfolding situation. Her feet stayed rooted to the spot even when Sawyer and the men headed down the dune toward Lake Michigan.

"We need to be ready," Mrs. Calloway urged. "The survivors will need warm, dry blankets."

Only then did Fiona notice the first spits of rain. Somehow she followed, her legs moving though her mind was still on the embattled ship. Surely they would survive. God would not take the life of one so young. Yet, she could name many who had died even younger. Mama had lost a boy who lived less than one day on this earth.

"Mary Clare," she whispered into the windy night. "I failed you."

If she had found a husband sooner. If she hadn't gotten entangled with that vindictive Evanston in New York. If only she had cast caution to the wind and taken in Mary Clare at once rather than head off on this quest to find a husband well off enough to give her niece all she deserved. What did it all matter now, when the little girl was sick and frightened on a sinking ship?

She looked back but could see only darkness cut by the beam of the lighthouse. This fretting was useless, borrowing trouble from the future. She had to trust Sawyer and the men. She needed to trust the ingenuity of the officers aboard the imperiled ship. Most of all, she needed to trust God. Turning back to the task at hand, she hurried to catch up to Mrs. Calloway.

They covered the distance in little time, pushed forward by the steady wind. Mrs. Calloway stomped her feet on the lighthouse stoop to knock off as much of the sand as possible. A coiled rope mat helped remove more before they stepped inside.

"Jane! We've brought blankets," Mrs. Calloway called out.

A girl of perhaps twelve appeared. "Mother said to leave them on the hall chair."

"Thank you, dear. Is there anything else you can use?"

Fiona set her stack of blankets on the chair, which was situated opposite the entry table. A simple pewter card receiver sat on the end of the table nearest the door. She couldn't help wondering how many callers Mrs. Blackthorn got. The tray was empty. The hall stand was not. It bristled with coats, hats, scarves and gloves. A number of umbrellas filled a brass urn beside it.

Mrs. Calloway handed her the rest of the blankets. Fiona had to rearrange a bit to keep the stack from toppling.

"Mother said there could be dozens of passengers," the girl said. "She's making soup, but we don't have enough bread."

"Don't go begging these kind folk," came a voice from the back of the house.

"It's no bother at all, Jane," Mrs. Calloway called back. "I've got plenty left over, and we can get more on the rise in no time."

Fiona wondered why Mrs. Calloway didn't just go back to the kitchen, but then she looked down and saw the sand coating their skirts and coats. No woman wanted that tracked through her house. A considerate visitor stayed in the entry. Fiona recalled all the times she'd barged straight into the boardinghouse parlor without shaking out her skirts. Mrs. Calloway never said a word, but it must have made her sigh with frustration.

"Anything else we can bring after we get the dough ready?" Mrs. Calloway asked loudly.

Jane Blackthorn appeared at the end of the hall, hands covered in flour. "No need to go to that trouble,

Mabel. I've got a batch ready to go. We might need bandages."

The two women proceeded to discuss preparations while the daughter returned to the kitchen and Fiona waited. Her thoughts drifted back to Sawyer and the men. What had they encountered at the lakeshore? The waves must be huge in this wind. Their crashing could be heard inside the keeper's quarters.

"Do you know what they plan to do?" she blurted out.

The two women stared at her.

"Some of the men went down the dune toward the lake," she added.

Mrs. Calloway looked to Jane before answering. "I expect they wanted to have a closer look-see at the situation."

Fiona prodded. "What will they do?"

Mrs. Calloway shook her head. "They're probably seein' what they can do to save those people on the ship."

The lump grew in Fiona's throat. "Then they are wrecked."

"Samuel says they're stuck on a sandbar," Jane said. "The waves could tear the ship apart."

Samuel must be her husband, the lighthouse keeper.

Icy fingers of dread wove their way around Fiona's heart. "Then there's little hope."

"There's always hope," Mrs. Calloway said. "All things are possible with the Lord."

The paraphrased scripture would normally settle Fiona's nerves, but not tonight. "But how will anyone get to them in these waves?"

The two older women looked at each other.

Mrs. Calloway answered. "Apparently your Mr. Sawyer—" she often added *Mr.* to a man's first name "—said during the war he saw someone send a line out to sea using a mortar."

"A cannon?" Fiona gasped. "You have one?"

Jane shook her head.

"If the ship's close enough," Mrs. Calloway said, "they're going to try tying a lead weight on the end and throwing it."

That sounded far-fetched, but Fiona wasn't going to say that, not with the ladies' husbands involved.

"If that doesn't work," Mrs. Calloway continued, "they'll use the mackinaw boat to try to get to the foundered ship."

Boat meant small. Fiona's head spun, and she leaned against the wall for support. All she could envision was Mary Clare's lifeless body dragged from the icy water. Just hours ago, she'd been upset that her designs on Carson Blakeney had come to naught. What were her plans compared to people's lives? Innocent people faced death on that ship, and brave men would risk their lives to try to save them. Sawyer in the lead.

"Now there," Mrs. Calloway said, "no one's gonna do anything foolhardy. They've all got a good dose of common sense."

Jane nodded. "Samuel knows better than to send anyone out in impossible conditions."

Even worse.

"But if no one tries to reach the ship…" She couldn't fathom that. "They must try. They must."

Again, the women stared at her.

"Now, what's got you all upset, dear?" Mrs. Calloway asked. "The good Lord will take care of everyone."

Fiona had always thought her faith strong, but she was no longer sure. Not sure at all.

* * *

Sawyer had seen the lake rough, but tonight was about as bad as it could get. When the waves and the cold were put together, the chances of rescuing anyone were slim. But they had to try. A little girl, Fiona had said, her eyes filled with an emotion he had never seen from her—fear.

Sawyer recalled the little girl who had held out her hand to him when he marched south from Atlanta during the war. Rail-thin, her lips had barely moved, but her eyes had told a terrible story. All she'd wanted was food, but he didn't have any. That failure still haunted him. He could not fail Fiona's niece.

A line of waves crashed and rolled ashore, pushing inland nearly to the edge of the dune. The men huddled there, just out of reach of the water. For now. With the wind steady, the waves would build. Soon there wouldn't be any beach.

The ship was lodged on the sandbar. The lights aboard, likely lanterns since the engines had failed, vanished behind towering waves and then reappeared in the trough. Otherwise, they hadn't budged. Blackthorn figured the sandbar—and now the foundered ship—was roughly a hundred yards offshore. Not impossible if they had a solid steam tug. She would pitch and roll like crazy, but they could get to the ship and get passengers onboard. It would take several trips, and hauling the passengers, especially the women and children, from ship to ship wouldn't be easy, but it could be done.

The mackinaw? Impossible. The shallow-draft sailboat was designed to carry a lot of cargo, not weather heavy seas. It would flip over and fill with water in minutes.

"Maybe the ship will last till morning," Garrett Decker yelled into his ear.

That was their best hope. That and the wind dying down. But if the passenger ship started to break up, they'd have to attempt the impossible. Sawyer could swim. But not a couple hundred yards into huge seas in icy waters. The ship might attempt to launch its boat, but that would be just as precarious as the mackinaw.

If only he had a cannon. They could attempt to fire the rope, attached to a shot, toward the ship and then rescue folks using that line. He'd seen it accomplished once, during the war, but the unit had resources that Singapore didn't.

Sawyer rubbed his arms. "Let's try heaving the line."

They'd practiced a few times, failing miserably. This time Sawyer put Edwards on the spot. The man had boasted of his prowess. Let him prove it.

The wiry crew chief warmed up by swinging his arms several times. Then he grabbed the lead weight, reached back as far as he could and threw. The weight arced in the light from the lighthouse and then splashed into the water. Tuggman hauled it in.

"It's useless," Blackthorn said. "No one's gotten near the ship."

That was a kind way of saying they'd all fallen short by at least half.

"I'm praying she doesn't break up," Roland stated.

Sawyer shivered, though it wasn't terribly cold. The southwest wind was warm, but the cold sweats had started coming on ever since he first saw the situation. Fiona's desperate plea only made them worse.

"She's breaking up!" Tuggman shouted.

Sawyer gulped. The worst had just arrived.

* * *

Fiona paced the small hallway in the keeper's quarters after helping Mrs. Calloway haul bandages and liniments from the boardinghouse to the light station. The boardinghouse proprietress had vanished into the kitchen after asking Fiona to wait out front for word from the men. Nothing more could be done until survivors arrived.

Mrs. Calloway and Mrs. Blackthorn reappeared, busily calculating how many bed linens were available throughout town.

"The empty bunkhouses," the latter suggested.

Mrs. Calloway shook her head. "It's all at the boardinghouse. If only the hotel was open. There would be plenty there."

"The VanderLeuvens would understand if we borrowed some," Jane Blackthorn replied. "It is an emergency."

Fiona couldn't count blankets and bedding when lives were at risk. In addition to Mary Clare and the rest of the passengers, now Sawyer and the men attempting a rescue were in peril. When Samuel Blackthorn returned to check the light, he'd informed them that Sawyer and a few of the mill workers had gone to launch the mackinaw.

Blackthorn had shaken his head. "It'll take the grace of God to bring them back alive."

Fiona's stomach churned. She was no sailor, but even she knew that a little sailboat didn't stand a chance in such angry seas.

Mrs. Blackthorn returned to the kitchen, leaving Fiona alone with Mrs. Calloway.

"I can't wait here." She plucked her cloak off the

wooden peg and threw it over her shoulders. "I'm going down to the beach to help."

Mrs. Calloway stopped her with a firm hand on her arm. "Now, what do you think you're gonna do that those men can't do?"

"Something." She couldn't stand to wait.

"Do you think your Sawyer wants to be worrying about a woman when he's got a boatload of people to rescue?"

Fiona didn't miss the wording. Mrs. Calloway figured Fiona was upset because she feared for Sawyer's life. She didn't know that Mary Clare could be on that ship.

"Let them do what needs to be done," Mrs. Calloway added. "And you be ready to help here when it comes our turn."

"How can you be so calm when your husband's part of the rescue party?"

"Faith in God above, child. Ernie is in God's hands, and that's the best place to be."

Deep down Fiona knew Mrs. Calloway was right, but she couldn't shake the fear. "My niece might be on that ship. My sister sent her here."

"Oh, child." Mrs. Calloway embraced her in a motherly hug. "God's got hold of her. You have to believe that."

Fiona was trying. "It's so hard. What if…" She couldn't finish the thought.

"Hush now. You just turn that precious girl over to the Lord's care." Right then and there, Mrs. Calloway prayed over the ship, the rescuers and the passengers, including Mary Clare.

A smidgen of peace wove through Fiona. Everything would be all right. She hoped.

Footsteps sounded on the stairs coming down from the tower. Both women looked toward the door to the tower. Fiona held her breath.

Mr. Blackthorn pushed open the tower door. His face was ashen. "The mackinaw's gone under. They're lost."

Fiona gasped. Sawyer. All this time she'd been worried about her niece, who might not even be on the ship, when she should have prayed fervently for Sawyer. She had sent him out, had begged him to rescue her niece. Now he was gone? Guilt crashed over her. She moved her lips, but no sound came out of her mouth.

She'd sent Sawyer to the grave.

Chapter Four

Sawyer spit out a mouthful of water and coughed. The cold lake had shocked him for a moment, and he hadn't been able to move. It took aching lungs and an iron will to swim for the surface. The icy air rushed into his lungs even as the frigid water slowed his limbs. He had little time to get out and warmed up, or he would be the first casualty.

Where was his crew? He spun, but in the darkness it was difficult to see.

Shouts came from all around. Someone hung a lantern over the water, and Sawyer spotted one, two, three heads bobbing on the surface. All the crew had survived, but the overturned hull of the mackinaw drifted farther and farther away with each wave.

Again the light shone toward him, and the shouted words became clearer.

"This way!"

The rolling waves splashed against his face. He rubbed the water from his eyes. That cost him effort. His legs were growing sluggish. Soon he wouldn't be able to move them any longer, and he would sink beneath the seas.

Fight!

Something inside him pushed him to move toward the lantern. It must be on another boat. Maybe even the steamship. Their lanterns wouldn't have survived the capsizing.

"Grab hold!"

A life ring landed nearby. Sawyer grabbed it as best he could, but his fingers wouldn't grasp it. He slung an arm through the center and felt himself moving through the water toward the light.

"My crew!" He couldn't accept rescue while his crew languished in the water. He let go of the life ring.

"Hang on! We have them," the voice from above shouted.

Sawyer threaded his other arm through the ring and tried to hang on, but he kept slipping off. Then someone grabbed onto his arms and lifted him from the icy water. Sawyer clawed and scrambled as best he could until he ended up on the slanted deck of the doomed steamer.

"Tuggman, Calloway, Edwards," he croaked.

"Here, sir," each said in turn.

Sawyer closed his eyes in gratitude as a heavy blanket was wrapped around his shoulders and a mug of hot and painfully strong coffee was put in his hands.

"Some rescue." He drew in a ragged breath as he recalled the moment they'd capsized.

They'd been near the steamer, ready to hand over the rescue line when a wave caught the mackinaw and flipped it over in a second. Sawyer hadn't had time to react. One moment he was completing his mission, and the next he was in the water.

"We got the line you brought," said an unfamiliar voice.

The rescue line had made it, but what good would

it be without the mackinaw? Unless one of the ship's boats could be launched.

"Your boat," he gasped.

"Already preparing for the first passengers."

Passengers! Sawyer's eyelids shot open. Fiona had been upset about her niece. "Is there a young girl on board?"

An older gentleman stepped into the lantern light. By his somber and simple attire, he was either a preacher or part of one of those clans who advocated simplicity.

The man tucked his thumbs under his suspenders. "Well, there are several young women under my care, but they are already spoken for."

Sawyer couldn't fathom what the man meant, but it wasn't what he needed to know. "I'm talking about a little girl. Seven years old."

"Oh." The gentleman's manner eased. "No children aboard."

Sawyer heaved a sigh. At least Fiona could rest easy on that account.

The deck shook and slanted more severely. Sawyer slid toward the deckhouse and caught his balance before he slipped back into the water. This wreck was in a precarious position.

He pushed to his feet. "We have to get the passengers off now. Women first."

If God heard prayers, the rest of them would make it to shore alive.

"The first survivors are ashore!"

The hurried shout came from a windblown mill worker who opened the door to the keeper's quarters.

"Survivors?" Fiona pulled herself from gloomy thoughts. "Who?"

"Passengers." Having delivered his message, the man left with a slam of the door.

"Mary Clare. It has to be," Fiona whispered. "Maybe Sawyer." At Mrs. Calloway's grim expression, she added, "And Mr. Calloway."

"They'd send the women and children first. If your niece was on board, she's here now." Mrs. Calloway grabbed a stack of blankets and piled them in Fiona's arms. She then took the rest. "Regardless of who it is, they'll need warmin' up, and that's our job. Follow me."

The girl who'd first greeted them opened the door to let them out even while her mother assured them that she wouldn't be far behind with the hot coffee.

The moment Fiona stepped outside, the wind slapped the breath from her. Sand stung her face. She squinted against it and could make out a small group huddled atop the dune. They were all standing. If survivors, they must be freezing in this wind.

Mrs. Calloway plowed toward them. Fiona followed.

Each step felt like slogging through knee-deep snow, thanks to the force of the wind coming at them. They hadn't far to go. Shuttered lanterns and the light cast from the lighthouse guided the way. Mrs. Calloway arrived first, but she didn't hand a blanket to anyone. Fiona hastened her step. Moments later, she too reached the small group of men and women. She recognized each one as a citizen of Singapore.

"Where are they? The survivors?"

"Not here yet." Mrs. Calloway point to the blackness in front of them where the dune dropped off toward the angry lake.

Sawyer had disappeared down that dune. For the last time. Fiona caught herself. Assuming the worst wouldn't help the situation. She would be needed soon, and one of those survivors might well be Mary Clare.

She strained to see into the darkness, but shouts met her ears before anyone crested the dune. Though the words weren't distinct, the intent was clear. Someone needed help.

"We're right here," Mrs. Calloway shouted. Her strong alto was well-practiced in giving orders that could be heard throughout the boardinghouse. In this case, that voice cut through the howling gale and gave comfort to the survivors.

Fiona tensed. Soon she would know.

Long minutes passed before the first figures appeared. The light was too poor to make out faces, but it was obviously a group of women with two men. No children.

"Mary Clare." Her niece's name slipped from her mouth. Had she drowned, or was she not on the ship?

Fiona raced to meet the group, Mrs. Calloway on her heels.

The men took the blankets, one at a time, from her arms and gave them to the women. Even in this poor light, Fiona could tell they were all young, perhaps eighteen to twenty years of age, and dressed in simple dark gowns. Each one gratefully wrapped a blanket around her shoulders as Mrs. Calloway directed them out of the wind and toward the keeper's quarters.

"Is that everyone?" Fiona asked the men, who were heading back down the dune.

"No, ma'am," one oilskin-clad man responded. "Just the first of 'em."

Fiona tried to ask more, but the men sprinted down the dune. Before she could follow, Mrs. Calloway called for her in that strident tone of hers that allowed no argument. Fiona worked her way back to the women, who were huddled sipping steaming mugs of coffee in the shelter of the lighthouse.

"Take them to the boardinghouse," Mrs. Calloway instructed. "Pearl and Amanda will be there to help you get them situated."

"But—" Leaving the rescue scene was the last thing Fiona wanted to do, but Mrs. Calloway shot her a look that reminded Fiona of her mother. That look meant there would be no negotiation. Fiona was expected to obey. But so many questions were unanswered. "Sawyer," she began.

Mrs. Calloway cut her off. "If he lived, you'll see him soon enough. If he died, he's in God's hands."

End of discussion.

Fiona turned to the ladies, who had followed the conversation with wide eyes. By Fiona's count, there were six of them, all dressed identically.

"Are you able to walk?" Fiona asked.

Each woman nodded.

"We're going down the dune into town. See the two-story building with all the lights in the windows?"

One of the women followed Fiona's outstretched arm and nodded.

"It's the boardinghouse," Fiona explained. "You can warm up there and have a place to sleep."

"And soup and bread," Mrs. Calloway interjected. "Jane sent a kettle there with her oldest. We'll take care of the rest here before sending them on." She squeezed Fiona's arm and shouted in her ear. "Don't fret. God has Mr. Sawyer and your niece in his care."

As Fiona headed down the slope with the ladies, she hoped that care left them both on this earth. While watching the young women converse with each other, she realized the opportunity to find out if Mary Clare was on the ship stood right in front of her. She hurried to join them.

"Excuse me, but were there any children on board?" Fiona asked rather breathlessly.

The women looked at each other and shook their heads.

"A little girl?" Fiona prompted. "About seven years old. Dark brown hair." She began to indicate her niece's height, but it had been a long time since she'd last seen Mary Clare—longer than mere months, more like a year. The girl could be much taller by now.

"No, ma'am," the oldest looking one said. "No children at all."

Fiona breathed out a sigh of relief. God did answer prayer.

Sawyer was shaking by the time he got into the lighthouse keeper's quarters. Even sitting next to the kitchen stove didn't warm his fingers and toes. The pea soup and buttered bread did more to shake off the chill. The men buzzed in and out, boasting about the perilous rescue and the fact that they'd saved everyone before the ship broke up.

He didn't have the strength to boast. Instead he ate more of the soup and tried to soak in the heat from the stove.

"Out, out." Mrs. Blackthorn and Mrs. Calloway waved their arms as if shooing crows from a cornfield.

"You men must have someplace better to tell your tales than in the middle of the kitchen," Mrs. Blackthorn added.

Mrs. Calloway nodded in agreement. "Mr. Roland brought dry clothes for those of you who are wet through to the bone."

"You can change in the parlor." Mrs. Blackthorn led them away. "The drapes are drawn, and the stove's got it toasty as can be. You'll feel a whole lot better once you're dry."

Gradually the kitchen cleared out except for Mrs. Calloway, who gave Sawyer a sharp look.

"That applies to you too, Mr. Sawyer. Go and get into some dry clothes."

The woman reminded him of his nanny when he was a boy. Mrs. Dougherty didn't take one bit of nonsense from Sawyer or his brother, Jamie. The memory brought a chuckle to his lips.

Mrs. Calloway braced her hands on her hips. "There's nothing funny about freezin' half to death. Get into some dry clothes. That's an order."

The smile died on Sawyer's lips. He'd heard his share of orders during the war. Whether they were foolish or wise, he was expected to obey without question. Mrs. Calloway clearly envisioned herself as the field general. But Sawyer was so exhausted that his legs could collapse if he tried to stand. Until the soup revived him, he preferred sitting right where he was.

He tugged at his thick wool shirt. "Everything is pretty dry already from the stove's heat."

"Nonsense. You men don't know what's good for you. Now, hurry along." As if to emphasize her command, she walked toward the kitchen door, where she waited expectantly.

"If you don't mind, ma'am, I'll finish the soup first. It's taking off the chill."

Mrs. Calloway sighed. "Can't talk sense into a hardheaded man."

"I promise to change into dry clothes once I finish eating." Sawyer placed a hand over his heart as a pledge.

"I suppose that'll have to do." An odd smile twisted her lips. "I expect one other thing'll help warm you right through." She lowered her voice from a shout to normal volume. "I oughtn't be tellin' you, but Miss Fiona pretty near fainted when she heard your boat had gone down."

"She did?" Sawyer found that difficult to believe. Fiona was not prone to fainting spells. In fact, she was the strongest woman under trying conditions that he'd ever met.

"Of course." Mrs. Calloway waved a hand. "A woman who thinks she's lost someone she loves can lose her head."

"You mean her niece." Sawyer couldn't believe he'd forgotten to relay the information to Fiona. "Tell her that there weren't any children aboard."

"I'm not talkin' about her niece. By now, she'll have heard that the little one wasn't on the ship." Mrs. Calloway moved close. "You know exactly who I mean. When the word came in that the rescue boat capsized, she was beside herself."

Sawyer grimaced at the matchmaking attempt. "Must have been concerned for everyone. After all, everyone can see she set her cap on Carson Blakeney."

"The Carson Blakeney who dashed out of town without bothering to say goodbye? Balderdash. He's not worth the clothes on his back."

Sawyer knew that, but Fiona didn't. Her shock when he told her of Blakeney's departure made that clear. The biting retort that followed still stung. "She made it perfectly clear that I don't measure up to her standards."

Mrs. Calloway clucked her tongue. "Do you always believe everything a woman tells you?"

Sawyer swallowed the memory of Julia's hidden attraction to another man. That was another woman and another time. Fiona was different. "Shouldn't I?"

Mrs. Calloway laughed and threw up her hands as she left the kitchen. "Young people these days."

Sawyer savored another spoonful of pea soup while her words sank in. Mrs. Calloway believed Fiona liked him. The idea warmed his heart. Then again, her obvious desire to marry coupled with the arrival of her niece could bring a whole lot more attention than he was prepared to accept. He couldn't take on a wife and family. Not now. Not even for Fiona.

Chapter Five

Louise had dressed and gone downstairs by the time Fiona awoke. She'd stayed up late making sure each survivor had enough to eat and a place to sleep. None of them could tell her if Sawyer lived. Guilt gnawed at the back of her mind even while she helped with blankets, nightgowns and hot tea.

Only when Mrs. Calloway returned in the wee hours of the morning did she get her answer.

"Chilled to the bone," the boardinghouse proprietress had said. "Won't surprise me if he catches a cold."

"But he's alive." Fiona had leaned against the wall, exhausted.

"That he is." Mrs. Calloway had said that with a twinkle in her eye. "No doubt he'll come a callin' soon as he can."

Fiona had made a flippant comment, trying to allay the woman's matchmaking efforts, but deep inside she was truly grateful. At least she hadn't caused his death by insisting he rescue her niece, who wasn't even on the ship.

"But they did manage to rescue everyone," she'd commented.

"That they did. My Ernie was right there at the fore-front, bringin' them up the dune to safety."

That must be why she was so relieved. Everyone was safe. Not just Sawyer. Then why did his face keep popping into her mind? Why recall the grace of his fingers moving across the piano keyboard? He never hit a sour note and never touched a piece of music. The first time she'd hummed a tune, and he then played it with harmony and bass notes included, she'd called him a modern-day Mozart. His face had actually gotten red.

She smiled at the memory, but that's all it was—a pleasant memory between two friends. Nothing more than that.

Reassured, she had retired to the comfort of her stiff and somewhat lumpy mattress. It didn't even bother her that Louise was already asleep and snoring softly.

This morning, Fiona stretched her arms with a big yawn. Once she'd dressed and completed her toilette—all without seeing a soul—she headed downstairs. Just how long had she slept? The six ladies, who had received the upstairs rooms, were either still sleeping, or they'd been awake for some time.

She got her answer the moment she set foot on the main floor. Giggling and excited exclamations came from the direction of the parlor. They were definitely awake.

"Good morning, Miss Fiona." Mrs. Calloway breezed from the kitchen with a platter of cinnamon rolls driz-zled with sugar icing.

Fiona's stomach rumbled. "You're serving break-fast?"

"More like morning tea at this hour, but everyone woke at different hours. You're the last."

The last. With a sigh, Fiona followed Mrs. Calloway

into the dining room. An older gentleman—perhaps forty or so—and his wife sat across from each other at the table. Otherwise the room was empty.

The man rose. "Good morning, Miss O'Keefe. You look lovely this morning."

Fiona accepted the compliment with a smile, though she scrambled to recall their names. They had arrived at the boardinghouse not long after she'd settled the young women in rooms.

"I'm sorry I didn't save a room for you," she said as she took a seat. "I wasn't thinking clearly."

"Understandable." The gentleman settled back in his chair. "The situation was soon rectified. Miss Eaton and Miss Geneva agreed to share."

So he had taken care of matters himself. Fiona had never excelled as a hostess. Her talents lay elsewhere. Her mother would have realized the need from the start and doubled up everyone. Pearl and Amanda would likewise have assessed the situation correctly, but Pearl was helping the passengers clean up while Amanda manned the kitchen. Fiona assigned sleeping accommodations and distributed nightshirts and nightgowns, but her mind had gotten stuck wondering if Sawyer was alive.

Fiona lifted a roll from the platter with the serving knife and set it on the plate in front of her before passing the platter to the husband and wife. If only she could recall their names!

She forced a smile. "Are you familiar with the young women, then?"

The wife chuckled, but her husband answered. "We are their escorts."

"Is one of them your daughter?"

"No." The woman laughed, but again she let her husband explain.

He set down his cup of coffee. "We are escorting them to our community on Low Island."

Fiona had to admit ignorance. "Where is Low Island?"

The man smiled graciously. "In northern Lake Michigan."

"I see. Forgive me, but I'm not from this area. I was born and raised in New York City."

"Is that so?" the man said while his wife made a surprised sound. "I have never been to that great city. How does it compare to Chicago?"

Fiona had no answer for him. "I spent little time in Chicago before taking passage on a steamboat similar to the one you took here."

The man's eyebrows lifted. "You were stranded here also?"

"No. Not at all." She didn't feel like explaining the mail-order advertisement that had brought her here. "This is…a promising town." The words stuck in her throat. It might have been if Roland Decker's glassworks or Carson Blakeney's new mill had gotten off the ground, but both ventures failed—though for entirely different reasons. Roland could not be blamed. A fire had destroyed his building before it was finished. Carson, on the other hand, was a coward and a liar. She suspected he had little intention of starting a new mill in a town that already boasted two sawmills.

"I was hoping another ship would call here soon," the gentleman was saying.

She'd gone and let her mind drift again.

"I'm sure one will." She took a sip of her tea, which was piping hot. Mrs. Calloway always brought scalding hot tea to table this time of year since it cooled rapidly in the colder-than-normal dining room. "What is the name of the community, Mr...?"

The man wiped his mouth with his napkin. "Forgive me. I should have realized you couldn't possibly remember everyone's name given the frantic nature of matters last night. I am Mr. George Adamson, and this is my wife, Bettina."

Even while completing introductions, a shriek of joy came from the parlor, followed by exclamations of "mine" and "no, mine."

Mr. Adamson frowned and set aside his napkin. "My apologies for their unseemly behavior. It will be put to a stop at once."

Mrs. Calloway, who could hear across town even when standing next to a running saw, breezed into the room with some of her apple chutney. "Never you mind, Mr. Adamson. It's a pure delight to hear young ladies' high spirits."

His frown didn't ease. "I can't imagine what they're carrying on about."

"Something in the local newspaper, I presume. The weekly arrived bright and early this morning, and they've been reading it front to back ever since. Now have a bit of my chutney. I'm rather proud of it, if I don't say so myself."

Fiona stared at the departing Mrs. Calloway while Mr. Adamson resumed his seat at the table and dished some of the chutney onto his and his wife's plates. She had read the *Singapore Sentinel* many times. There wasn't one thing over the course of months that would elicit that sort of reaction from young women with no connection to the town. The newspaper typically droned on about the number of board feet cut, who visited whom for Sunday dinner and which ships had called or were expected. It was a perfectly fine medium for inducing sleep.

After the initial outburst, the women quieted. That appeased the Adamsons, but it didn't quell Fiona's curiosity. Like a small child, silence brought suspicion, not comfort. Until now, they had made no attempt to hush their voices. Those ladies were up to something.

Fiona finished her tea and rose. "Forgive me, but the day is long and much remains to be done."

The Adamsons graciously released her, but they could not have known her purpose. Once out of the dining room, Fiona walked to the parlor. There she found all six ladies huddled around the sofa, four of them on their knees, though definitely not in prayer. The newspaper was spread out on the seat of the sofa, and six faces peered intently at the newsprint.

"He sounds wonderful," the blonde said, sighing.

Her high voice and petite figure only made her youth more evident. If Fiona was to guess, she would place her as the youngest. Other than hair color, height and weight, little distinguished the women, who were again dressed in the matching navy blue dresses.

"More than wonderful," countered the brunette who'd acted as the leader of the group from the moment they arrived. "He is everything a woman could want in a husband."

A husband! This sounded very much like they were reading an advertisement for a wife, but there had never been such a thing in the *Singapore Sentinel*. What on earth were those girls up to?

The other five ladies nodded, hanging on every word their leader said.

"Perfect." The blonde sighed.

The redhead echoed the sentiment.

"However, he is just one man, and we are already pledged," the brunette pointed out.

Already pledged? Fiona stared. This was unseemly behavior for women engaged to marry. Moreover, not a one had mentioned traveling with her betrothed. Fiona mentally counted the rescued passengers. There were not enough men of the appropriate age to match to the six ladies. Moreover, the Adamsons said they were escorting the ladies to some island far to the north. This got more and more peculiar, and Fiona intended to get to the bottom of it.

"Excuse me." Fiona glided across the room, ignoring the guilty looks on the ladies' faces and their quick attempt to refold the newspaper. "I could not help but overhear. Am I correct that you found an advertisement for a wife in the newspaper?"

The girls relaxed, and the leader reopened the paper. "There it is, as plain as day."

Fiona couldn't see it, unless she got on her knees and crouched with the rest of the ladies. That might be all right for some, but not for a star of the New York stage. She held out a hand, and the leader passed the newspaper to her.

It didn't take long for Fiona to locate the unlikely advertisement. The wording stunned—no, shocked—her.

Up and coming industrial magnate seeks cultured wife gifted in the social and musical arts. Must be willing to entertain and manage a home. Skill in baking highly valued. Prospective groom has brunette hair and a comely visage. Apply at the Singapore Mercantile.

Fiona let out the breath she'd been holding. Industrial magnate? Lover of music? Reasonably attractive? He did sound perfect, but why on earth would someone of that stature need to advertise for a wife? Even if circumstances did prompt such desperation, why seek such a woman in the least likely place? For a second she thought of Carson, but he had sandy blond hair, not brunette. No, this made no sense.

"This must be a joke," she announced. "There aren't more than a handful of unmarried women within miles. No one would advertise in Singapore for a bride."

"Maybe this isn't the only place he advertised," the brunette suggested.

Fiona couldn't deny that possibility, but the result was the same. She refolded the newspaper. "If you are already promised, I suggest you focus on your beau, not some foolishness published in the newspaper."

She then carried the newspaper—and source of the ladies' excitement—from the room.

"What am I going to do now?" Sawyer shook the newspaper in front of Roland Decker. As he'd feared, the advertisement had made its way into print.

Roland shrugged. "It's a good way to catch Fiona's attention."

"I'm not the one bent on catching her attention. You and Pearl are."

"Now, Sawyer. Anyone and everyone can see that you've had your eye on her for a long time."

Sawyer had no idea he was giving that impression. "She's pretty but only interested in someone whose wallet is fat."

"That's why the advertisement highlighted your potential."

"Potential?" Sawyer raked a hand through his hair. "Every word is completely false." Well, not completely. He could be an industrial magnate if he chose to ride on Father's coattails and obey the man's every demand, but Roland didn't know that.

"Then make it true."

"How? I can't become a wealthy businessman over-night."

Roland leaned on the mercantile counter, that grin of his not budging. "I didn't see anything in the advertisement about being wealthy."

Sawyer read the offensive points. "Up and coming industrial magnate."

"Doesn't say what you are now."

Sawyer moved on. "'Must be willing to entertain and manage a home.' If that doesn't point to wealth, I don't know what does. The poor don't entertain. Moreover, I don't have a home."

"You will. Now that you're manager at the mill you can afford one."

"But I don't have one now, and even if I did lease one, none of the houses here are big enough to require managing. That implies a servant at least, possibly a whole staff."

Roland chuckled. "That's a stretch, I'll admit, but can't you just see Fiona bossing the servants around?"

The problem was, he could. Sawyer let out a sigh.

"Besides," Roland continued, "there's no harm done. No one knows who is looking for a wife, only that applications are accepted here."

The doorbell tinkled, drawing Sawyer's attention. He lowered his voice. "And you think no one will ask who it is?"

"Not likely."

Mrs. Wardman approached.

"Good afternoon, ma'am," Roland said. "How are you doing this fine day? Anything I can get for you?"

"I'm curious about this advertisement. My girls are far too young, naturally, but I have a cousin over in Allegan who might be interested. I'd write and suggest she send a letter, but I'd have to know who the prospective groom is."

"Now, that's strictly confidential, ma'am. You must understand."

Mrs. Wardman leaned over the counter to whisper, "Is it Mr. Stockton?"

Roland gave her a conspiratorial grin. "You know I can't say."

"It is him, isn't it? Well, I thought that he'd never remarry after losing his wife." Mrs. Wardman chattered on, never once looking at Sawyer.

Maybe Roland was right. No one would think that the prospective groom was him. Like Mrs. Wardman, they'd think it was Stockton. Wouldn't the dour entrepreneur think that was funny? Well, maybe not.

Before Sawyer could get another word with Roland, woman after woman came into the store with the same question. Who was looking for a wife? Each bought something, making Roland beam. Apparently this little scheme had at least improved business. It sure didn't make Sawyer feel good, though.

When the last lady departed, Sawyer asked, "Any of them say they were going to apply?"

Roland's grin broadened. "Not yet, but it's early."

Sawyer groaned. He was ready to make his escape when the doorbell tinkled again. This time Mrs. Vander-Leuven walked in. Sawyer stood up straight. The hotel proprietress must be coming back to reopen. Either that or she'd gotten word about last night's shipwreck.

"Mrs. VanderLeuven!" Roland exclaimed. "I didn't know you'd come back to town."

She waved a hand. "Soon as we heard about the wrecked ship, we packed up the wagon and drove the old road down from Holland."

"News got to Holland that quickly?" Sawyer was astonished. Though people often traveled the ten miles between the two towns, the VanderLeuvens would have had to race to get here this quickly.

"They saw it up at the lighthouse."

That made sense. From the Holland light tower, the keeper could easily see off the shore from Singapore. The wreck hadn't gone under but sat like a great hulk on the sandbar.

"Though I'll miss my family in Holland," Mrs. VanderLeuven was saying, "I had to come help. People might be needing a place to sleep and something to eat."

While she and Roland discussed what would be needed to reopen the hotel, Sawyer pretended to browse the display of oilskins. The VanderLeuvens' return could mean resuming the concerts. That meant time with Fiona. Though marriage was out of the question right now, he loved making music with her. He'd never heard a clearer soprano.

When Roland and Mrs. VanderLeuven finished their business transaction, Sawyer caught the woman's attention. "Perhaps I could talk Fiona into a concert in the dining room to encourage business."

"I'm afraid I can't pay," Mrs. VanderLeuven responded, "not until we've started turning a profit."

That was disappointing. Sawyer wouldn't mind adding to his savings, but a bit of goodwill might improve business enough for the VanderLeuvens to once again pay them for playing. "Consider it a gift."

The portly woman's cheeks flushed. "Why, Mr. Evans,

what a kind gesture. Of course we would welcome a concert. The usual time?"

After Sawyer assured her that Saturday evening would be perfect, she left.

Roland's grin spread across his face. "Not interested in Miss O'Keefe?"

"This is strictly business." Even Sawyer had a hard time believing that.

When Fiona overheard the blonde young woman talking about the advertisement later that afternoon, she put a stop to it.

"Shouldn't you be thinking about your fiancé?"

The blonde sighed. "I can't think on someone I ain't met."

The girl's atrocious grammar and cheap muslin dress marked her as poor. Fiona had once been exactly the same. Changing her speech took practice, but improving her dress took money. She'd worked long and hard before she could afford her first pretty gown. Until then, a kindhearted singer had given Fiona one of her cast-offs for the stage. Away from the theater, Fiona had hidden in the shadows so no one would connect the poor girl with the singer on the stage.

Fiona stared at the young woman. "Are you saying you've never met your fiancé?"

The girl shrugged. "Ain't been no chance to."

"None of us has met our beau yet," the bubbly redhead said, "but we'll meet them soon. We're going to Harmony to get married."

Fiona drew in a deep breath. The similarities to her arrival in Singapore didn't drift past without notice. "You're all answering advertisements for a wife?" She hoped they weren't all going for the same man.

The leader shook her brunette locks. "No, ma'am. We each got a husband waitin' for us."

"I see." But she didn't. "Then you've written to them already."

Again the leader shook her head. "Mr. Adamson chose us."

"Chose?"

"Yes, ma'am. He held an interview, and we got picked. Dozens applied."

The whole process appalled Fiona. "Do you know anything about the man you're going to marry, Miss…?"

"Clara." The leader straightened her spine. "Call me Clara." She then proceeded to introduce the rest.

Fiona forgot their names in an instant except for Dinah, the blonde, who wasn't yet eighteen years of age.

"We all got a description," Clara finished up. "My fiancé's name is Benjamin. He's twenty-eight and tall with dark hair like mine."

The other ladies then described their future mates, all of whom were older and whose hair color came remarkably close to their own. When their matching dresses were taken into account, there was something odd about this whole situation.

"What do they do? Their occupation?" she asked.

Clara gave her a blank look. "They're all farmers, of course. We're creating a community free of strife and vice." She reeled that off as if quoting something she'd been told to memorize.

Fiona was appalled. "Surely you had another choice."

Each girl shook her head.

"Marry a drunken bum," Clara stated frankly. "We've been workin' in the shirtwaist factory after getting thrown out of the orphanage."

"Thrown out?" Fiona could hardly believe what she was hearing.

"Because we're too old," the redhead, Linore, explained. "That's why we're getting married."

"Next ta Bleek Street, Harmony sounds like paradise." Dinah sighed. "No drinkin' or brawlin'."

That did sound too good to be true.

"Then they are all upright men of God?" Fiona prodded.

"That's what Mr. Adamson says," Clara answered.

Each woman nodded in affirmation.

If what Mr. Adamson claimed was indeed the truth, Fiona could understand why these women had agreed to go to this island community. But what if it wasn't?

"Can you leave if your fiancé doesn't turn out the way he's been advertised?" Fiona would definitely have made certain that option was available. She'd held on to it when answering the advertisement that brought her to Singapore. Even now, that possibility remained, though it would get much more difficult once Mary Clare arrived. She had not set aside the fare for two to travel to Chicago.

The women all stared at her as if she were mad.

Clara vocalized their response. "Why would we leave? It's better than what we got now."

Fiona recalled the newspaper that had so gripped their attention. "Then why the interest in the advertisement for a wife?"

The women looked at each other and giggled.

This time the one with the chestnut-colored hair answered, her jaw thrust out. "A girl's gotta dream, don't she?"

"Well, I can tell you for certain that this advertisement is only a dream. There's not a man in this town who fits that description."

Instead of solemnly nodding, like she'd expected, the ladies grew quiet, their eyes wide, and stood as one, smoothing their plain skirts as if they wore silk. A hush came over the room.

A man cleared his throat behind Fiona.

She whirled to see Sawyer standing in the doorway, hat in hand. "Sawyer! Mr. Evans, that is. I'm glad to see you're well."

His complexion reddened as if—no, it wasn't possible—he were blushing. He stepped from foot to foot, clearly uneasy. "I'm fine."

"So I see."

The ladies giggled behind her.

Fiona left the room and led Sawyer to the front porch where they might have a bit of privacy. The chill air bit into her, and she hugged her arms close for warmth.

"You had something to tell me?" she prompted.

Sawyer cleared his throat again, though his eyes darted toward the parlor windows. "I just wanted you to know that the VanderLeuvens are back in town and are opening up the hotel. We can begin the concerts again."

Fiona breathed out. She hadn't realized how much she would miss the income she'd received from her concerts. Almost three months without pay had stretched her funds very thin. "That's wonderful. An answer to prayer."

"You've been praying to have a concert?"

"I've been praying for an income."

The color left his face. "An income?"

"I do need to pay for room and board," she pointed out.

"Of course." His color returned, this time to a bright red. He avoided looking directly at her.

"All right. What's wrong? Spit it out." Fiona hated when a man wouldn't express himself outright.

"Um." Again he cleared his throat. "I'm sorry to say that at least for now we'll have to do them without pay. Mrs. VanderLeuven said she needs to start turning a profit first."

Fiona's temper rose. Under that rationale, the Vander-Leuvens would never pay them. She'd heard the rumors of unpaid debts and heavy loans on the property. But it did no good to rail at the messenger. It also wouldn't help pay the bills when Mary Clare did arrive. She needed steady employment. The thought of cleaning rooms or scrubbing dishes at the hotel left a foul taste in her mouth. She'd clawed her way out of poverty. She would not descend back into it.

"I see." The terse reply was the best she could manage.

"Then you'll do it?" The hint of hope in his voice gave her pause.

He wanted her to sing at the hotel again. Maybe he looked forward to it. She did too, and not just the singing. Sawyer was surprisingly handsome and charming. And his piano and violin playing made her want to close her eyes and drink it in. Too bad he was only a sawmill foreman. Still, a concert couldn't hurt. Maybe she could persuade Mrs. VanderLeuven to give them a percentage of profit from the meals ordered that night.

"I will," she confirmed. "For now."

The faint sound of women's giggling reached her ears. She turned to see the ladies glued to the parlor windows. They weren't watching her. No, every eye was fixed on Sawyer. No wonder he'd looked so uncomfortable. It wasn't her at all. Drawing the attention of six women left him unnerved.

She glanced back at Sawyer. Granted, he was a fine specimen of masculinity with his broad shoulders, height, muscular build and shock of dark brown hair. Brunette for brunette. That's how Mr. Adamson had matched the girls. Under that criteria, Clara would go with Sawyer. The woman did have a proprietary gleam in her eye.

Sawyer looked away. "Are those the women we rescued? I didn't realize they were so young."

He didn't say they were pretty, but he thought it. She could tell.

Something fiercely protective rose in Fiona's breast. "Yes, and they are all engaged to marry. Every last one."

There. That ought to douse the spark of interest in his eyes.

Chapter Six

Sawyer had never been nervous before a concert in the past, but Saturday he tugged at the collar of his good shirt. The tie was choking him. Or was it the fact that the whole town knew about the advertisement? Fiona was bound to say something, and he had no idea what he'd tell her. He couldn't come right out and reveal that he was the bachelor supposedly seeking a wife. He certainly couldn't tell people that he hadn't placed the advertisement and had no intention of marrying right now. That hadn't worked for Garrett Decker, and it wouldn't work for him.

Still, as the days passed without a single response, he began to wonder what was wrong. Was it the advertisement or him? Had Fiona figured out that he was the prospective bridegroom?

As always, he stopped at the boardinghouse an hour before they performed. The brief walk to the hotel left them plenty of time to warm up before many guests and diners arrived.

She wore the emerald green gown—her favorite and the one she seemed to think most like those worn by the upper class. He couldn't bring himself to tell her that those born to wealth most often chose conservative colors and styles. The worst of them would look down their noses at Fiona's exuberant attire. He found it refreshing, for her gowns matched her temperament perfectly.

"I expect a large crowd," she said as they walked the boardwalk between the two businesses. "It's been a long winter, after all."

"We did perform a few times at the boardinghouse."

"It's not the same, and you know it. The hotel is roomier and more…professional."

Sawyer was again reminded of the talent and perseverance that brought her to the New York City stage. Many dreamed but few reached that lofty goal. Fiona had. Again he wondered why she would leave her blossoming career to answer an advertisement for a mail-order bride in a lumber town. According to Pearl, Fiona still searched the personal advertisements. Yet she had not responded to his.

He held the door of the hotel for her and escorted her into the dining room. A smattering of applause greeted them, and she flitted from one table to the next, thanking them for their gracious response to her return.

That left Sawyer to warm up on the piano. After a couple months of inactivity and icy temperatures, it was slightly out of tune. He could fix that but had forgotten to bring the tools with him. He'd been preoccupied with the looming catastrophe caused by that advertisement. Even if Fiona wrote to him, he couldn't mislead her into thinking he wanted a wife. Not now. And she seemed determined to marry as soon as possible.

The lovely lady returned, her cheeks aglow with pleasure that people had gathered to hear her sing.

"The piano's a little flat," he announced. "Would you prefer I play violin?"

She wrinkled her nose. "Play a little. I'll let you know if I can compensate."

He launched into a tune while she hovered over his shoulder. How he'd missed having her at his side this winter. A few concerts at the boardinghouse hadn't compensated for the fact that she barely noticed his existence if Blakeney was in the room.

Tonight he felt her closeness. Her rich soprano sent delightful shivers up his spine. To hear that every day... He shook away the thought. Marriage had to wait until after he started his own venture. He'd set aside every dollar he could, but he'd need a lot more to open a business.

Fiona listened to him complete the major and minor scales and declared the piano's flatness manageable. Having made the decree, she left his side to go through her music.

This was part of her usual preparation, but he hated her absence. "Do you want to warm up your voice?"

"I warmed up for over an hour at the boardinghouse."

"Then went out in the cold. It won't hurt to run through one of the tunes."

She glanced at the gathering crowd. "One set of scales will do. We don't want to set a precedent of giving them something at no charge."

Once again she'd focused on money. She must be in difficult circumstances for her to keep hinting about getting paid. Sawyer wished he could slip her a little, but she was too proud to receive it. He'd tried to buy her supper once and got an icy glare for his trouble. So he played the scales. She warmed up her voice and declared herself ready.

Only after the concert ended and the applause had died down could he talk with her. They sat together for late supper.

"I'm paying for this." He quickly added a reason that didn't hint of charity. "I want to celebrate getting promoted to sawmill manager and can't think of anyone I'd rather celebrate with."

She blinked in surprise. In the past their meals had been given to them, but Mrs. VanderLeuven had made it clear that she couldn't afford even that this early in the season.

"I shouldn't accept," she began.

He covered her hand with his. "I'm also grateful to be alive. That's worth celebrating."

She withdrew her hand and looked away. "I'm sorry. I thought my niece was on the ship. My sister wrote that she was sending Mary Clare. That's my niece. But she didn't say when. For all I knew, she'd sent the letter one day and my niece the next. I was terrified."

"I know." And he did. He'd seen the terror in her eyes and responded the only way he knew how, by risking his life to rescue the little girl.

Fiona set her jaw. "I should never have asked so much of you."

"I would have gone anyway. The passengers needed help." He swallowed back the hard memories of the war. "In the past I wasn't always able to help those in need."

Her delicate fingers touched his. "You don't need to hold on to your glass so tightly."

Sawyer released his grip and flexed his hand. "I didn't realize I was doing that."

"Bad memories?" she asked softly.

He gazed into her green eyes, highlighted by the color of her gown. The edge of the iris was darker, as if more of the pigment had pooled there. "I'd rather dwell on good memories."

She didn't respond for a moment and then nodded. "There's no use holding on to things we can't change."

He let out a breath he didn't realize he was holding. "True. Look forward, not back."

"Exactly." But she looked uncomfortable.

"Manager at the mill is good, but I have much bigger plans than that. My own business. Once that's established, I'd a like a big house with a family." He halted at the odd look she gave him. Why'd he gone on blathering like that about his plans and dreams? "Someday," he added. "I'm working on it."

Her expression was taut, cautious. "I haven't been fair to you." The words came out one at a time, as if too painful to say at once.

Sawyer held his breath. He'd heard that sort of prelude before. It was usually followed by something unpleasant.

She kept running a finger up and down one of the red stripes on the tablecloth. "You're a good, decent man and deserve a woman who loves you with all her heart."

"Good thing I'm not looking to marry, then." Though he kept the words light, an unexpected heaviness settled over him.

She looked startled. "Yes, I suppose it is." She stared at the windows, which were black due to darkness. "I wanted you to know that I need to take much into consideration. My niece for instance. I hope to give her a solid home."

"Home?"

She lifted her chin. "Yes, I will be raising my niece."

That explained her desperation to marry. Perhaps she thought a husband would be easier to find in a lumber town. It was true that men outnumbered women ten or more to one. But it didn't say much about her opinion of those men or why she was being so selective.

One thing was certain. Sawyer wasn't good enough for her even in a crisis.

A week of the same nonsense and no ship in sight had Fiona at her wit's end. Apparently orphaned young ladies rescued from the shirtwaist factory could think of nothing else to discuss than every man who walked past. Each one they compared to that ludicrous advertisement. Worst of all, Sawyer topped the list for Clara and Dinah. She'd told them that he had no intention of marrying, but that didn't put an end their speculating about him.

"It's ridiculous," Fiona complained to Mrs. Calloway in the sanctity of the kitchen. "Won't they ever stop?"

Fiona had resumed baking breads and pastries to the delight of guests and for her own sanity. The kitchen was the only place where none of the survivors ventured.

"Now, now, they're young women. That's what they talk about." Mrs. Calloway grabbed a tray of sliced bread.

"They're engaged to marry."

"Come now. What harm is a little sighing over a man here and there? They'll be gone soon anyway. This wind is bound to die down before long, and the ships will be sailing again."

"Not soon enough," Fiona grumbled as she threw her weight into kneading the sweet dough.

Saturday's concert had been her only respite. Though the hotel's dining room had been full of guests, few ordered supper. Mrs. VanderLeuven had grumbled about the pitiful receipts, so Fiona hadn't dared to ask for a percentage of the profit. Most likely there'd been no profit. Singing again to Sawyer's accompaniment was the only benefit she could take away from the night. If anything, his talents had improved over the winter, and she'd enjoyed the meal he insisted on buying for her. Until he got personal. What did he mean by talking about getting a house and family one moment and the next saying he didn't want to marry?

The man confounded her.

She sighed. At least Mary Clare hadn't arrived yet. Fiona had scoured her sister's letter again, but found no date for her niece's travel. It was impossible to tell if Fiona's niece had already been sent or would be sent her way in the future.

"They're bored," Mrs. Calloway was saying. "If you want to divert the ladies' attention, give them something to do."

Fiona stopped kneading the dough as her thoughts returned to the problem at hand. "Something to do... what a good idea. They need to be occupied. House-cleaning and laundry would be a good start."

Mrs. Calloway clucked her tongue. "Have you ever met a cleaning girl who didn't gossip and speculate whenever she could? Give them something more exciting to do than gape after the menfolk. Something that keeps their minds busy. Something they would enjoy."

Having finished her suggestion, Mrs. Calloway exited with the tray of bread.

Fiona absently kneaded the dough as she tossed around the idea of teaching the ladies. She had taught a few days of school, but that was for children, not grown women. What would she teach them? She couldn't sew like Amanda or direct a play like Pearl. She couldn't even lead them on a nature walk like Louise, who was always traipsing over the dunes, botany book in hand. Her sole talent was singing. Even her piano playing left much to be desired.

Perhaps she could teach them to sing.

Mrs. Calloway bustled back into the kitchen with an empty platter. "Ate every last bit of ham. At this rate, there won't be any left for Easter Sunday."

"Easter! That's it."

"That's what?"

"I've found a purpose for our female guests. We will form a ladies' choir and sing for Easter Sunday service."

Mrs. Calloway's brow creased. "Do you think they'll be here that long?"

"It's only a little over a week away. If they take instruction well, we can sing this Sunday also."

Her mind swirled with ideas. They couldn't possibly learn something as complicated as Handel's *Messiah*, but they could learn some traditional hymns. In fact, they probably already knew the melodies and words. She would only have to teach harmony.

"That's what we'll do. It's the perfect solution."

Sawyer hurried to the mercantile, eager to get Roland's opinion. His friend would know whether this venture was trouble or a great opportunity. The price was impossible, but Roland might have some ideas on that front. He'd gotten investors for the glassworks he'd begun building last fall.

Sawyer burst through the door, sending the bell jingling.

Roland looked up from his position at the counter. "Hi, Sawyer. Do you want to read the applications that have come in?"

"Applications? What applications? Garrett's still doing the hiring at the mill."

"Not the mill." Roland's grin should have cued him in. "For the, ahem, *position* in the advertisement."

Position? Oh. For a wife.

"I don't want anything to do with that, and you know it." Sawyer glanced around the store and saw no one. Nevertheless, he moved to the counter to make his next statement. "I don't care about any applications."

A week had gone by without any responses. Not that he cared, other than curiosity if Fiona would write. She'd made it perfectly clear that she didn't consider him marriage stock, so if she guessed he was the supposed groom, she would not write. Given the way the advertisement was worded, he doubted anyone would make the connection.

Except now someone had written.

"Is it from Fiona?" Sawyer asked tentatively. Part of him wanted it to be from her, while another part dreaded reading what she might say.

"I don't know. I wasn't here when they arrived, and Jimmy couldn't tell me a thing." Roland slid two envelopes across the counter. "See for yourself."

"Two?" Sawyer stared at the envelopes.

"That's right."

There weren't many women in the Singapore area of marriageable age. Most who came of age married right away to someone they'd known their whole lives. One or two had gotten sweet on a lumberjack, but parents tended to discourage those liaisons. Two letters increased the possibility that one was from Fiona. Who else would write? The widow, Louise Smythe?

He scanned the first. The handwriting was nearly

illegible, the spelling atrocious, but he could make out the signature. "Dinah? Who is that?"

"I believe it's one of the ladies we rescued off the wrecked ship."

Sawyer shot Roland a nasty look.

His friend stuck up his hands in surrender. "I had no idea there would be women of marriageable age stranded here."

"Likely story." Sawyer ripped open the second envelope and looked at the signature. "Clara?"

"Another one of the rescued women, I believe."

"See? This is exactly what I said would happen. I get responses from every unmarried woman in the county. For that matter, letters could come pouring in from far and wide. It only takes one person bringing the newspaper on a ship or train to cause chaos. Now someone has to tell the ladies that there is no groom."

"Oh, no. Not me."

"You and Pearl concocted the whole thing. It disappeared from your store. I think the duty falls to you."

"I'm already married," Roland pointed out.

"Then it will be easy to point out that it was just a mistake."

Roland shook his head. "It's not that simple. These women have put their hearts on the line. They deserve a letter in return. It can be simple. Maybe Pearl would help with the wording."

Sawyer recalled the letter his former fiancée had sent him. Brief and to the point. "No matter how it's worded, it's going to sting."

"Not when you've never met. They can't have expectations."

"They're expecting a rich man."

"Up and coming," Roland said with a shrug. "Answer right away, and it'll only be a mild annoyance, like a mosquito bite."

Sawyer had experienced his share of those, not to mention hornet and wasp stings. He didn't care to inflict the pain on anyone, even women he didn't know. "You and Pearl work out the wording...a generic note of regret, and I'll copy it."

"I'll ask her." Roland hesitated. "Can you write?"

Sawyer chafed at the inference. Lumberjacks and sawmill workers were often illiterate. He was not. Far from it. But admitting he'd read Shakespeare and Dante would shatter the workingman image he'd striven to create.

One of his crew entered the store.

"I can write well enough," Sawyer said in a low voice.

He pocketed the letters. They could wait. He had more important business to discuss, and Roland was the only man in Singapore qualified to answer his questions.

Even though the store was nearly empty, Sawyer kept his voice low. "VanderLeuven said he wants to sell the hotel."

Roland's eyebrows lifted. "That so? Well, I suppose it makes sense. It takes a lot to run a hotel, and they're getting up in age. With their children living in Holland, I can see why they might want to move there."

Sawyer nodded. All that was well and good, but he needed advice. "I've been saving up for years so I can open a business of my own. I'm thinking this might be the opportunity I've been looking for."

Roland whistled low.

When the customer looked up in curiosity, Sawyer leaned casually against the counter and chuckled, as if Roland had just said something witty. The man resumed his business.

Sawyer turned back to Roland. "You know about investing. The first thing I need to know is if it's worthwhile or not?"

"Well, you need to consider the outlay—what you'll need to spend—not only to purchase but to refurbish and repair. Look over the property carefully and make a list of needed repairs. Then estimate costs. Get an idea of past revenue—money they took in—and take your best guess at whether that will increase or decrease in the future. Measure costs against income, and you'll have your answer."

Sawyer knew all that. He'd spent too much time as a youth under his father's tutelage at the company offices not to understand accounts, profit and cash flow. Of course Roland didn't know that. No one in Singapore did, and that's exactly the way he wanted things to stay. If anyone knew the truth, it wouldn't take much effort to take a ship to Chicago and tell dear old Father that his renegade son was posing as a sawmill worker across the lake in Singapore.

So he feigned lack of knowledge all while trying to get an answer to his questions. "Do you expect the town to grow in the next few years?"

That brought a spark in Roland's eye. "Absolutely. Once I get investors lined up again, I'm getting the glassworks built. We will make Singapore the new Chicago."

Sawyer had planned to seek investors to make up the shortfall between the asking price and his savings, but he didn't stand a chance of beating out Roland for them. To make this deal, he would have to get the property at a low price. Then he could turn Astor House into the finest hotel on Lake Michigan's eastern shore.

"I don't have to do anything you tell me to do," shouted Violet Burr, the chestnut-haired young woman whose contentious nature came out the minute Fiona announced the forming of a church choir. "My church doesn't believe in singing or music of any sort."

Fiona couldn't conceive of such a thing. "Why ever not?"

"Because it leads to pride." Violet jutted her chin.

Fiona was not going to argue. She'd done enough of it with her siblings to understand it was a way to get others to do what you wanted. Violet was testing her. Fiona wouldn't bite. "Then you may leave."

Violet cast her a withering look. "I don't need your permission."

"And you don't need to come back either."

Violet looked spitting mad and ready to spout off some vulgarity.

Clara stepped between them. "No one has to sing. Miss O'Keefe just wanted to give us somethin' to do to pass the time."

Fiona wished she had those diplomatic skills instead of losing her temper whenever challenged. It was a flaw that had cost her at home, where she was often at war with her equally volatile sisters. Witness Lillibeth's sending Mary Clare at the least convenient time.

With the ladies' choir, Fiona held the advantage, and she wasn't relinquishing it. After all, the women would soon be gone to their island with its impossibly perfect village of Harmony. There they would discover the realities of marriage to men they'd never met. For a moment, Fiona's heart ached for them. Still, maybe it was better than sixteen-hour days in a factory.

"There has to be another way," she muttered aloud.

The six women stared at her. If Violet hadn't possessed the best soprano voice of the lot, Fiona wouldn't care if she stayed or went, but the feisty young woman reminded her too much of herself. She was a fighter, and she had talent. It would be wasted homesteading on some northern island.

Fiona drew in a breath and calmed her temper. "I would like you to stay, Violet. Your voice carries the soprano section and would uplift many a soul on Easter Sunday."

The girl's shoulders eased. "I'm sorry, Miss O'Keefe. I got a temper sometimes. Miss Henderson said it'd get me in trouble one day."

By now, Fiona had figured out that Miss Henderson had run the orphanage. Her immediate problem was getting this ragtag group together in three days.

"We will rehearse all day until nightfall, if necessary, but we—and by that I mean all of you—will be ready for Easter Sunday services. It's your sacred duty."

Apparently that struck a chord, for the bickering and protests abruptly stopped. In fact, the women assembled in their proper places without a word. Fiona was stunned until Clara's glance toward the doorway gave away the true reason for compliance.

Mr. Adamson nodded at her. "Carry on."

For the next half hour, practice went beautifully. With the exception of the pale, quiet one whose name Fiona could never remember, they even sang reasonably well. Thankfully, the pale woman's off-key voice was so weak that the others covered it. When they finally finished the piece, Fiona lifted her eyes to the heavens in thanksgiving. It wasn't perfect, but it was a start. In three days they might even draw closer to perfection.

"I have news, ladies," Mr. Adamson stated brusquely.

Fiona hadn't realized the man had stood in the doorway listening the entire time. Now he'd come into the parlor, and the ladies quietly gathered around him.

"Mrs. Adamson and I received a telegraph today by way of Holland stating that another ship will leave Chicago on Easter Monday, weather permitting, and arrive here the following day. Seeing as you have ample time to learn the songs for the Easter service, I expect you to listen to Miss O'Keefe's direction and do our Lord proud on Sunday."

Fiona watched the women's reactions. Though they remained stoic while Mr. Adamson was in the room, that changed the moment he left. A mixture of hopefulness and dread filled most faces, though the pale one looked as though she might swoon, and Violet crossed her arms in front of her.

"I don't wanna leave," whispered Dinah, the young blonde. She looked hopefully to Fiona. "Can we stay here?"

Fiona didn't know what to say. She couldn't promise anything. There were no jobs until the flow of logs increased and the second sawmill began operating. Even then the positions were menial or unsavory, like working the saloons. Fiona would not stoop to that type of work. She'd been asked to sing there and had turned down the owners every time.

"There isn't a lot of opportunity here," she said slowly.

"There's that rich businessman," Dinah retorted.

"The who?"

"That magnate who wants a wife. That's what Clara

said a magnate was. I thought it was something you used to pick up a lost needle."

The other women snickered, making Dinah blush.

Fiona felt for her. She was too young to be making this forever decision. "Why did you ever agree to marry someone you've never met?"

"Mr. Adamson assured us they're God-fearing, non-drinking men," Clara answered for the rest. "Can't do no better than that."

Perhaps not. But then again, maybe they could. What if there was another solution? What if Singapore boasted some way for women to earn enough to pay their own way? Wages for women were notoriously low. A decent wage could bring a woman a measure of independence and self-confidence.

If only there was a way.

Her old singing instructor had once told her that if there didn't appear to be a pathway to your dreams, you must make the path yourself. Somehow Fiona had to come up with a solution, and it had to happen before Tuesday. She couldn't live with herself if she didn't try to give the terrified girls another option than sailing off to an unknown future.

An excited murmur from the women broke Fiona from her thoughts. Yet another man stood in the doorway to the parlor, this one infinitely more attractive than Mr. Adamson.

Sawyer smiled and tipped his hat. "Ladies."

Dinah blushed furiously.

Clara pounced on him. "Come in and sit a spell."

Though the woman unceremoniously grabbed his arm, he didn't budge. "I was hoping to speak with Fiona—Miss O'Keefe."

"Oh." The disappointment rang clear in Clara's voice

but didn't last long. "Then when you're done, you can join me. I'll sing for you. If I knew how to play piano, I'd play for you, but there isn't one of us that can play."

"I can accompany you," Sawyer volunteered.

Fiona wanted to shout out what a bad idea that was, but the damage was done. All the girls crowded around him, begging him to play something for them. Like most men, he seemed to be dazzled by all the feminine attention and allowed himself to be dragged to the piano, where he proceeded to play not one song but six, while each girl took her turn singing.

Men. Why were they so oblivious to the machinations of women?

Or was he?

Sawyer had clearly forgotten that he wanted to speak to her. She might as well not even be in the room.

Fine.

Her temper high, Fiona stomped from the parlor and retreated to the kitchen. Surely some batch of dough needed pounding.

Chapter Seven

With six young women clustered around him at the piano, Sawyer didn't see Fiona leave the room. He spotted her absence when he wanted her to demonstrate a particularly difficult passage for the ladies.

For a moment he wondered where she'd gone, but then another of the ladies asked for a different tune. They had a seemingly insatiable appetite for singing, though only one of them had a decent voice. The rest were too weak, too bold, flat or sharp. Yet they'd sounded fairly good when he'd first approached the boardinghouse. Fiona was working wonders with them.

"Honestly, I do have to go," he said for the umpteenth time.

"Just one more," the pretty blonde with the long eyelashes pleaded. "We don't even gotta sing. I just love watchin' you play."

Blondes only reminded Sawyer of Julia. He avoided them, but this one was cloyingly persistent. When he hesitated, she took it as approval to go on and selected another song from the available music.

"D'ya know this one?"

Everyone knew the "Battle Hymn of the Republic."

Though it brought up painful memories, he couldn't wriggle out of it when surrounded by a chorus of "please, Mr. Evans."

"Last one."

He played two verses and rose. "I have work to do."

"At this hour?" the brunette asked.

It was nearly supper. That gave him an idea.

"You must need to freshen up before you eat."

"No, not at all," the ladies insisted.

The blonde even wound her arm around his. "You're gonna join us, aren't you? I been wantin' to ask if you know who put that advertisement in the newspaper. You must know who around here is a…a magnet."

The girls giggled.

The blonde corrected herself. "Magnate."

Sawyer forced a stiff smile. "Couldn't tell you, ladies."

Nor did he intend to *ever* tell them.

"Stop monopolizing him, Dinah." The brunette pouted.

So the blonde was named Dinah. One of the letters in his pocket was signed by Dinah.

"I ain't doing no such thing, Clara," the blonde shot back. "I'm only gonna show him to his seat at the table."

Clara was the other applicant.

"Maybe he doesn't want to eat with you," Clara said. "Maybe he has other plans."

Sawyer didn't mention that he often ate in the kitchen. Since he wasn't a guest at the boardinghouse, he didn't sit at the dining table but paid for and ate his meals at the kitchen table. Doubtless they would have insisted on joining him.

"Actually, I do have something to do." He extracted his arm from the blonde's grasp. He'd wanted to tell

Fiona about the hotel being for sale, but that would have to wait. He wouldn't get a moment alone with her with these ladies around. No, he needed an excuse that drew him away from the boardinghouse. "I need to check on progress at the mill."

He didn't really, but he'd find something to verify, even if it was just ensuring the machines had been properly shut down for the night. Anything to escape these ladies.

Thankfully, Mrs. Calloway called for assistance preparing the table, and an older gentleman appeared to shoo the ladies to the dining room. Sawyer plucked his hat off the sofa and nodded his gratitude to the gentleman.

The man surveyed him closely. "You're one of the fellows who rescued us."

"Yes, sir."

The man nodded. "Best not let the girls know that. They are all engaged to marry and don't need any… complications in their lives." Then, without so much as a thank you or a nod, he swept from the room, presumably to tend to those engaged women.

Sawyer gratefully left the boardinghouse and loped down the boardwalk toward the sawmill. As long as the young ladies were staying at the boardinghouse, he would have difficulty seeing Fiona. Unless she was in the kitchen.

He backtracked to the rear of the boardinghouse. Maybe that's where Fiona went. Maybe she was baking something. The memory of her flaky biscuits from this morning made his mouth water. Fiona didn't look like she could do one bit of menial labor, but her baking was exceptional.

The back stoop was sand-covered, which was unavoidable after a long day. No matter how many times a person swept away the sand, it returned. He climbed the stairs and poked his head into the steamy kitchen. No one was there, but he could hear banging and rattling.

"Fiona?"

Her head popped up above the corner of the stove. "What do you want?"

Though taken aback, he attributed her blunt response to frustration with whatever she was struggling to do.

"Can I help you?"

Her lips thinned. "I think you've done quite enough 'helping' for today."

He rounded the stove to see she had dropped a heavy pan on the floor. It took only a second to grab hold, and he would have lifted it onto the stove or the table or wherever she wanted it except she wouldn't let go.

"I have it," she said through clenched teeth.

Her red hair was in disarray, completely fallen out of its pins. With the high color in her cheeks and the spark in her eyes, she was utterly and completely attractive. It took everything in Sawyer's power not to kiss that frown off her lips. Instead, he set the pan on the stove.

As soon as he let go, she moved it to the table.

"See?" She wiped her hands on her apron. "I knew far better than you where I wanted it."

Sawyer raised his hands in surrender. "Just trying to help out."

"Well, you can 'help out' in the parlor and leave me to do my work."

"You're working in the kitchen?" Until that moment, Sawyer hadn't taken her claim to need an income seriously. He'd thought she baked for pleasure.

Her gaze narrowed. "Do you have a problem with that?"

"Uh, no." He searched for something that would lighten her mood. "Your biscuits this morning were delicious."

Her hands left her hips, and she began wiping the pan she'd just set on the table, though it was perfectly clean and dry. "I'm glad you enjoyed them."

"Roland said you're an excellent baker."

She looked up sharply and then resumed wiping the pan. "I used to bring bread for Roland and his brother when they were bachelors living above the store."

"You felt sorry for them?"

The dots of color hadn't left her cheeks. "Some." She didn't look at him.

Then the truth hit him. What a fool he was! She'd baked the bread to demonstrate her skill to Garrett Decker, in an attempt to prove she was the one he should marry. But that didn't explain her baking and working in the kitchen now. Unless Blakeney had somehow talked her out of funds. He'd heard rumors the man had gone through the area seeking "investors" for his new sawmill. If Fiona would bake to lure Garrett Decker, she might agree to whatever Blakeney suggested in order to claim his attention.

"Tell me Blakeney didn't bilk you out of money."

Again she looked up sharply. "I am no fool, Sawyer Evans."

Yet her jaw was tense and her eyes flashed with anger. Sawyer felt a sinking sensation in his stomach. That rogue Blakeney had not only abandoned her, he'd stolen money from her. Fiona must be in desperate straits, especially with her niece due to arrive soon. He swallowed the lump that was forming in his throat.

"Don't look at me like that," she said sharply. "I

don't need your pity. I'm fine. Just fine. And don't you forget it."

Sawyer choked down his sympathy. She didn't want it. She didn't want anything from him. What could he do anyway? Even if she would accept help, the opportunity he'd been waiting for had finally arrived. He'd come here today to tell her about the hotel, but that news would only make things worse. If he was able to buy the place, he would have to close it for a few months to refurbish and renovate. That would cut into her income.

He backed away. "Sorry for bothering you."

She didn't stop him from leaving.

"You need to assign them chores," Fiona told Mrs. Calloway when she entered the kitchen. It was easier to dwell on the ladies than think about how easily Sawyer had figured out she'd invested a small amount of money in Carson Blakeney's sawmill. It wasn't much, but it was all the extra she had above the reserve set aside for passage to Chicago. The cheat had taken her money and whatever he'd coerced out of others to who knew where. Fiona hated that he'd duped her. Even worse, his lies had come on the heels of Winslow Evanston's deceit. She should have known better. She was usually a good judge of character. Those ladies, for instance, had no intention of waiting until they reached Harmony to snag a husband, and they'd begun with Sawyer.

"Who needs more chores?" Mrs. Calloway asked.

"Those girls." Fiona waved her hand in the direction of the parlor. "Singing can only occupy so much of their day. Mr. Adamson said they will be here through Monday at least. Can't they do something around here?"

"They are already cleaning their rooms and sweeping the public rooms, but I suppose we could do laundry tomorrow, considering Good Friday and Easter are coming up."

"There must be a lot of it."

"There is." Mrs. Calloway sighed. "We didn't get the half of it done on Monday. All right. It's settled. We'll do laundry tomorrow and bake on Saturday."

That wasn't how Fiona had planned to spend her Saturday, but it would have to do. At least the young women would be too busy to chase after Sawyer. Now, if she could just find something to keep Sawyer away from *them*.

Mrs. Calloway pulled a pan of chicken and dumplings from the oven. "I take it you're not so keen on keepin' them here now."

Fiona blew out her breath. She was being hypocritical. "I do sympathize with their plight," she said slowly, "but they only seem interested in marriage."

"That's what all young ladies want."

Was it? Fiona recalled those heady days of youth when she might well have fallen into the wrong man's clutches if not for her mother's stern warning and her older sisters' examples. She'd been cautious but still fell victim to the likes of Evanston and Blakeney. She seemed to attract the louts, whereas the good, decent ones, like Garrett Decker, didn't give her a second thought.

"Who wouldn't be interested in an industrial magnate?" Mrs. Calloway chuckled. "But they'd be mighty disappointed if they set eyes on Mr. Stockton. He's old enough to be their father."

No one else could be the mysterious man placing the advertisement. Fiona considered the newspaper tucked in the bureau in her room. Louise had noted it without comment. Perhaps she had already written a response. Ordinarily, Fiona would have ignored it, but she was desperately low on funds. Mary Clare could arrive any day. Fiona needed a husband.

Mr. Stockton wasn't the worst solution. He was wealthy and spent most of his time traveling. She needn't see him often. Men who placed such advertisements had practical reasons and modest expectations for the new wife. Yes, he might be just the answer she needed. Tonight she would write in reply to the advertisement.

"No and no." Sawyer placed the letters on the mercantile counter. "I've met the women, but, even if I hadn't, I'm not ready to marry."

"Even if a certain redhead answered the advertisement?" Roland had that silly grin on his face.

"Did she?"

"I'm sorry."

In spite of a wave of disappointment, Sawyer pretended disinterest. "Just as well. I have other things on my mind."

Roland picked up the envelopes. "Are these your responses?"

Sawyer had no idea what to say. "Did Pearl come up with a response for me?"

Roland shook his head. "She seems to think it would be more honest coming from you."

"None of this was my idea. Besides, what would I say? They're expecting a letter from a captain of industry."

"Up and coming industrial magnate."

Sawyer scowled. "Small distinction. You know as well as me that every woman is going to skip right over the 'up and coming' part and see only the rich and powerful part. They'll expect a reply to come on fine stationery embossed with a company name and dictated to a secretary."

Roland's eyebrows lifted. "For a lumberman, you know a lot about how a business office works."

Sawyer had let too much slip out. He tried to look nonchalant. "I've been in one in the past." That wasn't a lie. He'd been in Father's office many times. The secretary always gave him a look of sympathy before Sawyer entered the office and endured Father's wrath over some petty mistake.

"I see."

Though Roland looked skeptical, he didn't ask further questions.

Sawyer turned back to the topic at hand. "I'm not answering these. They'll be gone soon anyway. If you think they need a reply, then you can write."

"Should I answer for you if Fiona writes?"

"No!" Now Roland was jesting with him, but Sawyer was in no mood for it. "How long do I have to put up with this?"

"Until you choose someone or the applications stop trickling in."

"You mean there's no ending date on the ad?"

Roland just shrugged. "It wasn't ever supposed to be published."

He raked a hand through his hair. "What do I do?"

"Wait it out." Roland began stocking some creams and ointments behind the counter.

That was not the answer Sawyer wanted, but he couldn't think of an alternative. "I don't need this now, not with the sawmill ramping up production and the possible hotel purchase. Speaking of the hotel, I'd like your advice."

Roland turned, a jar of cold cream in his hands. "Are

you asking if it's a good opportunity?" He set the jar down. "Well, it's the only one in town, aside from the boardinghouse. That gives it value."

"VanderLeuven's asking too much, considering the place needs work. I haven't seen the rooms, but the dining room and lobby are pretty worn."

"Agreed." Roland looked up as the bell on the front door rang and a customer entered. "What's the question?"

"I plan to offer a lot less than he's asking, but I'll still need investors or a bank loan. Which way should I go?"

"Bringing on an investor could mean an active partner. Be sure you understand his expectations. Or hers." Roland grinned. "Fiona would be a good partner. She must have set aside a good amount during her career."

Roland didn't know that Fiona was strapped for money. Like everyone else, Sawyer included, he must assume her expensive gowns and jewelry meant she was well-off. Now that Sawyer thought about it, she hadn't bought anything new since coming here. Judging from her reaction to his suspicions about Blakeney, she'd lost a bit of money to the criminal.

"That's not the business partner I had in mind." In Sawyer's experience, women did not make good business associates, especially when he was far too attracted to her to maintain any objectivity.

"I was jesting," Roland said with a laugh. He then spent the next hour, between customers, outlining how he'd found—and lost—investors. "Of course you'd be starting with an existing business. That's more than I had."

"Except the receipts aren't good, and the property needs refurbishing. That's where I'm going to need additional finances."

"Anyone in your family able to help?"

Sawyer stiffened. For a second he wondered if Roland knew who he really was, but the man's expression was as open and honest as always. He relaxed.

"No." Nothing could induce him to go crawling to Father for money.

"Then approach the banks. I'd try Saugatuck first. Then Holland."

This would be a risky venture, to be sure, but Sawyer was tired of waiting. He needed to make his mark now, before Father found him. Maybe, in time, he could offer Fiona the kind of security she craved, the kind he could never give her as a mill foreman. He would visit the Saugatuck bank tomorrow morning.

Chapter Eight

Writing a response to the advertisement felt too much like agreeing to marriage with a man Fiona had never met. In contrast, the ad that had brought her to Singapore last August did not require her to write and tout her virtues. That's what had attracted her to it—that and the promise of a *substantial inheritance*, if she remembered the wording correctly.

False!

That had turned out to be a play on words, and she couldn't shake the feeling that this advertisement was exactly the same. Certainly Mr. Stockton could have placed it, but then why put it in the Singapore newspaper, which had a small circulation? He would know that the town had few eligible women available. It also was not the place to search for a wife familiar with social dictates.

Perhaps that's what unsettled her. For all of Fiona's pretensions, she knew very little about proper etiquette for teas and soirees and the such. She had attended many a celebration but had hosted none. A woman who'd grown up in the tenements and now lived in a boardinghouse did not host social events. Well, she'd muddle through somehow. If this advertisement turned out to be genuine.

Fiona placed the pen back in its holder and blotted her note. It took little time to read.

> Dear Sir,
> Please accept my sincere appreciation for and interest in your recent advertisement in the Singapore Sentinel. Though I am loathe to speak of myself, those of my acquaintance can vouch that I possess all the skills requested. Baking is a specialty, and music is my life. I would be honored to meet you.
> Miss Fiona O'Keefe

Hearing movement in the hallway, she folded the note and tucked it into her pocket just before Clara and her band of wives-to-be filed into the writing room. She would bring it to the mercantile later.

"It's time for practice," Clara announced.

Fiona glanced up at the clock. "Indeed it is. Practice your scales, and I will be right with you."

"We don't need to practice scales. We need to practice our songs."

Fiona had been through this argument before. "First you need to learn the notes so they are second nature."

"How are we supposed to match the notes when we can't hear them?" Clara's hands went to her hips. "We need a piano player."

Fiona knew precisely where this was headed. "I'm sorry that my skills don't meet your standards." She managed only the scales while Mrs. Calloway attempted to plunk out the tunes. Neither was anywhere close to Sawyer's ability.

"It's not my standards." Clara pouted and managed to get a couple more of the girls to join her.

Whenever the girls wanted something, they employed this technique.

Well, Fiona was not going to fall for it. "What we have will suffice until the service on Sunday."

"But you know…" Clara's voice trailed off when Mrs. Calloway entered the room with dust rag in hand.

Fiona did know. Mrs. Calloway played the piano as best she could, even though one in three notes was wrong.

"We have no choice," Fiona insisted.

"There's that gentleman." Clara said no more, but her eyes moved toward the doorway.

No one was there.

Fine. Fiona would play along. "What gentleman?"

Clara managed to look surprised. "Why, the one who played for us, of course."

Naturally, they wanted Sawyer to help out. That was not going to happen if Fiona had anything to say about it.

"Why, that would be the perfect solution," Mrs. Calloway crowed. "I've often said I'd gladly hand over the reins, and who better than Mr. Sawyer? Why his playing is the best in the whole area." She swiped her rag over the desktop—and Fiona's fingers. "And he knows your tempo and preferences so well." She leaned close and spoke in what she doubtless thought was a whisper. "He's taken a fancy to you, dear. Don't let this one get away."

As if Fiona had let any man get away! Garrett Decker, the subject of the advertisement that had brought her to Singapore, never gave her a second glance. After vowing he didn't intend to marry at all, he'd fixed his attention on Amanda Porter. Oh, he'd escorted Fiona to supper at the hotel a couple times but never with the slightest bit of genuine interest. Looking back, she suspected he'd either been trying to forget his passion for Amanda or to make the lady jealous. Whatever the reason, the moment Amanda began taking care of Garrett's children, he'd fallen for her. Fiona could never measure up. As for Blakeney, that coward and thief had played to her vulnerabilities better than Sawyer played the piano. Never again.

"Please, Miss O'Keefe," the girls pleaded.

Dinah even clasped her hands together, the knuckles white from her passionate plea. "It'd help us keep tune."

Fiona rubbed the bridge of her nose, where a headache was beginning to form. "All right."

"Thank you. Thank you," came the chorus of squeals.

Fiona rose. "I'll go tell him."

"No need," Mrs. Calloway said as she swept past with her dust rag. "He's waiting in the parlor."

"He's been waiting all this time?" Fiona glared at the young women. "Someone already asked him?"

Each girl shook her head.

Mrs. Calloway chuckled. "No dear, he's paying you a call."

A gentleman caller was a whole other matter, even if it was Sawyer Evans. Considering the girls' unfettered interest in the man, Fiona had taken a second look and found more to admire. He was handsome, honest and manager at the sawmill. She could do worse. In addition, he could be quite pleasant, but he'd made it clear that he had no interest in marrying. The ladies didn't believe it, but Fiona had seen his resolve and how it had strengthened when she mentioned Mary Clare. Sawyer

Evans was no prospect. Then why was he paying her a call? And why this irrational fluttering inside?

Fiona rose and smoothed her skirts. "When exactly did you plan to tell me?"

"When you were ready." Mrs. Calloway's laugh trailed down the hallway.

Sawyer paced the drawing room. What was taking so long? Silly question. Fiona was often late. When he escorted her to their concerts, he arrived a little early to prompt her to hurry her preparations.

There was no concert today. He simply wanted to tell her about buying the hotel. The Saugatuck bank had agreed to lend him a goodly amount at 5 percent interest. To complete the purchase, he needed to talk Mr. VanderLeuven down a bit more on his asking price. The negotiations would be difficult, but Sawyer was sure he could succeed. He'd learned a few techniques in his days at Father's office. Some he wouldn't employ against his worst enemy, but a few were simply good business practice that ensured a fair and equitable outcome.

First, he needed to see more of the property, especially those areas that VanderLeuven had carefully sidestepped during their tour. The man had excuses. The rooms were let. Those rooms hadn't been opened up for the season. Winter had taken its toll on yet another section. That last particularly didn't hold water, since the winter had been mild with little precipitation. In fact, the lack of snowfall might be why the spring rush was slower than normal. Without snow, it was tough to get the logs to the river.

If the spring rush stayed a trickle, then jobs would be slashed and wages cut. Sawyer shook that thought away. It did no good to speculate when he had no solid information. But it did make closing on this hotel deal imperative. He had to sign the papers before the big rush arrived. The heavy influx of logs meant opening the second sawmill and bringing in additional work crews. The hotel would be full. Most workers weren't picky about their lodgings. He could settle them in the best rooms and begin fixing the ones that needed repair. The income would fund the staff needed to operate the place as well as pay for the materials needed to refurbish. Yes, he had to move on this now.

The giggling and not so quiet whispers should have alerted him to impending trouble. Instead, he was so deep in his thoughts that the sudden appearance of the rescued ladies just inside the drawing-room door didn't register for a moment. He stared blankly, wondering why they just waited there whispering to each other behind their hands.

Sawyer swallowed. "Uh, is there anything I can do for you?"

"He speaks like a gentleman," the redhead declared.

From the first time Sawyer saw her, he'd compared her lighter, brassy red hair to Fiona's glorious locks. Surely no one on Earth had hair as brilliant and beautiful as Fiona.

"Must be," Clara said in reply, making no effort to conceal her opinion. "Looks might deceive, but the tongue doesn't."

Sawyer wanted to point out an example of a man whose rough exterior didn't match his cultured speech, but he couldn't think of one. On the other hand, his father appeared the gentleman and most decidedly was not. Yet the man's silver tongue could charm pretty near any lady. If that didn't work, Father's wealth always impressed.

Fiona pushed through the crowd of ladies and stood several feet away, back erect and head held high. "So, you are here."

Why was she irritated with him? He hadn't even said anything yet. He stood. "Good afternoon, Fiona. Mrs. Calloway said she'd fetch you."

"Yes, of course, but—" Fiona stopped midsentence. "Never mind. I'm simply glad to see you. Did you wish to discuss our song choices for tomorrow night?"

"Oh. Right." He felt heat creep up his neck. In all the excitement of securing funding to purchase the hotel, he'd forgotten about their Saturday concert. "I didn't know if you still wanted to sing, it being the night before Easter and all."

"What difference does that make?" Fiona shot the women a scorching look, but only the pale one slipped away. She then propped her hands on her hips. "Don't you ladies have work to do? All the silver must be polished and each dish spotless."

Grumbling set up among the women, who gradually drifted away. Only when the last had gone did Fiona turn her attention back to Sawyer.

"There now. That's better." She swept across the room to the piano. "You accomplished your purpose."

"My purpose?" Sawyer was mystified. Then it occurred to him that Pearl or Roland might have spilled the news of his hotel purchase. "I didn't realize you knew about my efforts."

She snorted. "How could I not know, when they were only too glad to promote it."

"They're promoting it? But I haven't even settled on the purchase price yet."

She stopped leafing through sheet music. "Purchase? What purchase?" Now she looked as mystified as he was. "What are you talking about?"

"Buying the hotel. What are you talking about?"

Her eyes widened, and then a laugh burst from her lips. She covered her mouth with one hand before exclaiming. "You thought—" She stifled yet another outburst. "Oh, my. I was talking about my choir, and you thought I was asking about buying the hotel. Is that what you said?"

He nodded. "The VanderLeuvens have put the hotel up for sale, and I plan to buy it if we can settle on a price."

"You?"

He shouldn't have been surprised at the skepticism in her voice. Fiona thought he hadn't a penny to his name, a perception he'd carefully crafted in order to squirrel away every dime he earned.

"Yes, me." He left it at that and watched her expression change from disbelief to hesitation and back to disbelief.

"You. Sawyer Evans. A saw operator. You have enough money to buy a hotel."

"Yes, I do." It felt good to throw her misperceptions upside down. He didn't need to mention the bank loan. "Once we settle, you're looking at the newest hoteli—" He caught himself just before he threw out *hotelier*, a word that was bound to raise suspicion that this sawmill operator wasn't what he claimed to be. "Hotel owner."

Her utter silence spoke more than words ever could. His news had stunned her. Though a grin wanted to tug up the corners of his mouth, he stuck to business.

"If you weren't talking about my purchase, then what were you talking about?"

That snapped her out of the stunned disbelief. "Oh. About accompanying the choir on Sunday. You did agree to play piano for them. That's what Clara said."

It took mere seconds to process the misunderstanding. "You thought I was here to talk the ladies into asking me to play the piano for your little choir? Don't I have enough to do already between running the sawmill, working out the details of purchasing the hotel and playing concerts with you?"

Red dotted her cheeks even as her back stiffened. "I'll have you know, Sawyer Evans, that my 'little' choir's songs at the Easter Sunday service are not insignificant."

Now *he* felt chagrined. "Of course it's significant. I'm sorry. That came out wrong. But I don't understand. No one asked me to play the piano."

"They didn't?" She spun and stalked to the window. "I cannot believe those women—if you can call them that. Such a childish, ill-conceived, selfish thing to do."

This time Sawyer let the grin curve his lips. Fiona was gorgeous when she was spitting mad—as long as that temper wasn't directed at him. He went to her side, drawn like a moth to flame. "I'll do it, but only if their director wants me to."

She whipped her head around. "Their director?"

"Or is it conductor?"

"No." She drew in a deep breath. "No, director is fine. You care about my opinion?"

"I do. You are the one in charge. Every decision needs to go through you."

Her frown changed to a smile, and the sparkle returned to her eyes. "You're right, of course. It is all my decision. Oh, thank you, Sawyer." She grasped his hands, sending a jolt through him. "Thank you for reminding me."

Sawyer pulled his thoughts away from the softness of her hands to what she'd said. "Then you want me to do it?"

"I suppose it would be all right this one time." She heaved a sigh and smoothed her hair, though it was perfectly in place. "They will be gone on Tuesday anyway."

"You'll miss them."

"No." She looked startled. "Well, maybe a little. But it's more that I'll miss the chance to help them."

"How could you help them more than you already have? You've taught them to sing together. You're encouraging them."

"But they're still going off to some island to marry homesteaders. I don't think they have any idea what that means."

That statement gave Sawyer pause. "And you do?"

"I know what it means to be poor." She turned away from him to stare out the window again. "I know, and I will never go back."

He'd clearly struck the wrong chord. He wouldn't have guessed she came from poverty, if she hadn't just told him. Weren't they an odd pair? He wore ragged clothes to disguise his wealthy upbringing. She wore fine clothing to hide her roots in poverty. If she knew that advertisement pointed to him, she would call it trickery and deceit. But she didn't, and he'd better keep it that way.

Still, he couldn't resist the topic. "Did you see that personal advertisement in last week's *Sentinel*?"

"The one for a wife?" She sniffed. "I don't believe one word of it."

"Why is that?"

"No man who was actually on his way to becoming

a leader of industry would bother to place an advertisement in the Singapore newspaper. It makes no sense."

Sawyer had to agree, but only Fiona had been intelligent enough to recognize it. "Then it must be a joke."

"At others' expense." She crossed her arms. "That is cruel, utterly cruel. If only you knew the desperation some women face. Why those advertisements are their only hope."

It sounded like she was referring to real people. Others or herself? Or perhaps the stranded brides.

"Don't worry about them," he assured her. "They'll soon be on their way to a new life."

"It's not just the ladies headed to Harmony. Louise, Amanda and I came here in answer to an advertisement that proved false. I don't want to see anyone hurt again."

"Like you." The words slipped out before he'd fully thought it through.

"I happen to have fortitude and a talent that pays the bills." Her eyes flashed. "Other women are not so fortunate. We are expected to marry to secure our futures. If we don't and the family can't support us, we must take employment at a pitiful wage. You can afford to buy a hotel. We must pray we earn enough to buy the next meal."

"It's a harsh world."

"One that could get better if influential people would act to solve the problem."

Maybe that's why she'd set her cap on marrying a wealthy man, so she would have the power to enact change. Sawyer not only didn't blame her, he couldn't help but admire her drive to help the plight of others. That's what his father could have done instead of the incessant drive to acquire more. Compared to Father,

Fiona was powerless. She was the sort that his father preyed on.

"You can't help everyone," he said quietly.

"I must help. Somehow. There's no choice."

He had a feeling she wasn't talking about the shipwreck survivors.

Fiona stared out the window without seeing the barren landscape. Sand and tufts of wiry grass filled the space between weathered buildings. It looked the same every day since her arrival. The only difference was the amount of snow and the shape of the drifts.

Today her thoughts drifted far from Singapore to the tenements in New York. Mary Clare had spent seven years in squalor. Only Fiona could give the girl hope of a different future. That meant writing in answer to every promising advertisement for a wife, including the preposterous one in the *Singapore Sentinel*. As soon as Sawyer left, she would bring her letter to the mercantile.

The prospective groom must be Mr. Stockton. Who else could it be? Then why place the advertisement here? He knew Singapore boasted few eligible women. Unless he had seen either her or Louise on one of his infrequent visits and developed a fancy for one of them. Considering the advertisement specified musical affinity, he must be sweet on her! A moment of panic was followed by amazement that a man of his prominence would go to such lengths to secure her interest. He could have stated his case and expected a positive response in return. Perhaps he was reserved by nature, and preferred to handle marriage in the same way he would handle a business deal. Just as well, for she couldn't summon an ounce of affection for the man.

If all this speculation was true, she would thrust

herself into a situation just as unknown as the brides bound for Harmony. The thought gave her pause, and Fiona was not prone to pausing.

"Maybe I can take your mind off things you can't change," Sawyer said.

Fiona jumped at the sound of his voice. She'd forgotten he was there. Then he'd gone and spoken to her exact need. Had he read her mind? Surely not. She searched her memory for what they'd been discussing before her mind wandered. Mary Clare. She had to take care of her niece. Sawyer's comment still made no sense, for she had every intention of changing Mary Clare's plight.

"I will do all in my power," she replied. "Without anyone's assistance." That wasn't quite true. She was about to throw away caution and place her hope in marriage to a man she'd never met.

"I'm sure you will." Sawyer's gaze softened. "You are a strong and capable woman."

She melted into those warm brown eyes. Men often complimented her appearance or her voice, but Sawyer was the first to acknowledge how hard she'd worked to create this life.

He gave her a schoolboy shy smile. "The real reason I called on you today was to ask your advice, but maybe it's not a good time."

"My advice?" Men never, ever asked for her advice on anything more serious than which handkerchief to tuck in a suit pocket. "It's perfectly fine. What did you want to ask me?"

"About the business deal."

Now he had her attention. Sawyer wanted her opinion on business? She could have fallen over from the shock. "What business?"

"The hotel."

She drew in a deep breath. She didn't know much about the hotel business aside from entering a hotel lobby on occasion.

"You're asking me for advice about buying a hotel," she repeated just to make certain. "You do realize that I'm a singer, and the only business I've managed is how to pay for room and board and necessities from the little they pay me." That included her wardrobe, which was small but stylish, created to project an image of prosperity and status.

"You also have a keen eye for potential. I've heard your choir. They sound good—very good—certainly better than I would have imagined in such a short time."

She basked in the compliment.

"And you are familiar with the Astor House…not to be confused with its namesake in New York."

She chuckled, having made the same comparison soon after arriving here. "I'm only familiar with the dining room. I've never stayed there."

"However, you must have stayed in New York City hotels."

She couldn't tell him that she hadn't. She'd only been able to afford a room in boardinghouses. She would never go to a gentleman's hotel room. Ever.

"Why is my experience with hotels so important?" she asked instead.

"Because if I buy the hotel, it will need repairs and renovation."

"Ah." Still not something she was qualified to remark upon.

She took a deep breath and tried to imagine Sawyer running a hotel. He was all wrong for the job. A hotel manager ought to display impeccable manners, speech and attire. Sawyer spoke well for a lumberjack, and his manners were good, but his attire left a great deal to be desired. On the other hand, Singapore's Astor House was rather dilapidated compared to a big city hotel and was located in a lumber town. Maybe he would get more of the workers to stay there if he looked more like them and less like a big city hotel manager.

"Well, it is an opportunity." Her mind tumbled to another thought. "But weren't you just promoted to manage the sawmill?"

"Yes."

"You would leave that?"

"A man can't make his mark under another man's thumb." Surprising passion rang through every word.

Something—or someone—had pushed Sawyer too much. Stockton? As owner, he was the ultimate boss over everyone working at the sawmill. Just like the theater owners had lorded over her. And the Adamsons held the final word where the young brides were concerned. Her mind landed on a brilliant thought.

"Wouldn't the hotel make a wonderful school?"

"A school? Why would you say that?" Sawyer frowned. "The new school building is already taking shape."

Fiona had forgotten about the replacement for the schoolhouse that had burned last November. With the warm winter, the foundation had already been dug and put in place. Soon the floor and walls would rise.

"Not that kind of school," Fiona said. "A boarding school."

Sawyer looked like he was going to laugh but stifled it. After a bit of throat clearing, he managed to choke out, "In Singapore?"

"Why not? Miss O'Keefe's School for Young Ladies." She could see the sign above the door, painted with fancy lettering like they used in the posters advertising her singing engagements in New York.

More coughing issued from Sawyer, and his face had grown red.

Fiona narrowed her gaze. "You think it's a ridiculous idea. Well, I'll have you know that there's a need. Take the girls from the shipwreck, for instance. Being married off to men they've never met."

"Like answering a mail-order advertisement."

Fiona felt her face heat. "At least with an advertisement there's an opportunity to meet the man before making the final decision."

"I see. And what would a boarding school do to improve the ladies' lots?"

Wasn't it just like a man to miss the obvious?

"Why, it would train them so they can better their lives. Didn't I tell you the other day about the pitiful wages paid to working women?"

"How would training improve their lot if owners still refuse to pay more?"

"Perhaps they could learn skills to run their own business."

By the expression on Sawyer's face, he found that impossible to believe. "Some women are forced to run their late husband's business, but to choose it?" He shook his head. "Is that what you want, Fiona? To open your own business? I thought you came to Singapore to marry."

The words cut to the quick. She had. She was guilty as charged. A response to that ridiculous advertisement still rested in her pocket. She was willing to tie herself to Mr. Stockton or whoever wrote that ad without knowing a thing about him.

"Sometimes women are forced to make that choice for the sake of others." Such as Mary Clare. "My school would give women hope that they could earn enough to live comfortably on their own."

He looked ready to dispute her yet again but changed his mind. "It's a worthy cause but not the sort of business I am qualified to run." His jaw worked. "Do I understand that you would be competing with me to acquire the hotel?"

The glorious dream evaporated. She could not afford to rent a room, least of all buy an entire hotel.

"No," she said softly. "I will not stand in the way of your purchase."

His smile returned, but her heart sank. Like most women, she must rely on the hope of marrying well to secure her future.

Chapter Nine

In the light of day, the hotel looked a lot more dilapidated than it did in the evenings when lamplight hid many of the defects. Sawyer descended the staircase the next day, having surveyed several of the guest rooms. Many of the furnishings needed to be replaced. That would be costly enough, but he'd seen evidence of leaks. Repairing the roof and the damage within could bankrupt him before he even started. VanderLeuven would not have shown him the worst rooms, so Sawyer had to surmise that those were uninhabitable.

"She's a fine place." The owner smoothed a hand over the banister. "With the right man at the helm—such as yourself—she'll turn a handsome profit."

The hotel needed more than a firm hand to turn it around. It needed a serious investment in order to return to profitability. Sawyer didn't have the kind of money that could turn Astor House into a hotel worthy of its namesake in New York. Not at the current asking price.

He quickly did the calculation in his head. The amount promised by the Saugatuck bank—ensured only because Sawyer was now manager of the sawmill—in addition to his savings less the purchase price would only leave enough to make a dent in the refurbishing that needed to take place.

"It'd take a wealthier man than me."

VanderLeuven blanched. "It doesn't take a mountain of money. A bright young man like yourself has the skill and connections to make things happen."

Sawyer was about to protest when he realized that he did have connections. The people he knew and called friends would step in to assist, but Sawyer couldn't afford to hire anyone. Not with those costs. Neither could he ask people to work or supply materials on credit. He could repair the door, recaulk the windows, paint and varnish the wood floors, but it would take forever by himself.

He shook his head. "It's still too much." He named a figure that would give him an allowance for materials.

VanderLeuven sputtered and protested, but came closer to Sawyer's price.

If Sawyer delayed some of the refurnishing or was able to buy some items on credit, he might be able to afford a couple workers. That would get the place in running order in time to take advantage of at least some of the spring rush, not to mention the influx of visitors for the launching of the new schooner this summer. But it wouldn't allow for any new furnishings.

"It's still too much."

"Name a price," VanderLeuven responded, his jowls red.

Sawyer didn't want to get pinned down. He'd already given his preferred price, which had been rejected out of hand. He had a figure in mind, but naming it would give the advantage to VanderLeuven, who could then push him higher.

"I already gave you my bottom line."

VanderLeuven mumbled as he worked figures on the scrap of paper he'd pulled from a pocket.

Sawyer's mind spun with ideas. He could oversee the construction and repairs, but he had no taste or experience when it came to furnishings. He needed someone with a keen sense of color. One face drifted to mind. Fiona. In spite of her penchant for overly bright clothing, she knew what a fine hotel ought to look like. Her backdrop for the nativity play last Christmas had shown proper restraint as well as talent.

Yes, Fiona would be the perfect choice. That meant working together, often very closely. Not an unpleasant thought at all. He'd come to appreciate her spirited conversation. She might even warm to him once she saw his determination to make a success of the place.

VanderLeuven shoved the paper at Sawyer. "This is the lowest I can go. What do you say?"

Sawyer eyed the lobby and main entrance. Heavy velvet drapes blocked what little light drifted through the grimy windows. A little cleaning and redecorating would take care of that, but what would he find when the light was better?

"It's a lot to take on," he said slowly.

"Not for an energetic young man like you."

Sawyer strolled to the front window and pulled aside the thick draperies. Dust sifted down, making him sneeze. The additional light revealed yet more needed repairs. The wallpaper was peeling in places. The ceiling bore the telltale signs of water damage. The porch roof must have pulled away from the main structure, letting in rainwater and snowmelt. It all added up to far more money than he had.

"I can't afford it." Sawyer let the curtain drop and

turned to face VanderLeuven. "It's going to take a lot of money fix up this place."

"Not so much if you do the work yourself," Vander-Leuven whined. "A little paint. A little hammering here and there…"

Sawyer fingered a piece of wallpaper that had curled down to within reach. "New wallpaper and carpets. Roof repairs, new mattresses and bedding, and that's just the beginning."

"Now, there's no need to do all of that right off. Why, you could make the repairs off your profits."

Sawyer ignored the man's wheedling tone. Vander-Leuven was desperate to sell. Perhaps his wife had given him an ultimatum to sell the hotel or run it by himself. She clearly wanted to return to Holland to be near her children's families. She'd talked about nothing else since last week's concert.

"I haven't even mentioned the kitchen." Sawyer shook his head to emphasize his dismay. "Most houses in town have a better cookstove than the one in this kitchen."

"It works just fine." The man's hackles rose. "You haven't turned down any of my food."

Sawyer couldn't counter that without insulting the man, who'd served as cook last Saturday night, or his wife, who cooked the rest of the meals when they couldn't hire on another cook.

"True. But you won't be here. No one else would be able to coax the same quality out of that stove."

The man puffed up. "That might be the case, but I'm saying it's good enough for now. You're wantin' to make everything new right off. That's not the way things go here."

It might not, but it was the way Sawyer intended to begin this venture. Father was wrong about a lot of things but not his philosophy on starting out in a new business—make sure you're the biggest, the newest, and the best.

"You might have a point." Sawyer looked Vander-Leuven in the eye. "But it's not my way. I'll buy the hotel, but not at your price." Finally it was time to name the price Sawyer had settled on before beginning negotiations. This figure took into account the cost of refurbishing the place.

VanderLeuven's eyes rounded. "That's ridiculous! An insult."

Yet after twenty minutes of haggling back and forth, they settled on a price very close to Sawyer's preference and shook on the deal. The papers still had to be drawn, and Sawyer would go into debt, but he was the new owner of Astor House. The idea put a bounce in his step as he headed across town to the mercantile.

Fiona drifted back into his mind as he walked past the boardinghouse. He'd ask her after tonight's concert if she would give him some ideas on furnishings. They could begin with the dining room.

He pushed open the mercantile door, eager to tell Roland his news.

The man looked up from his post at the counter with a grin. "It's here."

"It?" Sawyer searched his memory. "I didn't order anything."

Roland held up a folded piece of paper. "No. *It.* The response you've been waiting for. She delivered it this morning."

"Fiona?" Sawyer strode to the counter.

Roland nodded toward a woman across the store looking over the white goods. Mrs. Calloway.

Sawyer blew out his breath. Mrs. Calloway was the

biggest gossip and matchmaker in Singapore, and he'd just gone and spoken Fiona's name. Now she wouldn't stop until she'd successfully paired them. Even worse, she might put the pieces together and figure out that he was the one who'd placed the advertisement. If so, the news would spread through Singapore like wildfire.

The thought made him want to walk right back out of the store and keep going until he reached Allegan. But he was the new owner of the hotel—or soon would be. He was putting down roots, making his own way, and that meant enduring the matchmaking attempts of the local matrons. Unfortunately, those were bound to increase once they learned he was now a business owner.

He fingered the folded sheet of paper and tucked it into his coat pocket. One thing could quiet all that feminine speculation. If this letter said what he thought it did, he might stand a chance of courting Fiona O'Keefe.

Fiona regretted turning in the letter, but there was no taking it back now. She'd agonized over each revision last night. This morning she nearly tore it up. Before she changed her mind, she handed it to Pearl Decker, who accepted her excuse that she was bringing the sealed letter for a friend. But Pearl must know. Who wouldn't? Fiona's only unmarried friend was Louise, and she'd probably already written a response.

Oh well, it didn't matter. Soon enough Mr. Stockton would have her letter, and then he could decide if she fit his criteria. Since she matched the advertised list of requirements precisely, he must have written the advertisement with her in mind. She should be pleased. Instead, she felt like a weight was suspended over her head.

"Are we going to practice or not?" Clara asked.

"There's other things I'd rather do," added Violet with a giggle.

The other ladies joined in.

"All right. Attention!" Fiona had to shout and then clap her hands. "From the beginning."

But she'd lost them. Half the women didn't begin on the proper beat. The rest gave a halfhearted off-key effort.

"Stop!" Fiona shouted with a wave of her arms. "That was awful."

The women stared at her sullenly.

"You can do better than that. Remember, this is for Easter Sunday."

"In some backward little town," snorted Violet.

"That's enough," Fiona snapped. "Singapore has just as much right to beautiful music as Chicago or New York."

Eyes rolled and whispers were exchanged.

Fiona's temper strained. "Fine. If you want to act like that, then we're going to be here all day and night. I don't care how long it takes. We're going to practice until you get it right."

Naturally, protests rained down on her.

"I wanted to go to the concert," moaned Violet.

"I got me a beau," added Linore.

"Aren't you singing tonight?" pointed out the plain one with the brown hair whose name Fiona could never recall.

That reminder only made her angrier. Yes, she was supposed to give a concert tonight, and these ladies were ruining even that.

"If you don't get our songs right, there won't be a concert."

More protests rained down.

Clara shook her head. "But everyone's expectin' you."

"Everyone is expecting beautiful music from you," Fiona shot back. "From all of you. This isn't just for the people of Singapore, you're singing for the Lord."

The girls quieted and resumed their positions.

Fiona was impressed. At least the mention of God could get them focused. She'd have to remember that in the morning. "Now," she said with a smile. "Let's go through these from the beginning."

The remainder of the practice went smoothly. Apparently the ladies knew the songs and could sing their parts perfectly when their unruly temperaments didn't get in the way. Only Mr. Adamson or reminding them that they served God could get them in order.

After Fiona dismissed them, she spent a few minutes putting her music in order for the morning.

"Miss O'Keefe?" The shy voice pulled Fiona from her work.

"Dinah. What is it?"

The petite blonde looked distressed.

Fiona's thoughts immediately went to tomorrow morning's singing. "Is there something wrong? Does your throat hurt?"

"No." Dinah blushed. "There ain't nothin' wrong with me. Leastways, not that way. I was wondering about something." Her blushes grew more furious.

"About what?"

"You're an experienced woman."

Fiona didn't like the sound of that. "I am an experienced singer."

Dinah face was as red as a hot stove. "That's what I meant."

Fiona suspected it wasn't.

Dinah drew a deep breath. "I was wondering what you'd do if there was somethin' you really wanted."

Fiona relaxed. The poor girl had finally realized what a foolhardy thing she'd agreed to do and wanted out. She led the girl to the sofa. Once seated, she took Dinah's hands and tried to look in her eyes, but Dinah kept her gaze averted.

"If you really want something, you need to pursue it with all your heart."

Dinah's face scrunched with puzzlement. "But what if it ain't possible? What if…bad things happen if I do what I want?"

Fiona squeezed the girl's hands. "Sometimes the most important things we do come with a measure of risk. We must proceed with courage, trusting in the Lord that all will work out in the end."

"Will it?" Dinah raised scared, wistful eyes to look at her. "Or will things be worse?"

Fiona couldn't promise that. She could only give advice. "Ask yourself how you'd feel if you never attempted to follow your dream. That will tell you what you need to do."

Understanding dawned, and Dinah's expression gradually eased until a smile darted across her lips. "Oh! Thank you, Miss O'Keefe. Now I know what I gotta do."

Fiona wanted to tell her that she would be welcome here, but she couldn't. She had no authority at the boardinghouse and no means to help Dinah. Her idea of a boarding school was just a dream. Employment for women was scarce in Singapore. At least reputable employment.

"You do understand the consequences of going astray," Fiona cautioned. "Be sure to guard your reputation above all."

"Oh, yes, ma'am. I understand." Dinah hopped up as if nothing had ever troubled her and bounded from the room, giving Fiona one last smile before she disappeared. "I know now that everything'll work out just fine."

Fiona puzzled over Dinah's quick turnabout from gloom to happiness. Choosing not to go to Harmony would be a difficult route, yet the girl hadn't asked one question about how to do it. Surely Dinah didn't already have another means to avoid going to Harmony. Or did she?

Sawyer stopped at every table in the dining room after the concert to make sure the patrons were pleased and to ask what needed to be changed. The food wasn't up to its usual standards tonight. Several remarked on that. The linens could be cleaner. The room brighter. Sawyer anticipated each criticism and noted them.

Every concern would be addressed under his administration. The hotel would sparkle. The food would melt in the guests' mouths like, well, like Fiona's pastries.

He eyed Fiona, who chatted with Amanda and Garrett Decker while they waited for Mrs. VanderLeuven to bring out their meals. Did he dare ask if Fiona would cook at the hotel? She was an unlikely cook. True, she could bake delicious breads and confections, but to work in a hot kitchen day in and day out didn't fit the image of elegance that she portrayed. No, she seemed more suited for high society, which was doubtless why Pearl had worded that advertisement the way she did.

He patted his pocket where Fiona's letter was tucked away. He'd read it a dozen times but didn't know how to take it.

Dear Sir,
I would be honored for you to consider me for your wife. Perhaps you have heard of my musi-

cal talent, which graced the finest stages in New York City. On the other hand, you might have caught rumors about my baking prowess. I assure you, the comments were not exaggerated. For years I walked among the highest of society and know full well the rigors that a powerful businessman's wife must face with grace and elegance. Our first meeting will assure you of my qualifications. I await word of that meeting with the deepest anticipation.

Miss Fiona O'Keefe

Clearly she believed the potential bridegroom either lived in Singapore or had visited it recently enough to have heard of her. Most likely she, like many other women, believed the advertisement was for Mr. Stockton. The entrepreneur would be furious if he heard those rumors.

Fiona's letter left no room for him. She expected a powerful businessman, not one beginning a new venture in debt.

"Here you go, Sawyer," Mrs. VanderLeuven puffed as she carried two heaping plates of roast turkey and potatoes to an empty table.

Thick gravy smothered the whole thing and made Sawyer's mouth water. It had been a long time since he last ate. Breakfast, if he recalled correctly. He followed the hotel proprietress to the table and waved at Fiona to join him.

"No bother," Mrs. VanderLeuven said. "I can take her plate over to the Deckers' table."

That would not help his plan. He needed to converse with Fiona, not watch her eat with a recently married couple.

"No, she's headed this way," he reported with relief.

Mrs. VanderLeuven set down the plate and left to wait on another table ready to order some of her pecan pie.

"Well, that was interesting," Fiona said as she sat down. "Garrett Decker said that Mr. Stockton asked them to wait before painting the name of the new schooner on the hull. I wonder why." She settled back with a smug look and then proceeded to answer her own question. "Perhaps he's waiting because he hopes to name it after someone."

"I thought he was naming it after himself."

"Perhaps he has another person in mind."

Sawyer placed the napkin on his lap, all too aware who she thought that person should be. She didn't know he was the object of the advertisement and had read her letter. Though tempted to reveal the truth, the results could prove disastrous. She expected a wealthy businessman, not an indebted hotel owner. In her place, he would be furious that he'd been misled. Best pretend he didn't understand what she meant.

"Like who?" He tried his best to look innocent. "He's never mentioned any family."

"Perhaps he expects a new addition."

"A new grandchild? I didn't realize he and his late wife had children."

Fiona laughed. "Silly me, I should never have expected you to understand." She leaned close and lowered her voice. "Most people think Mr. Stockton is the one who placed the advertisement for a bride in the newspaper."

Sawyer tried not to choke. It was just as he thought, but the idea of her pursuing Stockton rubbed him the wrong way. That extra sparkle in her eye tonight wasn't because she enjoyed being with him. She thought Stockton would marry her. He clenched his fists under the table. This was too much like what Julia had done. When he'd enlisted in the war effort, she had shifted her affection to a man with even greater prospects than his.

"I suppose he can name his ship whatever he wants," he muttered.

"Well, of course he can, and why not name it after someone special?" Her cheeks glowed, and her eyes sparkled even brighter than earlier that evening.

Sawyer ground his teeth. She was excited about the future, but that future again centered on someone wealthy. Like Julia, Fiona thought the man beside her was not good enough. Never mind that he'd told Fiona he wasn't ready to marry. She could show a man a little consideration.

"Will you say grace?" she asked, her gaze wide and innocent.

Sawyer felt a twinge of guilt. She didn't know. She'd come to Singapore to marry and was simply following through on that desire. She didn't know he was the one behind the advertisement, not Stockton. She'd simply leaped to conclusions like everyone else, and he'd let disappointment cloud his reactions.

"All right."

She smiled, all artifice gone, and squeezed his hand. "Thank you."

For a moment he could see the real Fiona, the one she tried so desperately to hide. Deep down, she had the joy of a little girl visiting her first circus. Wide-eyed and eager. That's the Fiona that tugged so deeply on his heart. That's the one he wished would show herself all the time.

"You're beautiful," he murmured.

She started, and the little girl vanished again behind a wall of caution.

"Why, thank you." Yet she said it the way she would to any stranger who'd dare unleash such a compliment, as if she didn't believe it was true.

"You truly are. Not the dresses or the jewelry or the way you do your hair. You."

Her eyes widened for just an instant before she shuttered them. "My, I'm famished. Do say the blessing on our meal."

After Sawyer finished praying over their supper, the moment was gone. They ate and talked about insignificant things like small changes to make in each song.

When she finished, he gave her his news.

He leaned close so only she could hear him. "Mr. VanderLeuven and I have come to agreement. Before too long, I will own this property."

She dropped her fork with a clatter. "You will?"

Clearly she hadn't expected him to be able to purchase the hotel.

"Between my savings and the bank loan, I can afford it. But I will need help getting it ready."

"Ready?" She looked around the room. "It's already open."

"Not the way I want my hotel to run. It needs refurbishing."

She sucked in her breath and then frowned. "If it took a loan to buy the place, how are you going to afford to refurnish it?"

"I calculated in those expenses when seeking funding."

She gave him a peculiar look, as if he'd just said something odd, but he'd only explained what he'd done. Then it struck him. He'd spoken like his father, like an insider to the business world, not like a lumberman and sawmill operator. But there was no way to take it back.

He forced a smile and glossed right past the mistake. "I can make a lot of the repairs myself, but I couldn't pick out rugs and draperies that match. You have a good eye for color. Will you help?"

The plea successfully shifted her attention from his finances.

Her eyes sparkled again. "Are you offering me employment, Mr. Evans?"

He coughed. He hadn't planned to pay her. "Mister? I thought we were on a first-name basis after all the concerts we've done together."

That coy smile returned. "Sawyer, then."

"Actually, it's Paul."

"Paul?" Her eyes widened.

What had possessed him to say that? With a little effort, anyone could now trace him to his father, Winslow Evanston.

He leaned close and whispered. "Just between us. All right? Wouldn't want any of the guys at the mill to find out."

Her tight smile told him she both understood and appreciated the confidence. "All right, *Sawyer.* But my question still stands. Are you hiring me?"

He'd hoped to gain her assistance without charge. "It's not a position, more of an opinion."

"I see."

Her frown told him she saw nothing except that he wasn't willing to pay. Once again he wondered how dire her financial circumstances were.

"I could offer a small commission," he told her, hoping he could cut expenses short in another area in order to afford it.

Fiona's smile blossomed. "Why of course. I would

be delighted to offer my assistance." Her smile faded. "Will it be soon?"

For a moment he wondered why the rush. Then he remembered. "You expect your niece to arrive any day now?"

She stiffened, and her color heightened. "Yes, of course."

But that wasn't her real concern. Over the years, Sawyer had learned to read the unspoken message in a woman's reactions. She wasn't thinking of her niece at all. She expected a response from Stockton. Again, he considered revealing the truth, but that would only make her angry.

"All right," he said slowly. "Shall we meet Monday after the mill closes?" He hoped a rush of logs didn't arrive tomorrow, or they'd be running the mill around the clock.

"That would—" Fiona stopped abruptly as her gaze rose to look over his shoulder. "Dinah, what are you doing here?"

Dinah? Sawyer turned to see the blonde from the shipwreck.

She blushed furiously. "I was hopin' to speak to you, Mr. Evans."

"All right." Sawyer glanced at Fiona, who did not look pleased. "What's bothering you?"

"Oh, nothin's botherin' me," Dinah said with a gasp, "'cept I can't get you off a my mind. I'm in love with you, Mr. Evans, and I has to tell you. Miss Fiona said so."

Fiona choked and coughed on the tea she'd been sipping.

Sawyer felt like he couldn't draw a breath. The girl was in love with him? Why, she couldn't be more than seventeen, more than ten years his junior. This must be the infatuation of youth, but how did a man disappoint a girl without crushing her? He glanced again at Fiona, hoping for a clue as to what to say. Her taut expression gave him no ideas. All it told him was that she'd be furious if he said the wrong thing.

Sawyer turned back to the girl and cleared his throat. "I'm, well, flattered that you would consider—"

Before he could get to the part where he let her down gently, the girl threw her arms around his neck and began sobbing hysterically.

Sawyer froze. What was he supposed to do?

"Now, there's no need for tears," he said awkwardly.

"But I can't do it," the girl said between sobs. "Not now. Not after what you said."

Can't do what? What had he said? Sawyer scoured his memory. He hadn't said much of anything to the girls. He couldn't recall being alone with Dinah for one moment.

"I, uh," he stammered.

Fiona pushed away from the table, her eyes blazing with fury. She threw her napkin on the table and stormed away.

"Fiona!" He extricated himself from Dinah's arms and stood, intending to chase after the woman he loved.

The girl's sobs grew louder. "You don't like me."

Everyone in the dining room stared at him, and not one look was friendly.

Chapter Ten

"It's all a big mistake." Sawyer had managed to shake Dinah and catch up to Fiona, but the songstress was doing her best to outpace him en route to the boardinghouse.

"It's a mistake all right. She is *engaged*." Fiona veered to the right.

Sawyer had to step off the boardwalk and into the sand, slowing his pace. "Believe me, I know that. I have no idea what she's talking about. I never said anything that would lead her to think I had feelings for her. Why, you were in the room whenever she was present and heard every word."

Fiona whirled to face him. Light from nearby cabin windows illuminated her anger. "I left the parlor, if you will recall. Or maybe you were too preoccupied playing songs and soaking in the ladies' attention to notice. Or just one lady in particular, whom you treated cruelly tonight."

"If you hadn't stormed out of the hotel, you would have heard me apologize for giving her a false impression."

"And then you left her."

"In the care of Louise Smythe, who was listening to the concert from the lobby." He'd done everything he could. Surely Fiona would forgive him.

"Men!" Instead of accepting his explanation, Fiona turned her back on him and resumed her torrid pace.

This was too much like the fits Julia used to throw, except in that case, he *was* engaged to her. Moreover, her fits of temper hid the fact that her eye had wandered. He had remained true. She broke the engagement and wed another. His relationship with Fiona was entirely different, and she had no reason to get upset over a girl's infatuation with him.

He made up the distance between them by the time she reached the boardinghouse steps. There she slowed just enough for him to catch her attention.

"We are not engaged," he pointed out.

She met his gaze. "We certainly are not."

"Then you shouldn't care which ladies are interested in me."

Her shoulders stiffened. "Is that what you think? That I'm jealous?" Her laugh sounded forced. "I simply care about the reputation of a defenseless and innocent seventeen-year-old girl."

So Dinah was just seventeen. That made the difference between them a dozen years. More importantly, Fiona's reaction was far too pronounced to be explained away by the excuse she'd offered. Perhaps she was the tiniest bit jealous after all.

"Then you're saying that you think the worst of me," he pointed out, "even though we've known each other for months, and you've known her just a few days."

"I know men," she huffed, arms crossed.

"That's not fair." Her statement saddened him, for

it meant she'd suffered at the hands of men. "This isn't about Dinah, is it?"

She spun away from him but held on to the railing a bit too tightly for someone completely in control of her emotions. "What do you know?"

"Nothing. I can only say how sorry I am for what you went through. I promise I've done nothing to encourage Dinah. In fact, I would like your help finding a way to discourage her."

Fiona's shoulders trembled ever so slightly. "You would?"

"I'm at a loss. I had no idea I'd inspired such thoughts."

"Even though she hangs beside you when you play piano for the choir practices?"

"I should have realized, but it never occurred to me. You told me they're engaged. She's so young. Why would she give someone my age a second look?"

"Because you're handsome."

Fiona's whispered words sent warmth through him nearly to the tips of his frozen fingers. It was the most she'd ever admitted to him.

"And she's met you." Fiona finally looked at him. "She's never met the man she's to marry. She knows almost nothing about him except his hair color and age. Apparently the Adamsons matched the couples by their hair color."

Sawyer was appalled. "Why would anyone agree to such a thing?"

"Because they have little choice." The passion rose in her. "That's what I've been trying to tell you. They can't earn a living wage, even working sixteen hours a day at the shirtwaist factory. They're orphaned and have no inheritance or family. Only the poorest of men would consider marrying them. In Harmony, they envision the sort of life they read about in storybooks, with a house and a family to call their own. Dreams are powerful, Sawyer, and they aren't exclusive to men."

He felt like a fool, for he'd never once considered what a woman might dream about beyond marrying a handsome and wealthy man. Fiona's dreams were deeper. Moreover, she had revealed her cherished dream to him—to provide schooling so women could rise above their circumstances—and he had dismissed it. He'd been too enamored of his own vision to fully consider hers.

"Thus, your school."

"My school."

"I wish I had the means to provide it." Guilt bit into him, for he *could* have the means. He simply wouldn't accept the terms that came along with the money. Though he sympathized with her and the plight of the stranded ladies, he couldn't throw his future away on a losing proposition, for a boarding school for ladies established here in Singapore had no chance of attracting students. Her insistence on helping the indigent meant those students who would attend couldn't pay a cent toward their tuition. Only the wealthiest philanthropists could make such a dream reality. The wealth Sawyer knew did not come with any philanthropy attached. His father would rather burn a mountain of cash than invest it in a profitless venture. "You do realize it wouldn't support itself unless the students can pay."

She turned her face from him. "Of course."

But she didn't. He could hear it in the tone of her voice.

"I wish I had the sort of money it would take to open a school for the poor."

Fiona sighed. "I shouldn't have said anything. I know

you're just a sawmill worker. It'll take everything you have to redo the hotel. I wish you well, Sawyer."

That sounded too much like farewell, especially with the resignation in her voice. Desperation seized him. This couldn't be the end. Not now, when he had her letter in hand and a chance to prove himself worthy of her.

"We will still see each other." He had to remind her of that. "You agreed to help me select furnishings, and once I own the hotel I will hire you for the Saturday concerts."

A faint smile touched her lips for a moment before fading. "After your renovations are done."

"Yes." He should have realized she would figure out the inevitable delay. A thought occurred to him. "Those renovations will begin with the dining room so it can open first." The income from meals for the mill workers would help fund the rest of the repairs. "Let's come up with design ideas for that room on Monday. The mill might run late, so let's get together a little later, say around eight o'clock? We can meet at the hotel and discuss how to transform the dining room into an elegant room worthy of the finest hotels in New York."

The brief smile told him he hadn't succeeded in cheering her.

"A fine idea." She looked toward the parlor with its glowing windows. "I should get indoors. I want to be there when Louise and Dinah arrive."

The words proved where her loyalties lay.

Fiona's choir sang beautifully at Easter Sunday service, no thanks to her. She couldn't keep her mind on the music. Thankfully, they had rehearsed so much that the girls knew the songs by heart.

Fiona's heart ached—not because she believed Sawyer had any attachment to Dinah. His explanation swept that idea away. No, she could not believe he would in one breath condemn her idea as impractical and the next say he intended to make the hotel into something that would rival its grand namesake in New York. *That* was impractical. What visitor to a sawmill town could afford a grand hotel?

Only Mr. Stockton. And that got her to thinking about her letter and the step she was about to take. With Mary Clare due to arrive any day, she had no choice but to move forward with her plan and hope that this time the groom would select her for his bride. Marriage would solve all the problems she faced. Then why was she so despondent? Why had she hoped Sawyer would build on his statement that he found her beautiful by then declaring some sort of affection for her? A hotel owner was a great deal different from a saw operator. She could convince him to scale back his grandiose plans to something more fitting for Singapore.

She had tried to provoke him into saying something with all that talk about the naming of Stockton's ship, but Sawyer had just sat there like a fool. She'd given him the opportunity. He hadn't seized it.

Fiona couldn't wait any longer. Her niece needed a home. Fiona had almost no money left. She must marry as soon as possible. There was no other choice.

"This is for you, Maeve," Fiona whispered.

She would do anything for her late sister, who had suffered terribly, first at the hands of a violent husband who thankfully disappeared when she birthed a girl and then from the consumption that took her life. Every day the family lived in fear that Mary Clare's father would return. He'd appeared at the burial but vanished again after Ma upbraided him. Still, he could return at any moment. Lillibeth had promised both Maeve and Fiona never to give the girl to him, but each day brought a rush of fear that Fiona only managed to push down by entrusting Mary Clare to God.

She needed a husband now. As much as she wished it could be Sawyer, she couldn't wait until he was ready.

When Mr. Stockton appeared in the back of the church at the end of the service, every female eye had turned his way. He'd nodded curtly and left.

Peculiar. He hadn't attended the entire service but had arrived only long enough to scan the congregation and leave. It was as if he was looking for someone. Her? Then why not wait for her or greet her? Unless he preferred to wait until a more private moment. A prominent businessman couldn't afford idle rumors. That must be it. He would probably pay a call later that day.

Easter dinner with its smoked ham and buttery rolls, preserved green beans and almond cake should have been a delight, but Fiona could barely eat a few mouthfuls. She dreaded hearing a knock on the door. She'd hoped Sawyer would join them, but Mrs. Calloway said he'd told her he was spending the day at the hotel. A knock could only be Mr. Stockton. Fiona would be forced to face an unpalatable marriage.

"Are you feeling poorly?" Mrs. Calloway asked, pressing a hand to Fiona's forehead right in the middle of the meal. "No fever, praise God."

"I'm all right, simply preoccupied."

"With what? It's a day for rejoicing that the Lord is risen."

Joyful affirmations greeted the boardinghouse proprietress's proclamation. Fiona smiled, but her mind was far away. She couldn't bear the wait. How she wished she was at the hotel talking over designs with Sawyer.

She set down her napkin and was about to excuse herself when the ladies in her choir began to praise her teaching. She couldn't very well leave.

Perhaps that was for the best. She should focus on Mary Clare's needs, not on feelings that Sawyer Evans didn't have in return. He'd made it perfectly clear that he did not want to marry. She needed to forget him and the emotions that bubbled to the surface whenever she was near him.

She would resign herself to her fate and wait for Stockton to call on her. The remainder of that afternoon and evening she lingered in the parlor. Perhaps Stockton hadn't received her letter or hadn't had time to read it. The thought buoyed her for a moment until she realized he would inevitably read it, sealing her fate. She tried to read but couldn't focus her attention. She paced to the window and back a dozen times. Bored, she sang, but that only made her miss Sawyer. Once married, she wouldn't ever sing again. A husband like Mr. Stockton wouldn't want her to spend any time around a handsome man like Sawyer. Her heart ached. If only...

The following morning, she awoke with greater resolve. It was best to get things settled as soon as possible, before her heart hurt even more and before her niece arrived. She wandered to the hotel, where she spoke with Mrs. VanderLeuven. Sawyer was working at the sawmill, and Mr. Stockton had gone to the shipbuilding site to discuss the progress on the schooner with Garrett Decker.

Fiona chided herself. Naturally, both men would attend to business.

By late that afternoon, she could bear the wait no longer. The moment school ended, and the children streamed past on their way home, she headed for the church building, which was used as a schoolhouse until the new school building was finished. Pearl Decker, the teacher, would know if her letter had been delivered. No small part of her hoped it hadn't, but that was her foolish side. Mary Clare needed a good home that could provide anything she ever needed or wanted. It could be years before Sawyer made a profit at the hotel.

Fiona knocked on the door frame, though only Pearl was left in the building. The schoolteacher was seated at her desk, making notations in a book. Probably marking the children's grades. Fiona hesitated, but Pearl waved her into the room.

"I'll be just a moment."

"Take your time." Fiona noted the pile of slates, which could use a good cleaning. Spotting a rag and pail of water, she dampened the rag and began wiping them down.

"You don't need to do that," Pearl said. "The Bailey brothers were supposed to wipe them."

"They didn't do a very good job."

Pearl laughed. "They weren't here today. Either Easter dinner didn't settle well or they came down with a case of chore fever."

Fiona chuckled, recalling the times she had pleaded a sore throat to get out of an onerous chore. Her mama didn't stand for that. If there wasn't a fever, a child was well enough to do chores.

"Perhaps they're really sick."

A smile tugged at Pearl's lips as she shut the grade book. "Every time it's their turn to clean the slates?"

"Oh, it's a recurring illness, then."

"Very much so." Pearl joined her and dampened another rag. "What brings you here today? I suspect it wasn't to clean slates."

"I wondered if the letter I gave you reached the gentleman in question." Fiona couldn't quite bring herself to call him a groom or even a suitor. Not yet.

Pearl's grin was almost as infectious as Roland's. "It did, to my knowledge. I gave it to Roland, who would have ensured it was delivered to the man who placed the advertisement."

Fiona slowly let out her breath. Then Mr. Stockton had her letter. The next question was even more difficult. "Do you know if he replied to anyone?"

"You can check for incoming mail addressed to you at the mercantile."

"I did already. I wondered if he wrote anyone else."

"I can't divulge what others have received even if I knew. Correspondence must be private."

Too often, from her experience in New York, it wasn't. Anything that arrived at the theater was opened by the house manager. At the boardinghouse, the proprietress often opened the mail, claiming it was her right as owner. Fiona had hoped to hear that Mr. Stockton had written to someone else. It wouldn't help her make a home for Mary Clare, but it would ease the pain in her heart.

She felt uncharacteristically vulnerable. Her funds had dwindled to the point that she would have to beg Mrs. Calloway to let her work off her room and board. And then, with her niece's imminent arrival… "I don't know how I will make ends meet."

Pearl enveloped her in an embrace. "If it's any consolation, I believe you have a fine chance of attracting his undivided attention."

Fiona should be glad, but she struggled to muster a thank you. "Now if he would just pay a call." At Pearl's puzzled expression, she added, "Or write. Anything to end this suspense."

"I'm sure you'll hear from him soon."

That reassurance only made the pain worse. Too soon she would step into a marriage as barren of love as the ones facing the ladies headed to Harmony.

All day Sawyer looked forward to his meeting with Fiona. In the morning, Stockton breezed through the sawmill listening to Garrett Decker's report. When Sawyer was introduced as the new foreman of mill operations, the man peered at him so long that Sawyer began to worry that he'd been recognized. After all, Stockton could easily have run into Father in Chicago. When Stockton finally moved on without comment, Sawyer breathed easier.

The rest of the day dragged but passed without incident. Just before seven o'clock, Mrs. VanderLeuven showed him into the empty dining room.

Sawyer was surprised. "No diners tonight?"

"The only guest is Mr. Stockton, and he takes his meals in his room," Mrs. VanderLeuven said with a harrumph. "No one else came by. Probably because it's the day after Easter."

Sawyer hadn't considered that—or the imposition he'd put on the VanderLeuvens. "Thank you for staying open for me. I'd love some of whatever dessert you prepared today."

That brightened the hotel owner's outlook, and she bustled off toward the kitchen. "Will Miss O'Keefe be wantin' any?"

He didn't know, but he was hungry enough to eat both if necessary. "Bring two."

The woman whistled a tune as she disappeared into the kitchen.

A moment later, the front door opened with a gust

of wind. It had increased steadily all day until it was now blowing a gale.

Sawyer helped Fiona from her cloak. "Blustery day."

"Too blustery."

She was clearly cross about something. Sawyer need only wait, and Fiona would tell him why. Sure enough, before Mrs. VanderLeuven reappeared with dessert, she noted how the weather would likely cause yet another delay of the ship that would take the Adamsons and their six charges to the community of Harmony.

"They are still here for who knows how long."

"That must be a boon to the Calloways' business," Sawyer offered.

Her look told him that was not the case. "They aren't *paying* guests. They lost everything in the shipwreck."

"I didn't think about that."

Fiona's look told him she wasn't surprised. "That means we're condemned to enjoy their company even longer."

Condemned was a harsh word. "Why does their presence bother you?"

The direct question drew a bit of a gasp, followed by yet another look that labeled him as a fool. "You, of all people, should know."

She was jealous. In the two days that followed Dinah's enraptured announcement, Fiona had been cross and out of sorts. Maybe the beautiful redhead did feel something for him. It would go nowhere, though, as long as she thought he liked the girl.

"I assure you that I have no interest in her." He worked hard not to smile. "My sights are set on a beautiful, spirited woman, not a girl."

"Oh?" That had caught her attention. "Anyone I know?" Color flooded her cheeks, and she uncharacteristically averted her gaze before looking up again with what appeared to be a hopeful expression.

Sawyer's heart pounded. Was he reading her correctly? He'd been wrong about Julia. He would be more cautious with Fiona. "I'm certain you do."

"Oh." Her lips curved downward. "Louise?"

Sawyer was tempted to tease her, but she seemed uncharacteristically vulnerable. "I wouldn't ever consider her spirited. More like reserved."

Fiona brightened. "Yes, she is. Very quiet, peaceable and...educated."

"Unlike the lady who interests me?"

Fiona's eyebrow quirked upward. "She's not educated?"

He'd blundered. "No...that's not what I meant. She's educated." But he could feel the embarrassment creeping up his neck. "Well enough."

Her color heightened, making her positively irresistible. Add in the way she drew back, eyes ablaze, and he longed to calm that temper with a kiss. Some men preferred the quiet types. Not Sawyer. Give him a woman with spirit any day. He'd had enough stoic silence from his former fiancée to last a lifetime.

"You think I'm educated *enough*?" She spat out the words. "Or were you referring to someone else? And what qualifies you to judge anyway?"

"Nothing." Sawyer had blundered yet again. "I can't seem to say the right thing. Can you forgive me? I was trying to tell you—"

Mrs. VanderLeuven's ill-timed return broke the moment before he could explain that Fiona was the one whose spirit intrigued and delighted him.

"Here we are, two slices of my apple caramel cake.

Oh!" The woman drew to a halt. "Am I interrupting something?"

"Not at all." Fiona opened her bag and began looking through it.

Sawyer paid for their cake and tried to ignore the delighted gleam in the hotel proprietress's eyes. She clearly hoped not only for a sale, but also for a romance. Sawyer did too—if Fiona could wait for marriage. By his estimation, the hotel business was not good. Every guest in town except Stockton was staying at the boardinghouse. Sawyer was going to have to make some changes to turn the place around.

He set his plate of cake across the table from Fiona and took a seat.

"Are you finished assessing my character?" Fiona asked, her fork hovering over the cake, which she had not yet tasted.

Sawyer's spirits sank even further. He'd upset her with his silly joking. "I could spend a lifetime and never grow tired learning about you."

At first she looked surprised, but then she gave him an odd look. "You speak like someone out of a novel."

Sawyer could kick himself. He'd let down his guard and acted like himself. Better be careful. He responded with a question, the best way to divert attention. "Is that a bad thing?"

Her brow knit, and she picked at the cake. "I wouldn't say it's necessarily a bad thing. More that it's…unexpected."

"I happen to like to read."

"You do?" Again her surprise was evident.

Sawyer was having so much fun that he decided to push it even further. "When I was in school, I even acted in a play."

She stared at him. "I could almost believe I'm seated across from an entirely different man. Aren't you the Sawyer Evans who fells trees and muscles huge logs through the big saws at the mill?"

"The same." He loved this interplay between them. "I'm also the man who accompanies you on piano and violin."

"Though not at the same time." She chuckled.

He laughed. "That did sound like I could play both simultaneously."

"There you go again. Where did you learn such... language?"

He leaned forward, as if to reveal a secret. "My parents taught me English."

"You are impossible."

"Precisely."

She laughed again. "You always manage to lift my spirits. When life seems unfair, you make me smile." She got serious. "Thank you for the cake."

"Thank you in advance for the advice about refurbishing the hotel." His mind turned away from the pleasant time with her and onto business matters. "Let's begin with this room, so it can reopen as soon as possible. What would you recommend for colors, fabrics and furniture?"

"Who do you expect to frequent it?"

A good question. "Locals. Perhaps some from Saugatuck. Those passing through or stopping on their way to Holland."

She nodded slowly. "Consider them and what would make them comfortable."

"I also want to grow."

"That can come later, but Singapore is not a final

destination for most travelers. You must first attract those customers most likely to eat here."

Sawyer leaned back. "Miss Fiona, you have an astonishing head for business."

That brought a smile to her lips. "Perhaps I shall open that boarding school one day after all."

"No doubt you will." Sawyer took a bite of the cake, which was indeed delicious. Back to business, which was much less fun than verbal sparring. "You are just determined enough to make it happen."

"All I need is the funding."

"They didn't pay you well in New York?"

Her gaze averted longer than it took to take another bite of cake. Sawyer waited until she answered.

"Well enough to live but not to build a school."

"Then why leave? Singapore is a little rough for the kind of school you're considering."

"You know what brought me here. Everyone does."

He didn't miss the trace of bitterness in her voice. "What happened? A beautiful woman like you could have captured the attention of any man."

Instead of appreciating the compliment, her jaw tightened. "Do you know what some men think of a woman in my profession?"

Sawyer swallowed hard. He knew all too well. "But that's not you."

"Would that matter to that type of man?"

Sawyer's father leaped to mind. "No. It wouldn't."

"So, I came here."

He still found it mystifying. "Why? To marry a man you'd never met?" It didn't make sense.

After a pause, she answered, "I have responsibilities."

The truth hit him. "Your family. Your niece."

She nodded but said no more.

He covered her hand with his and softened his tone. "Whatever the reason, I'm grateful you came here."

That brought her gaze back to his. "Because you now have someone who shares your love of music?"

"Your voice is beautiful, but I appreciate getting to know you even more."

She flushed and withdrew her hand. Then she fussed with her napkin before meeting his gaze again. "I am grateful for your skill on piano and violin. Our concerts have been…pleasant."

Not the response he'd hoped for.

"But?" he prodded.

She looked at the walls, as if examining the papering or the framed magazine covers that passed as artwork.

"Like I said, I have responsibilities," she repeated. "My niece."

"You plan to take care of her?"

"I will. I must. Surely you understand." She looked at him with such hope that it broke his heart.

He hadn't been mistaken. She needed a husband to help take care of her niece. As much as he wished that man could be him, he couldn't possibly take on a wife and child. Not now. Not with the debt he'd just incurred. It wouldn't be fair to Fiona or her niece. They deserved better.

"We all have responsibilities," he murmured, avoiding her gaze.

She pushed aside the remainder of the cake. "I see. Then you understand that responsibilities sometimes come with certain…requirements." She stood. "Good night, Sawyer. I wish you well with the hotel."

Sawyer shot to his feet. "Forgive me, Fiona. I shouldn't have brought up personal matters."

"That's right. You shouldn't have."

"You came here to help me." His voice actually shook, and he rubbed a hand across his mouth to hide how nervous he was. "I'd still like that help. Please."

Chapter Eleven

Disappointment flooded over Fiona. She'd given Sawyer a chance to step up and help her. He'd not only shied away but had turned the whole conversation back to what he needed from her for his precious hotel. Couldn't he see how desperate she was with Mary Clare soon to arrive? She'd all but told him outright that she needed to marry. The specter of marrying a man she did not know was raising such dread in her that she'd pinned her fading hopes on Sawyer Evans. A lumberjack. A man foolish enough to take on a faded and failing hotel. Even he had rejected her.

"I never meant to upset you," he said, those brown eyes of his as soft as a puppy's.

Her frustration vanished. How could he twist her around his finger so easily? One woebegone look, and she would give him another chance.

This lumberjack had a sensitive side. When he played violin or piano, he sank into the music, eyes closed, oblivious to the world. That's the man who tugged at her heart and made her want to cast aside any hope of wealth in order to be with him. But that wouldn't be fair to Mary Clare.

He stood before her in obvious anguish, thinking he'd ruined their friendship.

She needed more than a friend. She needed a husband, someone who would help her raise the girl she would soon take in as a daughter. Mary Clare needed a father as well as a *mother*.

The word sent a wave of panic through her. She knew nothing about mothering. Oh, she could feed a child and change a diaper, but the really important things didn't come naturally to her. Though she had four younger siblings, she'd stopped her ears to their howls for attention and sang loudly to blot them out. Ma and her older sisters watched over them. Even Lillibeth was better at watching the youngest. After Reginald rubbed coal dust all over the walls while Fiona practiced singing in the other room, Mama stopped leaving any of them in Fiona's care. More than once her mother had shaken her head and declared that Fiona hadn't a mothering bone in her body.

Fiona had taken that as fact and moved forward as a singer.

Now she had to raise a little girl, and she hadn't the slightest idea how. Neither did she have the money. Sawyer had asked for her assistance redesigning the hotel. He would pay. She mustn't cast away much-needed income over a perceived slight.

"I will sketch out my designs for this room tomorrow." She tugged on her gloves. "You may pick them up after supper."

Sawyer visibly relaxed. "Thank you. I appreciate it more than you can know. And I'm sorry I upset you."

She let the last part go unanswered and concentrated on the first as she swept through the lobby. "I could also come up with some ideas for this room. Clean, simple yet tastefully elegant, something to appeal to all guests, no matter their—" She lost her train of thought as Mr. Stockton descended the staircase.

The gentleman caught sight of her and waved her over.

Fiona's heart pounded as she crossed the room. She must make a good impression for Mary Clare's sake. "Mr. Stockton." Her mouth had gone dry. "It's a pleasure to see you again."

"Yes, yes. Enough of that bother. Get me another pillow. I can't sleep without at least three pillows. Make sure they're down, mind you. I don't want to get poked in the neck by a feather."

His demands laid out, he turned without another word and ascended the staircase.

Fiona stared, mouth agape. Mr. Stockton thought she was a maid. A maid! Or a housekeeper. Yes, she had worn a rather plain gown in muted goldenrod, but it had cost a month's wages and had been sewn by the finest seamstress Fiona could hire. In no way did it look like a common housekeeper's dress.

No doubt Sawyer was snickering behind her back. But he couldn't know the worst of it. Stockton had not placed that advertisement with her in mind. No doubt he'd crumpled her letter or was laughing over it. A pillow!

"I'll get it for him," Sawyer said, not a trace of humor in his voice. "You head on home."

The unexpected kindness sent a twinge of guilt through her, followed by a wave of gratitude. Sawyer wasn't laughing at her. He cared. "Thank you. I don't know why—"

He stopped her with an upraised hand. "Perhaps his vision is poor at that range. It's the only excuse I can imagine. Clearly, you are no housekeeper."

She couldn't hold back a smile. Sawyer Evans had a

good heart. "If you have a moment tomorrow evening, we can go over the sketches and discuss future plans."

His shoulders squared even as his expression softened. "I'd like that."

So would she. More than he could know.

Sawyer had never been this nervous, even when he was courting Julia. Then again, both sets of parents had assumed for years that he and Julia would one day marry. Mother had spoken of it often, with a dreamy look in her eyes. Father had stated it as he would any business deal. The Spencers owned a dozen hotels. Father owned railroads. The match would bring the two together into an empire that would one day control America.

Sawyer ruined that by tiring of Father's machinations and enlisting in the war. Unlike other engaged women, Julia hadn't wept or proclaimed undying love at the news. In retrospect, she hadn't given him a great deal of affection at all. She'd never once looked at him the way Pearl looked at Roland or Amanda looked at Garrett. Sawyer dreamed of one day seeing that starry-eyed gaze that told everyone the couple's world began and ended with each other, while still keeping God at the center. He'd even hoped that Fiona would be the one.

At the appointed hour the following day, he paid a call at the boardinghouse and was greeted at the front door by Dinah. She was scrubbed clean with her hair pulled up with a ribbon.

"Good evening, Mr. Evans," she said slowly, enunciating each syllable. "How are you tonight?"

That was rehearsed.

"Fine. I'm here to see Fiona."

Dinah's smile vanished, replaced by a pout. "Don't

you like my new ribbon? A gentleman ought to say somethin' when his gal dresses up special for him."

Saturday night, Sawyer had tried to gently inform her that he was not interested. Apparently his words didn't sink in.

"I don't have a gal."

"'Course you do. You got me." She threaded her arm around his.

He extricated himself. "Is Fiona here? She said to meet her after supper."

Dinah's lower lip stuck out a bit farther. "In the reading room," she said with a huff. She then stomped off muttering, "Men can't see what's right in front of 'em."

Sawyer stifled a smile as he closed the front door and removed his gloves, hat and coat. This time Dinah had gotten the message. He was not interested in anyone but a certain fiery redhead whose letter in response to his advertisement still nestled in a vest pocket near his heart. The advertisement! Maybe Roland was right, and he should write a response to each inquiry. Then Dinah would stop pestering him. Then Fiona would know he was the one seeking a wife—eventually.

That gave him pause. She'd forgiven him. That much was clear, but she hadn't given any indication she liked him as more than a friend. The letter-writing would have to be confined to regrets. Last night she'd been humiliated when Mr. Stockton thought she was a maid. The man must be blind. Fiona was stunning, regal and exquisitely dressed. No man in his right mind would think her anything but a lady. Yet Sawyer had made his own gaffes last night, something he intended to remedy tonight.

"Sawyer!" Fiona swept into the hallway while he was

still making sure his boots were clean. "You're right on time. We just finished supper."

A wonderful aroma of roast beef filled the air. His stomach rumbled. The fare at the hotel dining room hadn't been as tempting.

"Did you get anything to eat?" She led him toward the room set aside for reading and writing letters.

"A little."

Fiona took that answer as a negative. "Mrs. Calloway! Sawyer will eat the leftover roast beef." She vanished into the kitchen and returned moments later with a plate heaped with thick slabs of beef, mashed potatoes and gravy. "Let's go to the dining room. It's more private anyway."

Once there, she extracted silverware and a napkin from the sideboard. She then assembled his place setting as if he were dining at the finest establishment in Chicago.

"Thank you. I didn't expect to be fed."

"Better than the food at the hotel?" Fiona had a twinkle in her eye. "Go ahead. Taste it."

Had she made it? Sawyer hesitated, suddenly awkward. "You're not eating?"

"Already done."

He stared at the plate. The meal smelled delicious, but what if taste didn't measure up to aroma? Best ask a blessing on the food—and on his choice of words. He didn't want to end up walking on tenterhooks the way he had last night.

After praying for God's blessing, he picked up his knife and fork. Fiona watched every move. He cut off a piece of beef. It was so tender he didn't need a knife. After swathing it in potatoes and gravy, he put the whole thing in his mouth. The flavors melted on his tongue. He leaned back in the chair, eyes closed.

"This is the best roast beef I've ever eaten."

She settled into the chair beside him. "It is?"

Her eagerness gave him the answer. He opened his eyes. "You made this?"

"I did. With a little coaching from Mrs. Calloway."

"My." That's all he could think to say. His mouth was watering for another bite. "This is delicious."

Then he dug in, and in no time devoured the entire plate of food. When finished, he leaned back with a satisfied sigh. "That was delicious."

Fiona chuckled. "You didn't need to rush so. I wouldn't have taken it from you." She sobered. "Did you have to compete with your brothers for food?"

Sawyer took a drink of water so he didn't have to answer right away. He only had the one brother, Jamie, who idolized Father. He always had. Sawyer's stepping down gave him the opportunity he'd hungered for since they were boys scrapping over toys and the best seat in the carriage. But food?

"No. I only have one brother, and he's three years younger than me."

"Only one." Fiona said that wistfully. "Any sisters?"

Sawyer wiped his mouth and hands on the napkin and then pushed his empty plate aside. "No. Shall we get down to business?"

"Don't like the personal questions?"

He supposed he deserved that. "They're all right. Do you have brothers and sisters?"

"Many. Both older and younger." She pulled out a sketchbook and opened it to a page marked with a ribbon. "Here are my ideas for the hotel dining room."

Sawyer wondered for only a moment about her brief

answer before the sketch captured his attention. He pulled it close. "You did this between last night and now?"

"Of course."

"And cooked supper?" He ran a finger over the exquisitely detailed drawing. "When did you have the time?"

"The nights and days are long at present."

At present. Once her niece arrived, her time would be occupied. "Since no ships have arrived."

She nodded.

"When do you expect your niece?"

Fiona heaved a sigh. "Lillibeth didn't say."

Lillibeth? Sawyer instantly had visions of a family holed up in the Appalachian Mountains. "Where did you grow up?"

"New York City." Her fierce gaze told him not to ask more personal questions, but he had to know one thing.

"Where did you learn to draw like this?"

All the tension left her. "First from Mr. McCarthy. He lived in the same building. Then the stage designers. At first they thought it peculiar for a singer to ask what they did and how they did it, but they showed me their work and then taught me how to sketch and design rooms."

Though she'd been careful not to say so, he suspected she'd grown up in the tenements. With her Irish name and the few bits she'd told him, she must have come from a deeply impoverished background. That only made her rise in the New York singing world more remarkable. It also explained her defensiveness.

"They might have taught you a thing or two, but you have real talent," he said.

She glowed under the compliment. "Do you like the design?"

He moved the sketchbook a little so the light fell directly on the page. "The furnishings are both functional and elegant without being osten—overblown."

She caught his near blunder with a raised eyebrow. "Ostentatious?"

"I heard someone say it recently." Hopefully she'd believe that.

"Louise. She's always spouting off long words."

Whew. He'd dodged that one. To distract her, he went back to the sketch. "I wonder if the wallpaper is too… frilly for a dining room."

She stiffened. "It's exactly what was used in a tea room frequented by the social elite."

"Ah." Just what he needed to avoid. "But, as you said, I'm not likely to have many of society's elite visit Singapore."

She relaxed and let out a brief laugh. "You're right. I did say that. Perhaps something more reserved."

"I believe Roland has some samples at the mercantile that we can look through. Shall we meet there at six o'clock tomorrow?"

"We?" She brightened even more. "You want to look at them together?"

She wanted to spend time with him. The thought made his pulse accelerate, but he had to keep his head and play the calm businessman. "It'll be faster that way. We can each choose our favorites and then compare in order to come to a decision."

"I'd like that."

The sigh in those words made him look her way. Was that a starry-eyed gaze she'd just given him?

* * *

Fiona spent the next day pondering the mystery that was Sawyer Evans. One moment he overflowed with compliments. The next he held her at arm's length. At times she could almost believe he felt something for her, but then he would make some comment to dash her hopes. If he wasn't so alarmingly handsome and gentlemanly, she could dismiss him out of hand and step into a loveless marriage with no regrets.

A day in the kitchen had distracted her from the looming problem of her charge's imminent arrival and her increasingly impoverished condition with no husband in sight.

Sawyer had lifted her spirits with his confidence in her abilities and tender concern over the way Mr. Stockton had dismissed her the night before. Moreover, she rather enjoyed spending time with him.

He did seem better educated than the average lumberjack or saw operator. He appeared to stick to a strict set of moral standards. From what she'd heard, he never entered one of the saloons and listened intently to the sermons on Sunday. He was always well-groomed, and his Sunday clothes were finer than any she'd seen on another lumberman. Oh, they were old and slightly out of fashion, but the cut was too good for ready-made.

All in all, Sawyer was a solid, upright man. Though Fiona had dreamed of giving her niece the finest tutors and vocal instructors, life in a hotel wouldn't be that bad. More and more, Fiona could picture it. Unfortunately, Sawyer didn't, and that left her waiting for an answer from the man who placed the advertisement, the man she'd once hoped was Mr. Stockton.

At six o'clock, she wandered the displays in the mercantile, waiting for Sawyer. The thought of him stand-

ing next to her perusing samples made her heart beat
a little faster.

"Are you certain I can't help you?" Pearl asked.

Fiona jumped, startled from her daydream. "I'm certain." Then she reconsidered. "Sawyer said that Roland
had some wallpaper samples. Perhaps I could begin
looking at them."

Pearl's eyes widened. "You and Sawyer Evans?"

"For the hotel." Fiona tried to ignore the heat flood-
ing her face. She could not remember the last man she'd
blushed over. A neighborhood boy who brought her a
tired wild daisy? She couldn't let Pearl think she was
sweet on Sawyer. "He hired me to help with the refurbishing."

"Oh. I see."

Fiona didn't miss the trace of disappointment in
Pearl's exclamation.

"Strictly business," Fiona reiterated. "Does Roland
have any samples?"

"Well, I believe he does. Let me go upstairs and ask
him. Tell anyone who inquires that I'll be right back."
She hurried through the back door and upstairs to the
apartment she and her husband shared.

Fiona waited near the counter for her return. None of
the customers appeared eager to purchase anything, but
she did have a good view of the front door. She would
see Sawyer the moment he walked through it.

"Did you see him?" The hushed statement, followed
by giggles, came from behind a nearby display of wa-
terproof raincoats.

Fiona knew the ladies well enough to recognize
Linore's voice. She was probably with Dinah. Doubtless they meant Sawyer, who would soon walk right

into their midst. In fact, the doorbell rattled that very moment, and Sawyer stepped inside.

The giggling increased, followed by fruitless attempts by Dinah to hush her friend.

Fiona had to stop Sawyer before he got to them, or the pleasant evening looking through wallpaper samples would never occur. She abandoned the counter and hurried to greet him.

His smile upon seeing her sent every concern fleeing.

"I got here as soon as I could," he said. "I hope you didn't wait long."

"Not long. Pearl went upstairs to ask Roland about the wallpaper samples. She should be back any moment." Fiona looked behind her, but neither Pearl nor Dinah and Linore were there. "We could discuss table linens while we wait." She guided Sawyer across the store and away from the giggling girls.

Though he didn't look thrilled about going over fabric, he didn't protest. Since the only other customers were workers from the mill, that section of the store was empty.

"Excuse me, Fiona, but I have to tell Tuggman something." Sawyer crossed the store in a few long strides, talked to the mill worker and returned just as Pearl stepped out of the back room, her arms laden with squares of wallpaper. She headed for the counter and set the paper on the end while she tallied Mr. Tuggman's purchases.

"The wallpaper." Fiona headed for the counter, but Sawyer didn't follow. She turned to ask why.

He was frowning, arms crossed and gaze directed across the store. What had upset him now?

She returned. "You've changed your mind?"

"You said you wanted to talk about tablecloths and napkins." His words were just as grumpy as his stance.

"That was only to pass the time. Now that the paper samples are here, we should go through them."

"How long can it take to decide on linens? If I even need new ones. The old linens look fine."

Yes, something had clearly upset him. "You might choose a different quality of fabric."

His frown deepened. "I can't afford to change everything. Not right away."

Fiona's heart sank. His means were as tight as she'd guessed. He must have sunk everything into the hotel. A man like Sawyer wouldn't take on more than he could handle. He wouldn't take on a wife and daughter.

"All right," Sawyer said suddenly. "We can look at the wallpaper now."

Startled from her thoughts, she looked up to see Sawyer already heading across the room. No one was at the counter. Aha. It wasn't that he didn't want to look at wallpaper samples, he didn't want to do so in front of his coworker—now his subordinate since he was manager at the mill. Fiona recalled the way Pearl had brightened when she told her that she was going to look over samples with Sawyer. People made assumptions. Sawyer must have realized that. She should have recognized how awkward this would be for him. As far as she knew, most people weren't aware that he was buying the hotel. If they saw him looking over wallpaper samples with her, they would assume he was courting her.

If only that was possible.

When she reached the counter, she stood close to Sawyer and watched as Pearl laid out the first set of samples.

"Too flowery." Sawyer pointed at two of the samples.

"I agree." Fiona could practically feel his breath on her cheek. "But the striped one might work."

"It might, if it was a different color. It's too…"

"Pink?"

"Exactly."

"Does it come in other colors?" Fiona asked Pearl even as she heard movement behind her.

"Let me check." Pearl stepped to the side. "May I help you, ladies?"

Fiona turned to see Linore and Dinah, just as she'd suspected.

They quickly averted their gazes and muttered, "No, ma'am."

"Oh, Dinah, I have a letter for you." Pearl turned to the cubbyholes that served as mailboxes and pulled out an envelope.

Dinah appeared surprised at first and then overjoyed. She and Linore scooted out the door, speculating about the letter.

"I wonder what that was all about?" Fiona said.

Pearl glanced at Sawyer and shook her head. "I wouldn't know."

She then smiled at Fiona, as if to say that it was nothing of concern.

"Shall we look at the next samples?" Pearl asked.

Time flew past while Fiona and Sawyer looked over each wallpaper sample. In the end, they both agreed on a simple pattern in ivory with a narrow china blue stripe. Sawyer didn't even ask about the cost. When Pearl gave him some figures, he told her he would place an order once the purchase of the hotel was complete.

Sawyer reached the door first and held it open for Fiona. "I enjoyed working with you."

"And I with you." If only it wasn't over. "I could come up with ideas for the other rooms, if you want."

"Maybe later." Sawyer opened the door and extended his arm. "I'll walk you to the boardinghouse."

She threaded her arm around his and drew near. The winds still cut through her cloak, and she was grateful for his warming presence.

"Thank you."

"For what? I always walk you home."

Home. A pang of sadness wove through her heart. For years now, one boardinghouse after another had become her home. None echoed with the joy and laughter of family.

"I hope to have one someday."

"One of what?" he asked.

She didn't realize she'd spoken her thought aloud. What did it hurt to say it to Sawyer? He was a friend. "A real home. A house."

"Instead of the bright lights of the theater?"

"Those lights may be bright, but they don't keep you company at night or encourage you when your spirits are low."

He didn't reply for a while. "I suppose you're right. I spent many a lonely night while on the march during the war. There were men all around, but I'd never been so alone."

"You understand."

He nodded, and her heart warmed. No one had ever understood before. They figured a mention in the newspaper was far better than an ordinary life. But she'd come to crave the ordinary.

"We always want what we don't have," she murmured.

"True." He stopped at the base of the boardinghouse steps. "But that doesn't mean we shouldn't try to reach for our dreams."

She caught her breath. Was he reconsidering what he wanted, or was he talking about the hotel? "Even when those dreams change?"

"Especially when they change." He stood close, holding her hands. "Sometimes it's for the better."

"Yes." She could barely get the word out.

He was so near that she felt each word whisper against her cheek. His touch warmed her from fingers to toes. In that moment, all the wealthy gentlemen who had sought her attention vanished into the recesses of her memory. There was only Sawyer, and she was beginning to feel things for him that she'd never felt for any man.

"Good night," he whispered so close to her lips that it felt like a kiss.

"Good night," she whispered back, eyes closed, hoping against hope that he would kiss her. Every man who greeted her after one of her concerts tried to seize that opportunity.

Sawyer did not.

He stepped back, still holding her hands. "Until tomorrow?"

She opened her eyes, disappointed. "Tomorrow?"

"Rehearsal for our next concert."

She let out her breath. "Of course. Tomorrow."

Only then did he let go of her hands, and the chill made her shiver. Still, he turned back to look at her and shout out, "Tomorrow," before hurrying along the boardwalk to his cabin.

"Tomorrow." Never had the word carried more promise.

Chapter Twelve

Never had Fiona so needed rehearsal. That morning, she learned Stockton had hired a buggy and left for Holland at dawn. No one knew if he would return. The similarity to Carson's departure couldn't be ignored. Though relieved for the moment, his departure made her situation more desperate. Rather than indulge in self-pity, she plunged into the day's work.

Still, she couldn't avoid the speculation that raced around the boardinghouse. Some thought Mr. Stockton had gone to the larger town to make arrangements before declaring himself. Others believed he wasn't the advertised groom at all, though those people couldn't come up with another prospect. For Fiona, every mention of the man's name sent a wave of dread over her. She, Amanda and Louise had come to Singapore hoping to marry a man none of them had met. The six ladies were going to Harmony to marry men they'd never met. Fiona had even more cause to marry. Then why now wish for love from a man, Sawyer, who refused to give it?

The rest of the morning, she kept to the kitchen to avoid Clara and Dinah, who were in foul moods and stomped about the boardinghouse like petulant adolescents. After the midday meal, Mrs. Calloway chased her out of the kitchen, saying she had done quite enough. Since the young ladies were ensconced in the parlor receiving instructions from Mr. and Mrs. Adamson, Fiona went to the writing room to work out several sketches of the hotel lobby.

About the time she finished, Dinah dragged herself into the room with Linore on her heels. The two plopped into chairs drawn close together to facilitate conversation, but Dinah's long face indicated any talk would be of the melancholy sort.

Fiona reviewed her designs for the lobby. One sketch was as elegant as Sawyer had described, but that would be beyond his means, so she did two other sketches in more affordable styles.

"What will I do?" Dinah wailed from across the writing room.

"Forget him," Linore counseled. "He's not worth the trouble."

"But I don't want to go," Dinah whispered loudly, likely so neither of the Adamsons would overhear. "I can't go there."

Linore shrugged. "Then go back home."

"I can't." This time Dinah's cry was accompanied by tears.

Fiona would have ignored the histrionics if she hadn't suffered through similar anguish when she'd endured her first crushing defeat in the singing world.

"I know it's not polite to listen to other people's conversations," she began, "but you need to have faith that everything will work out for the best. If you don't want to go to Harmony, then tell Mr. or Mrs. Adamson that."

Dinah's eyes rounded. Then she looked side to side

to ensure no one had heard Fiona. "I don't got no other choice."

"There's always a choice when marriage is involved." Fiona ignored the fact that she had placed herself in virtually the same position as Dinah. "Marriage is final. The time to turn back or change your mind is now."

"But what would I do?" Dinah's lip quivered.

That was the question. If only Fiona had the boarding school of her dreams. Then she would truly be able to help the girl. Now, she could only give advice. "Seriously consider who can help you, and then reach out to them."

The poor girl looked petrified. "Mr. Joyce—he's my new pa—would tan my hide if I showed up back there."

"Would Mrs. Joyce?"

Dinah shook her head. "But she can't do nothin' when Mr. Joyce is in one of his rages."

"Would he truly throw you out?" Fiona's family would take her in at any time. She was the one who couldn't bear to return to the tenements.

Dinah hung her head. "No, but it ain't no kind of life." She nibbled her lip. "I was hopin' for more. A real house with a fence and a pretty porch."

Fiona felt the tug in her own heart. "Keep praying for it. Get down on your knees and ask God to show you the way."

Dinah stared. "God will give me a husband?"

"If you trust Him, He'll lead you to the right man."

Listen to her, giving advice she didn't follow herself. Fiona scooped up her drawings and shoved them in the sketchbook.

"Where are you going?" Dinah asked with surprise.

"To my room."

It was time she got on her knees.

* * *

Sawyer fingered Fiona's letter and tucked it in his waistcoat pocket rather than leave it in his trunk. Maybe it was time to tell her that he was the one who'd placed the advertisement. She hadn't backed away when he drew close last night. Oh, he'd been tempted to kiss her. The desire nearly overwhelmed him. That flowery scent she wore, the sweep of her coppery hair, the long eyelashes. It was almost more than he could bear. Then he recalled her bitterness at men who thought she would agree to anything they wanted in order to further her singing.

He wanted to punch the louts who'd done that to her.

Chances were he'd never meet any of them. Fortunate for them. Sawyer couldn't stand the idea of any other man near Fiona. She was too good for the sort who came through Singapore. She deserved the best, better than he could give her. Stockton? Sawyer couldn't imagine Fiona with the man. He was a cold businessman, a lot like Sawyer's father. His money could give her the big house she longed for, but she'd soon learn that some things were more important than comfort and fine furnishings.

Sawyer's thoughts flitted to his mother, alone now in the large house with a man who gave her none of himself. He couldn't imagine Fiona settling for that sort of life, but he had nothing to offer her in return except debt and a family divided.

Sawyer took a deep breath and finished knotting his tie. He couldn't offer marriage, not yet, but he had to warn her about men like Stockton. He slipped on his Sunday jacket. Fiona seemed drawn to well-dressed men. If he hoped to convince her, he had to put his best forward. If only she could wait… She would be good for the hotel. Together they would create a warm, welcoming place known up and down the lake. Her elegance and beauty would be the perfect counterpoint to his practicality and business sense. Folks from Chicago might visit on hot summer days to spend time at the lakeshore. The possibilities were endless.

Except she felt that she had to marry now. For her niece. What could he offer her? Employment? A promise of the future? He wasn't sure, but he had to try.

Sawyer took one last look in the mirror. Freshly shaved, hair trimmed and dressed in his Sunday best. Tonight, Fiona wouldn't see a lumberjack when she looked at him. She'd see a gentleman who would soon own and operate a hotel. Perhaps that would be enough.

Nervous, he whistled as he strode down the boardwalk and climbed the boardinghouse steps. At his knock, Mrs. Calloway ushered him in with an appreciative sigh.

"Don't you look fine tonight, Mr. Sawyer."

"Is Fiona ready?"

Mrs. Calloway chuckled. "Have you ever known a woman to be ready on time? She'll be down right soon, I imagine."

"Now, Mrs. Calloway," Fiona purred as she swept into the front hallway. "I'm only late when—" She gasped softly and then gulped. "Is there a concert tonight?"

Sawyer fought the smile that threatened to drag up the corners of his lips. "Just rehearsal. We can have the hotel dining room, since it's past the supper hour."

She breathed out what looked like a sigh of relief, since they usually rehearsed in the boardinghouse lobby or the ice-cold church building. "Well, then, I will need my cloak."

Sawyer assisted her into the fur-trimmed cloak and waited for her to pin on a hat and pull on gloves. Then at last they were off and away from prying ears. Mrs. Calloway would never admit it, but gossip spread quickly from the boardinghouse to the rest of town.

"This is a luxury, practicing at the hotel," she murmured. "If I'd known, I would have brought my sketchbook."

"Oh?"

"I put together some ideas for the hotel lobby."

"Wonderful." He drew closer as they strolled together along the boardwalk. "You can show me another evening. Perhaps tomorrow?"

She laughed. "Sawyer Evans, are you trying to monopolize all my evenings?"

"Is it working?"

"I'm afraid it is."

"I do have a selfish reason, though," he added.

"The hotel."

"No." He squeezed her hand. "The company."

She didn't pull away or give him a scathing look. Though her hand trembled on his arm, she kept it there. "In that case, I can't possibly object."

Each step felt as light as air. She didn't object to spending time with him. At one time he'd never thought to hear words like that from her. She'd always been careful to tell him their relationship was professional only.

He helped her up the steps and opened the front door for her. Once they'd both entered the lobby, he took her cloak and gloves to the coatroom. After he removed his coat, he patted his waistcoat pocket. Yes, the letter was still there. Perhaps this was the time.

He glanced out at the lobby. Fiona was examining the wall fixtures and decor. Mr. VanderLeuven stood at the hotel registration desk. Since the paperwork hadn't been finalized, the VanderLeuvens still ran the hotel. Sawyer planned to ask them to stay on as employees for a week or so after the sale closed.

Now would not be a good time to tell Fiona the truth. Later. After rehearsal.

He reentered the lobby and extended his arm. "Are you ready?"

"Of course." She took his arm the way she always did during a concert, as if they were partners in life as well as on the stage.

Sawyer was beginning to think that would suit him just fine.

Tonight the dining room was empty. The oil lamps burned low. The VanderLeuvens wouldn't want to waste oil without customers. It didn't make any difference to Sawyer. He'd never used music. Couldn't read the notation. Since he was young, he could pick up an instrument, practice on it for a week or so and play it. His mother had put him in lessons, but, impatient at being kept indoors, he refused to follow the instructor's directions or play a single song for the man. The instructor quit, and Mother never tried that again.

"Which songs should we do?" he asked.

It was always better to let Fiona pick them since only she knew what her voice could and couldn't handle.

She named several tunes, and they ran through them with few adjustments.

"I believe we are ready," she stated after the last one.

Now was the time. They were alone, and she was in a good mood. His heart beat wildly. What if she thought he was interfering? What if he'd completely misread her, and she wasn't growing interested in him?

He stood. Too quickly, for he knocked into her music

stand and sent her sheet music flying. She jumped back and lost her balance. He caught and held her. Close. Too close. Her cheeks were rosy and her eyes wide. In the past she might have chided him, but tonight she looked deep into his eyes. He could hardly breathe, couldn't think of a single word. Her lips softened, and before she could say anything, he kissed her.

Briefly.

Then he stepped back, shocked. What had he done? He'd acted like a cad, taking what she hadn't offered.

"Forgive me," he choked out. "I don't know what came over me."

Her gaze narrowed. "You didn't mean to kiss me?"

"No. Yes." What was he supposed to say? That he fought the urge every time opportunity presented itself? "I, uh, don't want you to think I'm a callous lout. I should have waited."

Her brow pinched just above her nose. "Until when?"

Sawyer was digging a deep hole. "A gentleman is supposed to declare his intentions and get confirmation from the lady before, well, before he does anything." Yet he hadn't followed that progression in the past, except with Julia, who preferred to keep her distance.

Fiona looked like she was trying to stifle a smile but with little success. "Are you a gentleman, Sawyer Evans?"

"I, uh, well…" No answer got him out of trouble. If he said that he was, then he had no explanation for his behavior. If not, then he didn't belong in the lady's company. "I hoped to act like a gentleman. Forgive me for falling short."

She gave up any attempt to hide her amusement. "Don't look so disheartened. I appreciate the effort."

"You do?"

She nodded.

Sawyer felt a rush of something relatively foreign to his experience. Delight. Yes, that was it. Her approval delighted him.

One of her eyebrows arched. "Of course I must consider my niece's well-being first. She is my responsibility."

That was the big obstacle that stood between them. "That's why you came to Singapore, to marry Garrett Decker."

"I had hoped to do so."

"And now that you expect your niece to arrive any day..." He couldn't finish the sentence.

She knew. "Mary Clare needs a home—and a father."

A father. Not just a provider but a father who loved and cared for the little girl. What was Sawyer thinking? He had no idea how to be a good father. He'd only experienced the type of father no man should be.

He cleared his throat. "I understand."

"You do?"

She looked so hopeful that it broke his heart to not give her what she wanted. He was growing to like her a great deal, but he couldn't take the step that she demanded. He scoured the other possibilities that had crossed his mind of late.

"I could hire you—once the purchase is complete." He would delay renovating the west wing in order to pay her. Would she be willing to cook? At her frown, he choked back asking.

"Hire me?" The words came out in a screech.

Now he had truly offended her. "It would help you provide for your niece." Even to his ears that sounded weak.

She stiffened. "I can provide, Sawyer Evans. I'm looking for a man courageous enough to be a husband and father."

By that measure, he was failing miserably. But the thought of her settling for someone like Stockton, just because he was wealthy, made him ill.

"Don't trade love for a big house."

Her eyes pierced through him. "Are you offering me love, Sawyer Evans?"

Was he? He wanted to spend time with her. He wanted to protect her. He wanted to spend each day exploring the mystery that was her life. But marry and raise a child? "I would like to get to know you better."

"We have talked and sung concerts for eight months. How much more do you need to know?"

A lot. "You are a mystery to me."

She snorted with disgust and shook her head.

Before she could condemn him, the words burst out of his mouth. "I'd like to court you."

That stopped any retort. She stared, clearly dumbfounded. Then, as realization sank in, she sighed. "With marriage in mind?"

"One day, if all goes well between us." It was the best he could offer.

Her lip trembled ever so slightly before her fortitude reined it in. "I see." She gathered her music. "I believe I would like to return to the boardinghouse now."

That was it? No answer? He stood with his jaw slack. "Then you…?"

"I'm sorry, Sawyer." She looked out the window, her cheeks dotted with red. "Time is the one thing I don't have."

And he couldn't give up time. They were at an impasse.

* * *

Fiona still felt horrible long after she went to bed that night. While Louise slept soundly, she stared into the darkness, looking for confirmation that she'd made the right decision. Instead, doubts crowded near. She had prayed for God to lead her to the proper husband. Yet when Sawyer asked to court her, she questioned that it was an answer to her prayer. She needed a husband now, not "perhaps one day."

Then again, she had feelings for Sawyer. Turning him down might have ruined any chance for happiness?

Selfish fool! Her happiness was unimportant. All that mattered was Mary Clare's future. Then, why did her decision feel like she'd condemned her niece also?

Mr. Stockton might return looking for her.

Sawyer might change his mind and promise a future.

Or she might have ruined her only chance at marriage, no matter how far in the future it might be.

How could she be certain she'd made the right decision?

Fiona's mother hadn't faced such questions. Back in Ireland, she'd faced crushing poverty and few choices.

"Can't afford to be choosy," she'd often told Fiona. "God wills what He will, and it's our lot to accept with grace whatever may come."

For Ma, that meant leaving Ireland for the hope of a new country, only to find that poverty dogged America's streets just like back home. What sorrow and disappointment that must have brought. Yet Ma carried her head high.

Surely it wasn't wrong to want the best for Mary Clare. The girl had a beautiful, clear voice that was always on pitch. Fiona could only dream of such a voice. Her niece had little chance of ever using that God-given gift if she remained in the tenements. Fiona had wanted to take her in a year ago, but Winslow Evanston had destroyed that possibility. He had smeared her reputation across the gossip pages, calling her a woman of loose morals—all because she insisted on exactly the reverse.

Where was God's will in that?

Surely He did not enjoy seeing His children treated unfairly. Then again, had not Jesus endured false accusations? So too Paul and the apostles?

She heaved a sigh. They accepted the insults as proof they were furthering God's kingdom on Earth. She couldn't claim that noble purpose. No, her goals had been practical. For Mary Clare's sake, she had sought a husband in Singapore, Michigan, far from the vultures circling the bright lights of New York. Thus far her attempts had failed. Where could she turn now?

She flipped onto her side, frustrated.

"Are you awake?" Louise whispered.

Fiona fought back a pang of guilt. "Sorry I woke you."

"It's all right. I've had trouble sleeping lately too."

Fiona lay on her back again. "You seemed to be sleeping well to me."

Louise shifted to her side and rose on one elbow. "I can't help thinking about Clara and the rest of the ladies. I nearly walked into just such a marriage."

"Are you talking about Garrett Decker?" Fiona didn't recall Louise having much contact with the man beyond their first meeting.

"Yes. It would have been all wrong."

"You didn't know that then."

"I was desperate. I think they are too. There has to be a way to help them."

Fiona couldn't believe what she was hearing. "You think that too?"

At Louise's affirmation, Fiona explained her idea for a school for young ladies.

Louise instantly warmed to the idea. "I could teach reading and the natural sciences."

Those weren't the skills that Fiona had in mind, but now was not the time to mention that. "It's just a dream. The fact is that I don't have the money to make the school a reality." Sawyer's quick dismissal of the subject still stung. "Nor am I likely to ever get such funding."

"Oh. Maybe Captain Elder would invest in it, if they return this summer."

That was as far-fetched as anything Fiona had dreamed up. Dreams were all well and good, as Fiona's mother had often told her, but living meant taking things as they were, not like you wished they could be. Fiona couldn't make her dream a reality without money. The only way to get that kind of income was to marry into it. Her attempts thus far had fallen short. If Mr. Stockton had truly been considering her for his future wife, he would not have left town so suddenly nor treated her like a chambermaid. What was left? She'd already turned down Sawyer. No other prospects were in sight.

"I suppose we're back to marriage as the only solution," Louise whispered with obvious disappointment.

"I suppose we are." Fiona sighed. "If only I had more time."

"Why don't you?"

Fiona regretted not telling Louise sooner. "My niece is coming to Singapore." She paused but Louise didn't reply. "She's my late sister Maeve's only child. I promised to raise her."

"Oh. I see."

"She's just seven years old." Fiona felt cold and callous, but there was no way around the fact that another person would need the bed soon.

Louise understood. "Perhaps I'd better answer that advertisement that Clara and the rest are all stirred up about." But she said that with resignation, not hope.

Then Louise hadn't written yet. Perhaps Mr. Stockton had intended to reach out to Fiona after all. She couldn't understand his behavior around her, but no doubt he would explain everything once they met. She should be excited. Instead, the dread returned, followed by resignation. The time for hopeful dreams was over. As Ma said, she couldn't afford to be choosy. She must care for her niece. That meant making every effort to marry Mr. Stockton. First thing in the morning, she would write a second letter.

Chapter Thirteen

Sawyer whistled as he strolled from the sawmill to the mercantile. The VanderLeuvens had been so eager to close the deal that they'd agreed to his terms and arranged for the banker from Saugatuck to join them at the mill at the end of the workday. Minutes later, Sawyer had signed the paperwork.

The hotel was his.

The keys to the main entrance nestled in his pocket, making a comforting jingle when he walked. He now owned a business. What would Father think of that? More importantly, what would Fiona think? It might be enough to change her mind and accept his suit. Given her limited options, she could well see him in a new light.

There was a bounce in Sawyer's step. He nodded at every passerby, greeting him or her with extra friendliness. It never hurt to cultivate goodwill.

He mentally made a list of things that needed doing. First, he would clean the lobby, dining room and kitchen. The dining-room wallpaper could be ordered. He would go over Fiona's plans for the lobby and order necessary materials. Once the dining room and kitchen were ready, he would have to hire minimal staff. That all cut into what he could spend on renovations, but the income could more than make up for that shortfall. He hoped.

The terms of the bank loan made it impossible to leave his foreman position at the sawmill right now. He would need to hire someone to staff the registration desk on weekdays. The VanderLeuvens had agreed to do that while they packed their belongings, but they wouldn't be here more than a week.

His excitement slipped down a notch. Now the hard work began. He would need to lay out money before he got back a return. He had to hire help before any income came in. This was risky, but it was the leap of faith all entrepreneurs had to take. Sawyer had studied the options and had come up with some reasonable possibilities.

Fiona had turned down his offer yesterday, but she might change her mind if he asked for her help rather than suggest it as a solution. She refused anything that looked like charity. He would pay her well, of course. She deserved it. The other lady at the boardinghouse, Mrs. Louise Smythe, might be eager enough for work to accept a housekeeping position at a lower wage—once he had paying guests.

Sawyer pushed through the mercantile door, eager to tell Roland his news, only to hear the familiar voice of Mrs. Calloway. Her voice was always so loud that he suspected she had a hearing problem.

"I tell you, I know who it is."

"All right," Roland replied calmly, "but I don't listen to or pass on rumors."

"It's not a rumor. It's fact, and either he comes out and tells those poor women or I'm gonna."

All thoughts of his good news evaporated. Sawyer had a bad feeling this little discussion was about him and the newspaper advertisement. Mrs. Calloway could have overheard just enough to piece together that he was the prospective groom. He sure didn't want the boardinghouse proprietress spreading this around town.

He hurried toward the counter, ready to intercede, but Roland, spotting him, held up a hand.

"Now, there's no use upsetting anyone," the store manager told her calmly. "I have been assured that the gentleman in question will respond to each woman who writes."

Sawyer's spirits bottomed out. He'd written those difficult notes to Clara and Dinah, but he still didn't know how he was going to tell Fiona that he was the man in the advertisement. If she got upset when he asked to court her, what would she do when she learned the truth? Maybe he'd better wait until she accepted his suit. Until it was safe to tell Fiona, he had to do something to stop Mrs. Calloway from springing her news on her.

He approached the counter. "Good afternoon, Mrs. Calloway."

The woman whipped around, her expression so much like a girl caught sneaking candies from the jar that Sawyer had to steel himself so he didn't laugh.

"Oh. Hello." She ran a hand along the counter. "I was just tellin' Mr. Roland about how I heard the other day that rutabagas are good for rheumatism."

Sawyer knew a last-minute explanation when he heard one, but he didn't let on. "That's interesting, but I'd have to try it before passing that on to anyone. We wouldn't want to harm anyone, no matter how innocent our news seems."

"Right. Right." Color dotted Mrs. Calloway's cheeks, revealing she understood his hint. "I think I will, now that you mention it. My Ernie'd feel a lot better if it works." She edged away from the counter and shot a glance at Roland. "Just send Jimmy on over with my order."

"Yes, ma'am. I'll do that."

She hurried out of the mercantile, leaving Sawyer alone with Roland.

"Close call," Sawyer muttered.

"I doubt she'll stay silent for long. Have you written back to everyone?"

"All but Fiona. Writing seems too impersonal, but the right moment to tell her hasn't come up yet."

"You might want to hurry it up." Roland turned and leafed through the cubbyholes he used to sort the mail. After checking several envelopes, he set one on the counter in front of Sawyer. "She wrote again."

"She did?" Sawyer picked up the envelope, though it felt like carrying hot shot between the furnace and the cannons. Dangerous. He glanced at the address. Sure enough, that was her handwriting. He let out his breath slowly. "Maybe she felt the need to express her feelings." The thought of her and Stockton didn't set well. "Or maybe she's writing to say her affections lie elsewhere." He hoped.

"Could be." But Roland sounded skeptical. "I, uh, need to find Jimmy out back. If you don't mind, tell anyone who comes in that I'll be back in a minute."

The store manager disappeared into the back room. Even though Sawyer had heard Mrs. Calloway ask to have Jimmy deliver her order, he suspected Roland had chosen to leave so Sawyer could read the letter. He sure didn't have any privacy at the bunkhouse.

Sawyer ripped open the envelope. The same fine paper, lightly scented, slipped from inside. He unfolded it. The note was longer than he'd anticipated, but then it usually did take a woman longer to get to the point.

He focused on the words.

Dear Sir,
Under no circumstances do I mean to hurry you. An important businessman has far greater concerns than answering what must be a multitude of letters arriving in answer to your advertisement. I would like to reiterate my interest…

Sawyer's stomach turned. She wasn't writing to withdraw her interest, she was confirming it. Fiona thought Stockton had placed the advertisement. That's where her interest lay. She would not be reconsidering Sawyer's offer to court her. He should be pleased. He couldn't afford a wife and child, not with the debt he'd just accepted. But the memory of Julia's betrayal resurfaced. Julia had broken her engagement to him in order to marry a wealthier man. Fiona was doing the same.

His blood boiled as he crumpled the piece of paper.

Again the mercantile doorbell jingled. This time Fiona herself swept toward the counter.

Sawyer stuffed the crumpled letter into his coat pocket.

"Sawyer! How delightful to see you." Yet her attention shifted at once to Roland, who fortuitously popped out of the back room. "Did Mrs. Calloway stop in with her order?"

Roland covered the distance between them in seconds. "She just left. You should have crossed paths on the boardwalk."

"I didn't. Isn't that odd?" Fiona tilted her head just so, showing her profile to good advantage.

Wasn't that exactly what Julia had done when Sawyer was courting her? Except she didn't limit that flirtatious glance to just him. No, she'd cast her gaze on every man whose prospects surpassed his. That wouldn't happen this time.

Fiona once again turned to him. "I'll see you at the hotel tonight."

"Not tonight." He didn't trust himself to say more.

"Is something wrong? I thought you wanted to meet."

"Not tonight." Sawyer slapped his hat on his head. "Good evening."

"Good evening…"

Her voice trailed off as he strode through the store, eager to get as far away from her as possible. He needed quiet. He needed somewhere to think this through. He needed to get away from her before his temper caught fire and he blasted a hole in his future.

What had possessed him to think Fiona, of all women, would be different? She didn't hide her interest in climbing the social ladder. Her dresses were so brightly hued as to be considered gaudy. No doubt she'd drawn the adoration of men during her time on the New York stage. Men. Not just one. She was accustomed to getting whatever she wanted from a man. He'd been a fool to fall for her.

Fiona sat in the writing room attempting to read, but she couldn't stop puzzling over Sawyer's peculiar behavior. He'd been abrupt, almost as if he didn't want to see her. Fear stabbed through her. She'd seen that sort of behavior before. Men who'd previously doted on her suddenly wouldn't look her in the eye or would cast furtive glances toward the door. Invariably it meant they'd lied to her about their marital status and feared imminent discovery. That wasn't the case with Sawyer.

Something must have happened to upset him. Perhaps the purchase of the hotel didn't go through. Her chest tightened, making it more difficult than usual to draw a breath. He'd put everything and more into that venture. It had to work out. If there was anything she could say to the VanderLeuvens…

She rose, intending to march over there right now.

"Where are you heading off to?" Mrs. Calloway remarked as she swept through the room.

Fiona sat back down. "Nowhere." She'd reacted without thinking. Sawyer's distress might not have anything to do with the hotel at all. He might be sore that she'd refused his offer. In that case, their friendship was shattered.

"Haven't seen you wear that dress before," Mrs. Calloway said. "Did you borrow it?"

"No, it's mine."

"Imagine that!"

Fiona could see how people might not believe that she owned such a plain, poorly sewn gown. The old gray dress was a remnant from her days before the stage. She kept it as a reminder of how far she'd come. She also donned it whenever she got tired of the attention and wanted to vanish in the crowd.

Today was just such a day. She picked up the book again and tried to read.

The words blurred as doubts and regrets overwhelmed her. Writing to Mr. Stockton had taken great resolve. Each word burned, for the truth she'd so carefully guarded all those years in New York had been thrown away. She wasn't eager to meet him. She didn't want to marry him. She had to marry, and that was a lot different. If only Sawyer had proposed or promised marriage. She would have gladly accepted, but he had not. So she'd written to Mr. Stockton. Now the letter was in his hands. Roland had confirmed it when she inquired after Sawyer stormed out of the store. There was no turning back.

She set down the book and rubbed the bridge of her nose where a headache was forming. One of the girls plunked out a tune on the piano with painful results. Every measure included a wrong note, and the tempo was so uneven that no one could decipher what tune was being attempted.

Fiona took a deep breath and attempted again to focus on her book. Instead, her mind drifted. Perhaps something had happened at the mill and Sawyer wasn't angry with her at all. She hated to lose his friendship. That must be why her heart ached so much. But she'd had no choice. She had to write again to Mr. Stockton. She'd made the right choice. It had to be right. Mary Clare could arrive any day.

Please, Lord, for Mary Clare's sake if not for mine.

Her niece needed a real home, not a tenement and not a boardinghouse room.

"There's a ship coming into port!" The excited shout sounded like Linore's voice.

The squeals that followed were undoubtedly those of the rest of the young ladies, except perhaps Dinah, who still hoped to catch Sawyer's attention.

Mary Clare. Fiona's niece might finally arrive. She set the book aside and made her way to the front hall, where she found the girls and their escorts clustered. Mr. Adamson was attempting to quiet the group, who had pulled on coats and hats, presumably because they intended to go to the docks to see the ship for themselves.

Linore, cheeks rosy from the cold, was still bundled in coat and bonnet and mittens. How she'd managed to leave the boardinghouse at this hour was a mystery. The Adamsons kept a close watch on their charges.

After holding up a hand for a good twenty seconds, Mr. Adamson was able to slow their eagerness. "First we must wait for any passengers to disembark."

Fiona's heart pounded. Was she ready for the added responsibility of a little girl? Louise had not yet moved out of their room, though she had packed her belongings.

"At the proper time we will walk together to the dock," Mr. Adamson was saying. "Mind you, I will escort only those young ladies who are quiet and well-mannered."

That sent the group into the parlor to sit quietly for Mr. Adamson's direction and cleared the way for Fiona. She donned her cloak and swept from the boardinghouse. If that precious little girl was on board the incoming ship, Fiona needed to be on the dock. Mary Clare must see a friendly face, even if it was only in the glow of the lanterns lining the wharf.

Sawyer's bunkmates left the cabin to meet the incoming ship. Doubtless they hoped to snag a treasured commodity at a cut-rate price or dazzle any incoming young ladies. Their initial hopes for the Harmony-bound brides had been cut short by the Adamsons' vigilance. Chester had apparently managed to see Linore earlier tonight before she had to run back to the boardinghouse. Though he bragged about it, Sawyer suspected the couple had been interrupted by Mr. Adamson.

"You're better off without her," Sawyer had counseled the young lumberjack.

Maybe he'd better take his own advice. He'd taken a risk by asking Fiona if he could court her, and she'd refused him. Not only that, she'd written again to the advertised groom that she believed was Stockton. Fickle woman! Just like Julia. Inconstant as the breeze. He couldn't trust any of them.

In the light of the oil lamp, Sawyer smoothed out her offensive letter. He held a corner to the flame. Fiona's elegant hand was perfectly straight, as if she'd used another sheet of paper as a guide for each line. The corner caught on fire. The flame burned downward, toward her beautiful script. He suddenly had a vision of Fiona cornered by fire and blew out the flame.

His hand shook. What was wrong with him?

He held the letter up to the lamp again. This time he let the flames devour her letter, just as her single-minded focus on marrying a wealthy man had destroyed his love for her. Love? Was it possible this hurt so much because he'd come to love her?

A ship's whistle blew, and he shook off the unwelcome thoughts. Dwelling on the past would get him nowhere. An incoming ship meant passengers. Passengers could be hotel customers.

His romantic life might be in a shambles, but he could take pride in the fact that he was the new owner of Astor House. He wasn't just a saw operator or mill manager any longer. He owned and ran a hotel. Yes, the VanderLeuvens were still there, but he needed to take the lead, not sulk in his cabin over a woman.

He took off at a brisk pace for the hotel.

Fiona peered into the gloom of dusk. Night was falling faster than the ship could get moored at the dock. It would be dark before any passengers disembarked. She scanned the railing, looking for any sign of a young girl.

Would she recognize Mary Clare? It had been over a year since she'd last seen her. First, the family agreed that the girl needed both a mother and a father. Fiona would support Mary Clare while seeking a husband. Then Lillibeth claimed Fiona kept disreputable company. Considering the way things turned out with Winslow Evanston, Lillibeth had a point. Fiona thought Singapore would be the answer, but more than seven months here had not produced a husband.

She focused on the incoming ship. The girl had dark hair, like Maeve's husband, who'd disappeared shortly after the girl was born. Mary Clare was short—or had been—for her age. The child might have grown over the past year.

Many passengers stood at the promenade railing, watching those ashore as intently as the residents of Singapore watched them. The lamps cast them as featureless silhouettes. Fiona couldn't spot any who appeared to be children, and Lillibeth had said she was sending Mary Clare west with a group of orphans. If they were still together, Fiona should see several children. They might have parted company, though. Her sister had not explained if the orphans were proceeding north by ship or west by train.

She blew out her breath in frustration.

The ship slowly came alongside the dock. Thick lines were cast ashore, and men from the mill wrapped the lines around heavy pilings. Only after that long process was complete did the ship extend a gangway.

At last passengers began to disembark.

Fiona moved toward the gangway with the rest of the crowd, but she couldn't get close or see over the men.

"It's always exciting," said a familiar voice at her elbow. Pearl Decker. "It was when we arrived."

"Yes, it was," Fiona said absently. She searched the scant number of people disembarking. "Looks like more workers for the sawmill." Sawyer would be busy. An ache settled into her heart.

"Yes, it does. Roland said he expected an influx about now. The bulk of the spring rush should be here soon, and they'll get the second mill up and running."

The words floated over Fiona's head. She scanned the gangway over and over. No children. None at all.

"She must not be on this ship," she murmured.

"Who?"

Fiona had forgotten that Pearl was still at her side. "My niece. My sister is sending her here, but she didn't say when."

"How exciting. Is she of school age?"

Naturally, Pearl's thoughts would wander that way since she was the schoolteacher. Fiona supposed Mary Clare would need to attend school here, though that thought hadn't crossed her mind. My, oh, my, how was she ever going to be a decent mother when she couldn't recall the most basic things?

"Yes, she is," Fiona admitted. "She's seven."

"Perfect. We'd be delighted to have her join us. She can tell us about growing up in the city."

That was exactly what Fiona did not want Mary Clare telling people. No one needed to hear about the cramped quarters, the rats, the filth and the illness. She would have to school her niece on what was appropriate to say and what was not.

A woman appeared at the top of the gangway. With her was a small girl. Fiona's heart leaped in her chest. Was it Mary Clare?

She stumbled forward. Now that the bulk of passengers had disembarked, the crowds ashore had thinned. The new mill workers had met their cohorts. After introductions, they'd left to settle into their new quarters or to whet their thirst at one of the saloons. Fiona could walk all the way to the base of the gangway.

"Auntie!" cried the girl.

Fiona extended her arms, overwhelmed by a wave of affection for the little girl. "Mary Clare!"

The girl left the woman and ran down the gangway, straight into Fiona's arms.

Fiona knelt, oblivious to the wet, dirty docks. What was a little dirt when her darling niece had arrived safely?

"Let me look at you." Fiona held the girl at arm's length.

In the light of the lanterns, she could make out the dark, straight hair and an impish smile.

"My, you've grown." Fiona again embraced the girl, who soon squirmed so much that Fiona released her from the hug. "Where is your bag?"

The girl shrugged. "I got lots to tell you. There was this huge horse that brought me to the ship." The little girl chattered on, hopping from one marvel to another without much connection other than that all these wonders had occurred during her trip from New York to here.

A man dressed in a long, black coat tapped his cane impatiently on the gangway. "Do you plan to block the way all night?"

Fiona's blood ran cold. That voice was painfully familiar. Winslow Evanston. The man who'd ruined her reputation after she refused to become his mistress. The railroad tycoon was rich enough and influential enough to sully her name in a large city. Here he could destroy her. She instinctively drew Mary Clare away from the lantern light and wrapped her arms around the little girl.

Please God, don't let him recognize me.

"Do you know that man?" she whispered into the little girl's ear.

"No, Auntie."

"Quiet now. We don't want him to see us."

"Why?" This time in a whisper.

This was not something Fiona could explain to a little girl. "He's a wicked man."

Fiona had left New York to get away from this man. What was he doing in Singapore?

Chapter Fourteen

The ship's arrival had not brought a rush of guests. Sawyer saw men heading for the saloons and bunk-houses, but no one stopped at the hotel. He didn't need the light from the lanterns hanging on the porch to know the new arrivals were sawmill workers.

"Afraid that's the way it is most times," Mrs. Vander-Leuven said as she wiped a season's dust from the nearly empty bookshelves in the small lobby.

"You could have passed along that piece of information before I bought the hotel."

Mrs. VanderLeuven burst into laughter. "You're a funny man, Sawyer Evans. Right funny."

That lightened his mood a little but didn't solve the problem at hand. He couldn't afford to pay the Vander-Leuvens for the week, least of all hire basic staff if there weren't any guests or diners. Worse, with the influx of mill workers, he wouldn't have much time to devote to the hotel. Things were going from bad to worse.

Trust no one. Father's words echoed in his head. Father had repeated them daily, like a creed. Sawyer couldn't live that way. He needed to trust someone. In spite of Father. In spite of Julia's betrayal. In spite of the heartache of war. Somewhere there was a person he could trust.

Fiona.

Except she'd pursued another relationship rather than accepting his suit. The refusal crushed him. Couldn't she see how much he'd given? He wasn't prepared to provide for a family, and she came with a child attached. Offering courtship had been a big step, one he couldn't afford. It should have touched her. Instead she'd gone after Stockton.

While Sawyer grumbled to himself, Mrs. VanderLeuven removed cobwebs from the windows. He couldn't stand to look at the empty boardwalks, so he flipped through the registration book. Far too few guests stayed here. Based on the dilapidated state of the place, it wouldn't garner many recommendations or repeat stays. Those who returned to Singapore probably stayed at the boardinghouse. Except Stockton. That man consistently frequented Astor House. Unfortunately, he visited only in the spring and fall.

"Oh!" Mrs. VanderLeuven said with a great deal more excitement than usual. "Someone *is* coming our way, and he looks like he has money." She practically rubbed her hands together with glee.

No wonder guests preferred to move on. Sawyer had never seen this side of the former hotel owner.

The woman crossed the lobby until she stood directly before Sawyer. In a low voice, she instructed, "Charge four dollars a night."

"That's more than double our usual rate. Does it include meals?"

"Of course not." Mrs. VanderLeuven looked shocked that he would even think such a thing.

Sawyer was appalled. "Well, it's my hotel now, so the fees are up to me."

Mrs. VanderLeuven shook her head and moved away from the registration desk. "Won't be my fault if you fall short before summer shows its face."

Movement past the hotel drew Sawyer's attention. That looked like Fiona, and she had a child with her. Her niece must have arrived.

"That man stopped to watch Miss O'Keefe," Mrs. VanderLeuven reported, her face nearly flattened against the window.

Though Sawyer couldn't see much beyond the lit hotel porch, he could make out the gentleman's lean figure. Sure enough, the man, dressed in a long coat, had paused to watch Fiona pass. She was a lovely woman. Anyone could see it, but the thought of another man watching her sent a stab of jealousy through Sawyer.

Surprised by the reaction, Sawyer drew in a deep breath and shook his head. He needed to concentrate. His first customer was on his way. He couldn't afford to be rude to the only passenger wanting a room.

He tugged his waistcoat into place and made sure his cuffs were proper.

The front door flew open with a rush of cold air. The man halted without closing the door behind him.

Mrs. VanderLeuven hurried to shut it.

The man pulled off his top hat and stared. "Paul?"

Sawyer stared back, his mouth dry. Impossible. What was Father doing in Singapore?

Mrs. VanderLeuven bustled toward the counter. "Ain't no Paul here, but I can ask Sawyer here to run out and ask around."

"Sawyer." Father's lip curled into a sneer. "How... pedestrian."

Sawyer's gut knotted. Not only was Father here, but he hadn't changed. He was still the arrogant, self-serving autocrat he'd always been. That meant he was just as morally corrupt. And he'd cast a long look at Fiona. Sawyer fisted his hands. If Father so much as touched Fiona, Sawyer would knock him senseless. The command to honor one's father couldn't possibly apply to a man who squashed people like flies.

Father surveyed the surroundings. "So you've lowered yourself to working a menial position in a moth-eaten hotel."

"Astor House isn't moth-eaten," Mrs. VanderLeuven protested, apparently forgetting she no longer owned said moth-eaten establishment.

Sawyer was just glad she didn't look closer at his wealthy father's impeccable attire and Sawyer's comparatively threadbare suit. He'd taken the most worn pieces of clothing with him when he left home, but a practiced eye would still recognize the fine stitching of an expert tailor.

Father walked past Mrs. VanderLeuven without even a nod in her direction. As usual with those he deemed beneath him, he thoroughly and ably ignored her. Hopefully Fiona had slipped from Father's mind too. The idea of his philandering father anywhere near Fiona made Sawyer's skin crawl.

"Are you going to say anything, boy?" Father's jaw worked, the only sign that his temper was flaring.

Let it. Sawyer was no longer the young boy who'd cowered under Father's rages. After years wielding an ax and leveraging logs onto the log carriage heading into the circular saw, he was strong enough to defend against any physical attack, but that wouldn't protect him or anyone else against Father's spite.

A hundred questions raced through his mind. How had Father discovered that he was here? If so, why come now, ten years after their parting? He must realize Sawyer would never reconcile, even for Mother's sake. Mother. Had something happened to her? No. Filby, the family's butler, would have sent word. Father must have come for another reason.

As much as Sawyer wanted to ask the questions and demand the answers, he would not cause a scene in front of Mrs. VanderLeuven, who stared at him with jaw agape. She looked from Sawyer to Father and back again. Thankfully Sawyer resembled his mother, not his father.

Father glared at him. "Have you lost your voice?"

Sawyer tried to swallow, but his throat was dry. "Would you like a room?"

"Of course I want a room. I also want to know what you're doing here when you should be home learning the business."

Sawyer turned the registration book so Father could sign in while he considered what to say. The secret was already out. Mrs. VanderLeuven had heard every word, and by morning the entire town would know the truth unless he tried to cover it up.

Father signed the register. Though Sawyer was tempted to give the man one of the rooms needing repair, he heeded his conscience and chose the best room.

He set the key on the counter, not wanting their hands to touch. "Your room is at the top of the stairs. We will bring your baggage to the room when it arrives from the ship."

"I only have this small bag. Don't plan to stay long. Once you see sense, we'll be on the first ship headed back to Chicago."

Sawyer would not "see sense," nor would he be on a

ship to Chicago. Ever. But he didn't want to say that in front of Mrs. VanderLeuven, who pretended to dust but was listening to every word. So he stuck to business.

"Breakfast will be served in the dining room at seven o'clock unless you prefer to be served in your room. Dinner is at noon and supper at six."

Father stared at him. "Stubborn fool."

Sawyer took that as a compliment.

He kept the smile frozen on his face. "Is there anything else I can help you with, Mr. Evanston?" He spun the registration book around. Father's handwriting was as atrocious as always.

Mrs. VanderLeuven gasped slightly before resuming her dusting.

Father glanced at her and then back at Sawyer before ascending the staircase.

Only after Sawyer heard footsteps overhead, indicating Father was in his room, did he let the smile drop.

Mrs. VanderLeuven hurried over. "Is he your father?"

Conscience fought against self-protection. To deny it would be a lie. "Please don't tell anyone." He had to hope she would heed his wishes. "I need to work some things out with him before it's general knowledge."

From the look on her face, his secret wouldn't last long.

"This is Mary Clare," Fiona told Mrs. Calloway and Louise in the sanctity of the kitchen.

The latter stood promptly. "I'll move my things from the room."

"There's nowhere to go," Fiona pointed out, "not until the stranded passengers leave tomorrow."

"Well now, don't you go worryin' about that," Mrs.

Calloway said as she removed a couple cookies from the jar where she kept a few aside for herself and Mr. Calloway. "Wouldn't you like some sugar cookies and cold milk?" she asked Mary Clare, who vigorously nodded. "Then just set yourself down at the table, and I'll get you a glass of milk." She bustled across the kitchen, never having finished her thought.

"We could squeeze three into the bed," Fiona mused. "It would be tight but possible."

This time Louise shook her head.

Mrs. Calloway clucked her tongue. "Nonsense. We'll take some pillows and make a nice little bed for Miss Mary right next to yours."

"Mary Clare," Fiona's niece corrected her.

"Mary Clare, is it?" Mrs. Calloway cackled. "Like you're royalty."

"I am." Mary Clare held her chin high. "Mama always told me I was a princess."

Fiona had heard the same tale from her mother, how they were descended from some sort of Celtic royalty centuries ago. That didn't do much for any of them now, but on cold nights when her stomach ached from lack of food, it had helped her to dream of a better future.

"Now, don't you say," Mrs. Calloway said with a laugh. She patted Mary Clare's head before turning to Louise. "I've got extra pillows in the upstairs linen closet. Top shelf."

"Maybe I'd better get them," Fiona said. Though unwilling to leave Mary Clare, Fiona knew that Louise couldn't possibly reach the top shelf of the closet.

"We can work together and make short work of it," Louise added. "I wouldn't want to keep you from your niece for very long."

Fiona would have to tell Mrs. Calloway that Mary

Clare was staying, not just visiting, as the boardinghouse proprietress seemed to assume. Fiona had planned to be married by the time her niece arrived. That hadn't happened. Worse, her tormentor, Winslow Evanston, had arrived in Singapore, of all places. Why? To destroy her reputation here too? Surely he had more important things to do than follow her around the country. Whatever the reason for his arrival, he'd clearly seen her. If he made one move to destroy her reputation here, she must leave. She could not subject Mary Clare to the sneers and taunts that would inevitably follow. If only she'd been able to marry someone prominent enough to ward off Evanston's lies. That hope was gone now.

Louise led the way up the staircase. Fiona followed, her legs as heavy as lead. At least the young ladies were occupied in the parlor, discussing with their chaperones what would happen tomorrow.

When they reached the closet, Louise turned to her rather than open the door. "What happened?"

"What do you mean?"

"Instead of being excited by your niece's arrival, you've been pensive and melancholy. Mary Clare is a dear, and you clearly love her, so that's not the reason. What happened?"

Fiona closed her eyes and leaned against the wall. She was strong. All O'Keefes were strong. Then why this terror? "She wasn't the only passenger to get off the ship."

Louise simply waited.

Fiona blew out her breath. "What does a woman do when a man is bent on destroying her future?"

Louise squeezed her arm in sympathy. "Get on your knees and pray. With God, all things are possible. Then rely on those who know and love you. We will stand by you."

Fiona blinked back a rare tear. She was accustomed to snide comments and exclusion, not kindness. "Thank you." It came out raw, and she had to take several breaths before she could continue. "I recognized one of the men who got off the ship tonight. I met him in New York over a year ago. He ruined my reputation by spreading vicious lies that the only way I'd gotten on the stage was by—" it hurt to say it aloud "—giving myself to every man who could further my career."

"Why would he say such things?"

For a moment Fiona wondered if Louise thought her guilty also, but the woman's expression was open and honest.

"Because I refused him publicly. He expected me to become his mistress. I would not. Though few believe it, I refuse to compromise my morals."

Louise's eyes misted. "They misjudge you."

"Most do. I made the mistake of refusing the man in front of journalists. The newspapers published it, giving his name."

"So he struck back."

"By discrediting me." Fiona rubbed her temples. "And now he's in Singapore. Why? I'm almost certain he recognized me. And now Mary Clare is here. What a horrible mess. What am I to do?"

"We will stand behind you."

That was nice but not enough. "Winslow Evanston is rich and powerful. We don't stand a chance."

"Of course we do. God can be our strength, just like He helped David defeat the giant."

"It's going to take a lot more than a rock and a sling." Fiona shuddered. "Winslow Evanston is the reason why I came to Singapore, so I could marry respectably and raise Mary Clare away from the malicious gossip."

"You were wrongly accused. Couldn't you tell the reporters the truth?"

"Who would the columnists believe? A star of the stage or a respected businessman? I didn't stand a chance. Leaving New York was my only hope. I thought I had moved far enough away. I thought no one could hurt me here. Oh, why did he have to come to Singapore?"

Louise grasped her hand. "It was dark, and you had a child with you. Maybe he didn't fully recognize you."

Fiona shivered at the memory of the look he gave her as she made her way to the boardinghouse. She should have cut across the sand rather than follow the boardwalk, but she didn't want Mary Clare to stumble. Walking through sand was much different from walking along a city street. Mary Clare had done none of the former. So Fiona stayed on the boardwalks and came too close to Evanston. Lanterns lit the hotel porch so thoroughly that their glow illuminated the villain's face. Cold and hard and unfeeling, that's what Winslow Evanston was, as if he had no conscience at all.

"He saw me," she said dully. "He stared a long while but said nothing, probably because of Mary Clare."

"He would never hurt a child."

"I'm not sure of that."

This time Louise shivered. "Now you're frightening me."

"Good. Stay far away from him."

"What are you going to do?"

That was the question. Normally, Fiona took charge, but this man had rendered her powerless and broken. Now he was within reach of Mary Clare.

"I don't know."

Chapter Fifteen

In the dull light of early morning, Sawyer hurried to the hotel after a stop at the sawmill. Upon learning that a southbound ship had stopped during the night to load lumber, he hoped his father would leave today. The moment he arrived, Mrs. VanderLeuven informed him that Mr. Evanston had paid for another day.

Sawyer frowned. "Does he know that a southbound ship arrived overnight?"

"Wouldn't know. Neither me nor Lyle had a chance to strike up a conversation, what with cooking and serving breakfast and all."

Sawyer ran a hand through his hair. "I probably should have stayed through the night."

"Nonsense. You were tired as a boy after an outing to the circus. When I found you nodding off behind the registration desk, I knew it was time for you to head on home for a spell. Now you're back, and we can take our rest."

"You do that. Thank you for taking care of everything while I was gone."

"That's what you're payin' us to do." She hesitated. "Things all set at the sawmill?"

"Stopped by there first thing this morning and set up the day's work." It was going to cost him a day's wages, but that was the price he'd have to pay. "Is our guest still in his room?"

"Woke before dawn and wanted breakfast at once. Wouldn't listen to reason." She squinted up at him. "Difficult sort, if you don't mind my saying so."

Sawyer felt for her. Father had probably demanded every detail meet his high expectations. "Tonight I'll watch the desk."

She waved off the suggestion. "You need to spend time with your sweetheart."

Sawyer felt the heat rise to his face. *Sweetheart* was not a term he'd ever considered in connection with Fiona. She was fiery and strong, determined and confident. All that and more, but not exactly sweet. Moreover, she had turned him down in favor of Stockton.

Mrs. VanderLeuven chuckled. "I was young and pretty once. I know how it feels to catch a young man's eye." She winked. "Don't let this one get away."

Sawyer opened his mouth but nothing came out. She must have overheard his offer of courtship to Fiona but missed the part where the lady declined.

"No need to say a word. I have eyes." She pointed to them, winked again and then trundled off to the quarters she and her husband had long shared and would still share for the next week until they crated their belongings and moved to Holland.

Sawyer stood a long moment watching the door behind which she'd disappeared. Once he was managing the hotel, he would live there instead of in the bunkhouse. No more stuffing cotton in his ears to drown out the snores of his bunkmates. No more men coming home at all hours from the saloons, too inebriated to walk straight. It would be quiet. Perhaps too quiet, at least until he finished refurbishing the guest rooms and began renting them again. Until then, he would only have diners—providing he found a cook. Even then, once the diners left for the evening, he'd be all alone.

That thought sent a chill across his skin.

But the voice behind him drove that chill deep into his bones. "So you have a *sweetheart*, Sawyer."

The way Father emphasized "sweetheart" made it clear he disapproved. Sawyer could inform Father that Fiona had refused his suit, but even mentioning her name would put her in Father's sights. She was just the type of woman that he would prey upon. Sawyer could not let that happen.

He turned slowly, shoulders square and jaw set. "That is none of your concern."

Father stood at the base of the stairs. "You're my son, my oldest son. Everything you do is my concern."

"When I enlisted in the Union army, you told me I was dead to you."

For the briefest moment, Father lost his composure. In that instant, Sawyer saw an older, more fragile man than he remembered, and a wave of pity rose in him. Father had no one. A moment ago, Sawyer had felt alone when he considered running the hotel after the Vander-Leuvens left, but he wasn't truly alone. He knew every man and woman in Singapore. They greeted him by name and with a wave or shout of pleasure. He was part of the fabric of this community. Even if he never regained Fiona's affection, he had that.

Father had lost Mother's love long ago. She tolerated him but lived separately. Sawyer had been gone ten years. That left his brother.

"How is Jamie?"

Father flinched at the nickname. "James lost his head and married poorly."

Sawyer wanted to cheer for his little brother. Long spellbound by Father's manipulations, Jamie hadn't once stepped out on his own. Until now. "He's still with the company?"

Father scowled. "He's managing a stockyard."

The distaste was so obvious that Sawyer laughed. "Good for Jamie. How did he ever wander into that field?"

"His wife."

"Ah. That explains it." That also explained why Father had come to Singapore. He'd lost Jamie and now wanted to make peace with the son he'd cast aside ten years ago. "How did you know I was here?"

"I intercepted a letter you wrote your mother."

Sawyer cringed. Poor Mother. She must feel terrible that Father had found him, but it was bound to happen eventually. At least Sawyer had found his place in the meantime.

Father looked him in the eye. "Come home, son."

"I am home."

That look of distaste returned as he surveyed the dilapidated lobby in the light of day. "Working in a run-down hotel?"

"Actually, I bought it."

Father's jaw dropped for a split second before he snapped it back up. "I thought you were more intelligent than that. Didn't I teach you the principles of investment?"

"Yes, and I applied them to this purchase."

"Misapplied is more like it. Fine. Have your fun here." Father pulled out a cigar and lit it. "Hire a good manager under terms that ensure you make a profit. Then come home where you can run a real business."

"Under your oversight."

Father blew out a cloud of smoke. He always did purchase the finest cigars, the most expensive wines and equally expensive mistresses. "There's no one better to teach you the finer points of turning a business into an empire. They don't talk about me in the same breath with Carnegie and Vanderbilt for nothing."

"I'm not interested." Sawyer pulled a cloth from beneath the desk and began polishing the brass lamp next to the registration book.

"Not interested!" Father leaned close. "A thousand men would like to be in your shoes."

"Then pick one of them and give him a chance."

Father's face darkened. When dark clouds formed on the western horizon over Lake Michigan, it meant a storm was on the way. So too with Father.

Sawyer tried to cut it off. "Let me remind you that the VanderLeuvens are on the other side of that door. They can hear every word." And if they were like Mrs. Calloway, they were listening intently.

Father drew back, and the storm passed. In its place came sinister calm. "Your sweetheart might think differently. She might prefer a life of ease and distinction. She might want her children to bear a prominent name."

Sawyer's heart thudded in his chest. Fiona had grown up in poverty. Her every move indicated she placed wealth and a good name above other virtues. Naturally, she would want everything that Father had just listed. Did Father know that Fiona was his sweetheart? He had watched her intently last night. Mrs. VanderLeuven might have mentioned something to Father.

Sawyer did not want Father anywhere near Fiona.

Desire for wealth was her weakness. Father would ex-
ploit that desire to get what he wanted from her. The
very thought made him ill. Father could never respect
a woman like Fiona. Once he'd convinced her to do his
will and extracted everything he wanted, he'd cast her
away like rubbish.

Sawyer had to keep Father from her, but how?

"All right," he said slowly, hoping this bought him
time. "I'll listen."

"What are you going to do?" Louise whispered the
moment Fiona opened her eyes.

A restless night had finally brought slumber near
dawn, but Louise's stirring had awakened Fiona. Judging from the light streaming between the drawn cur-
tains, they had overslept. Fiona rubbed her eyes and
yawned, wondering why Mrs. Calloway hadn't knocked
on their door to wake them up and why Louise was
whispering questions in her ear. It took a moment for
her to recall what had happened the night before.

Mary Clare!

Fiona sat bolt upright.

The girl was still sound asleep. Winslow Evanston
doubtless wasn't. If he recognized Fiona last night, he
was probably searching for her now.

Fiona lay back down, her mind now churning. "I
will stay out of sight and see if he leaves this morning.
If not, I'm taking her north."

Louise's sharp intake of breath told Fiona what she
thought of that idea. "And where will you go? Captain
Elder said it's even more remote up north than here.
There aren't any cities. Where would you live?"

Fiona had thought this out during the wee hours of

the morning. "I'll go to Harmony. He would never follow me there."

"Isn't that rather drastic? They might not take you."

Fiona had to hope they would, because she had no other options. She couldn't wait for an answer to her letters to Mr. Stockton, which might never come. "They seem desperate for women."

"But what about Sawyer? He likes you a great deal."

Fiona closed her eyes. That was the part that hurt. Though he wouldn't give her what she most needed, she couldn't imagine never seeing him again. "The move would only be temporary."

"Would it?" Louise sounded doubtful. "Once there, how would you leave? It's an island, and from what the Adamsons said, it doesn't sound like they welcome many visitors. Will any ships even stop there?"

That gnawed at Fiona too, but she couldn't stay here. Evanston would spread the same false stories here as in the New York. He might have already begun the process. Mr. Stockton would never have her. Even Sawyer wouldn't be seen with her. No one would.

"Why did he have to come here?" she muttered. "He has railroads to run. A wife. Sons. The moment I learned that, I broke off all contact with him."

"That's when he started spreading the rumors," Louise said.

"And didn't stop until I was fired from my engagement and refused at every other reputable theater and teahouse." Fiona sat up and began dressing. She would wear the old gray gown and pull her hair back in a knot that could be easily hidden under a cap. "At least he didn't take a room here." She'd stayed up long enough to ensure that. "I can thank the shipwreck survivors for that."

Louise sat up. "Then he must have stayed at the hotel."

Fiona tugged on the gown. "I assume so."

"Was Sawyer there last night?"

Fiona's fingers paused while buttoning the bodice. "No. Maybe. I'm not certain." He had purchased the hotel, but did that mean he had taken over running it? "I think the VanderLeuvens are still here."

Louise nodded.

Mary Clare yawned noisily.

Fiona clamped her mouth shut and put a finger to her lips. All unnecessary, for the little girl slipped back into slumber at once.

"He must be at the sawmill," Fiona whispered. "He's manager there." And of the hotel.

The thought of Winslow Evanston speaking to Sawyer made her nauseous. Would he ask Sawyer about her? Sawyer didn't know what sort of man Evanston was. He would tell Evanston exactly where to find her.

Fiona dropped to her knees beside the bed and reached underneath until she found her carpetbag. The trunks would have to be packed later. First she needed to find out what the fare cost. If it was too much, she'd have to beg Mr. Adamson for assistance. She would plant fields, clean houses, whatever it took to provide for Mary Clare.

Louise scooted across the bed. "Talk to Sawyer first. Tell him what happened. He'll believe you over a stranger."

Fiona bitterly recalled the friends who had turned their backs in New York. She hadn't hurt them the way she'd wounded Sawyer. "Will he?"

"He will. He adores you."

"I hurt him."

"Nothing an apology wouldn't clear up. I've seen the way he looks at you. He wouldn't let anything or anyone hurt you."

Louise sounded certain. A spark of hope lit inside Fiona. Was it possible Sawyer could forgive her? Would he stand beside her through the storms that Winslow Evanston was sure to ignite? She had to hope he would. It was her only chance.

She looked Louise in the eyes. "Will you watch Mary Clare until I return?"

"Of course. Go to him."

Fiona hurriedly finished getting ready and slipped from the room, heart pounding. Words had wounded him. Could they also heal? It cost her nothing to beg Sawyer's forgiveness. She didn't deserve it for the way she'd treated him, but she must try. Her hand trembled. Louise believed he still loved her. Was it possible? She hoped and prayed it was.

Father's arguments hadn't changed in ten years. Oh, he added new twists, like doing it for the woman he loved, but every word led back to the end goal. Father wanted Sawyer home. And not just home but resuming his place as heir.

Sawyer couldn't agree, but he also couldn't oppose Father, at least not yet. Daylight streamed through the lobby windows. Everyone at the boardinghouse must be up and about by now. Father would get on the southbound ship, but only if Sawyer agreed to his terms.

Some men might make a promise, all the while intending to break it. Sawyer was not that kind of man. He kept his word. He couldn't tell Father he would return home when he had no intention of doing so.

He took a deep breath. "I'm sorry that Jamie decided not to take over the business."

"He never had a head for business like you did," Father wheedled. "You have the right instincts, boy. Always did."

"I have a conscience."

Father plowed right over Sawyer's statement as if he hadn't spoken. "With a little tutelage from the master—me—you'll turn Evanston Railway into an empire that stretches from coast to coast."

Sawyer had inherited more than his conscience from his mother. The Williams side of the family boasted height and strength. Sawyer towered over his father, and in that moment saw how desperate the man was. He'd succeeded in business at the expense of his family and was now trying to reclaim some small piece of what he'd lost. Sawyer was not that piece.

"My place is here. This is my business." He swept his hands wide to indicate the hotel.

"This decrepit place?" Father scowled. "Calling it Astor House won't save it. This town is too small. There's no reason for anyone to come here except to work the mills, and those people aren't going to rent hotel rooms. Trust me. This place will fail."

"Then it's my failure, and I'm willing to accept it."

"Then you're a fool."

Sawyer set his jaw. "Maybe I am, but I want to succeed or fail on my own terms."

Father stared at him, uncharacteristically silent. Sawyer waited for the tirade. It never came. Instead, Father's lips curled into a sneer.

"If that's the way you're going to be, then I want nothing to do with you." Father stalked from the hotel without a backward glance.

At first Sawyer was relieved. The man who'd denigrated and manipulated him since childhood was finally gone. Then, slowly at first, suspicion grew that Winslow Evanston had not played his last card. Father did not give up that easily, especially not when his back was against the wall. Sawyer would hear from him again.

Fiona hurried down the stairs and glanced at the grandfather clock in the front hallway. It read half past eight o'clock. The smell of eggs, bacon and cinnamon wafted through the house, making her stomach rumble. No time to eat now. It would have to wait until after she talked to Sawyer.

Muffled voices came from the dining room along with the clink of silverware on china.

Then Mr. Adamson directed, "Be ready to go to the dock at two o'clock."

"So early?" Linore whined.

"I won't have anyone late. The *Bayshore Clipper* sails at three." His voice then lowered again, and Fiona couldn't make out anything else.

She stepped into the front hallway. She kept her cloak on one of the pegs lining the wall. No fashionable hall tree here. Mr. Calloway had crafted a long board with pegs mounted on it every six inches. It usually had plenty of room for coats and cloaks, but the shipwreck survivors had added to the assembled outerwear so that each peg bore two or three coats.

Fiona moved down the line, checking each peg. If only she would get it into her head to remember where she'd hung her cloak, this hunting wouldn't be necessary.

"Aha!" There it was, buried beneath two threadbare coats that doubtless belonged to two of the brides-to-be.

She lifted off the old coats and set them on another peg temporarily. Then she grasped her cloak.

"I don't care if you're the president of these United States." Mrs. Calloway's loud voice easily reached Fiona from the parlor. "I'm not disturbing anyone from her sleep."

Fiona started. Who wanted someone awoken? Her thoughts scrambled back to Mary Clare, asleep on her makeshift bed, and her heart stopped. Someone wanted to wake Fiona's niece. She squeezed the fur-trimmed collar of her cloak, oblivious to its softness. The only reason to wake someone was to talk with them. Who would want to talk to Mary Clare?

"You can wait, or you can come back," Mrs. Calloway added.

"I'll wait." The masculine voice sent ice through her veins.

Evanston.

She would not let him anywhere near Mary Clare. It was too late to find Sawyer. She must protect her niece.

Fiona replaced the coats on top of hers, effectively hiding it. Evanston would recognize that cloak. Though she'd purchased it with her own earnings, it had been the subject of rampant speculation, thanks to Evanston's innuendos.

Then she crept toward the staircase. She must get Mary Clare out of here now. As long as Fiona still drew a breath of air, Winslow Evanston would not speak to her niece.

She hurried up the first few steps.

"There you are, Fiona dear." Mrs. Calloway had caught her. "There's a man here who wants to talk to you."

"I don't want to talk to him."

"But he's well off. He looks important."

"Looks can be deceiving. I'm going to my room."

"Running away again?" Evanston's voice grated on her nerves.

Fiona turned slowly, taking care to hold on to the railing. "I have no business with you."

"Is that so?" The snake stepped to the bottom of the staircase and put one hand on the banister. "I thought I recognized you last night, Fiona."

"I *knew* I recognized you."

Mrs. Calloway stepped away, but Fiona doubted she'd retreated beyond earshot.

Fiona fixed her attention on Evanston. "I see no reason to talk to you. Good day." She turned to head upstairs.

"Not even when I could tell you something important about Sawyer?"

She halted. Her heart pounded as if she'd run from the hotel to the boardinghouse. What could Evanston possibly know about Sawyer? They might have met at the hotel last night, but they came from different worlds.

She lifted her head high. "Sawyer will tell me all I need to know."

"Such as his time in the war?"

"He told me about that."

"And his childhood?"

She couldn't answer that question in the same way. "What could you possibly know about his childhood?"

The man had the audacity to laugh. The cruel sound snaked up the staircase and wound around her, squeezing the breath from her lungs.

"I know everything, *dear* Fiona." Triumph curled his lips. "I'm his father."

Chapter Sixteen

This detestable man was Sawyer's father? The tightness squeezing Fiona's rib cage made it impossible to breathe. Her head spun. She braced her other hand against the wall so she wouldn't plunge down the steps. Evanston cared for no one. He would have her fall to her death and count it a triumph.

Every instinct told her to run, but that would only trap her upstairs. With Mary Clare. He could easily follow her then. She tightened her grip. No one would get past her.

"Lies," she hissed, gathering courage along with the anger that had built up over the months. "Just like the lies you fed the newspapermen in New York."

The man's laughter echoed through the front hallway. "What a vivid imagination you have, my dear."

"I have proof. Eyewitnesses. The imagination is all yours. What was I to you anyway, just an average singer at best? I believe that's how you put it. You could have nearly any woman you want. Why me? I'm nothing to you."

"Conquest, my dear. Someone like you couldn't possibly understand. It's not about getting what's easy to acquire. It's about the challenge. You were untouchable. Everyone—friend and rival alike—insisted nothing could win you over. I told them that I could."

"Then this misery you brought me was just to feed your pride. How sick a man are you?"

He ignored her outburst. "I don't lose, Fiona. That's how a man builds an empire. I don't accept refusal, and I never give up. It's an Evanston trait."

With a sick feeling, she realized that same perseverance described Sawyer. He'd saved wages for years until he could buy the hotel. At least that's what he'd told her. If Evanston spoke the truth, then Sawyer could have gotten the money from his father. Lies. Why did every man deceive her? Evanston. Countless other men who promised a bright future only to vanish when she refused to give them what they wanted. Blakeney, who'd told her that he would invest her money and return it manyfold, only to steal away when she wasn't watching.

She'd thought Sawyer was different, a common man of strength and courage. Though she'd pushed him away, he never gave up. She'd admired his persistence, but what if it was only a guise? What if his motives were as foul as his father's? If so, then she didn't want Mary Clare anywhere near him.

And yet her heart told her Sawyer couldn't possibly be like this man claiming to be his father. While Evanston took what he wanted, Sawyer insisted on doing things properly. He never pushed for more than she would give. He'd always been a gentleman.

Mary Clare was nothing like her cowardly father. Fiona didn't inherit her mother's submissive temperament. Sawyer might be nothing like his father. If in fact he even was Evanston's son.

"You and Sawyer don't have the same last name."

She stared down the older man, hands on hips. "You're making up everything."

Evanston didn't even flinch. "For some reason Paul thought it beneficial to hide his real name."

Fiona gasped. Evanston knew Sawyer's first name.

"Yes, his real name is Paul Evanston," the man confirmed. "You didn't know that, did you?"

The steam went out of her argument, and she looked away.

Evanston added the crowning touch. "He probably changed his name to keep away fortune hunters."

The implication was obvious. He considered her just that sort.

She would not accept that unfair assessment. "Maybe he changed his name because he didn't want to be associated with you."

Fury slashed across Evanston's face. If she'd been close enough, he would have slapped her. Or worse.

She went up another step. "That is all I have to say to you, Mr. Evanston. You have no connection to my life now or in the future. Goodbye."

Before he could respond, she turned her back on him and climbed the staircase, head held high.

The man cackled, as if he had succeeded in driving her away, rather than the other way around.

When Fiona grasped the doorknob to her room, she knew beyond doubt that she must act now. The escape she'd sought with Sawyer had vanished. As Evanston's son, he could be just as deceptive. For months they'd played concerts and rehearsed. Never once did he mention that he came from wealth and such a cruel, ruthless father. Yes, he'd given her his first name, but nothing more. Nothing that really mattered.

She pushed open the door. Louise stood just inside, looking stricken. She lifted a finger to her lips and pointed to the bed, where Mary Clare slumbered. Louise motioned for Fiona to leave. Had Mary Clare overheard the dispute?

Fiona backed from the room. Louise followed and silently latched the door. Since Fiona didn't care to go downstairs and run into Evanston again, she motioned toward the linen closet.

Louise shook her head. "We can speak here. No need to go downstairs. I overheard what that man said to you."

"Did Mary Clare?"

"No. She was asleep."

Fiona let out her breath, but the relief was short-lived. Mrs. Calloway had surely overheard every word. Even if Evanston didn't spread vile rumors about her here, Mrs. Calloway wouldn't be able to resist passing on this bit of news. Soon the entire town of Singapore would believe she was a fallen woman. She stood no chance of finding a decent man for a husband or making a respectable life here with Mary Clare.

"I must leave today. I have to get Mary Clare away from here." The truth seared through her with the pain of a hundred bee stings. Her hopes had been crushed once again. There wouldn't be a home with a husband who loved her. She wouldn't spend evenings singing and teaching her niece to pick out a tune on the piano.

Louise touched her arm. "I'm guessing that Sawyer took another name because he didn't want to be associated with his father."

Fiona wanted to believe that. "I can't be sure."

"Are we ever sure? Measure a man by what he does, not what he says."

Such truth in those words, as if Louise had experience. "Your husband?"

Louise averted her gaze. "I should have known. People warned me, but no man had ever paid me such attention before. I didn't realize his real aim was my fortune." She looked up, stricken. "He squandered it all and then blamed me."

The pain in those words pulled Fiona from her own plight. Poor Louise had suffered too. She wrapped an arm around the woman who had become a friend.

"We don't always see the signs or heed the warnings. It's easier to overlook them." Fiona swallowed that truth. "I didn't recognize Mr. Evanston's true character at first. He seemed the gentleman with his fine suits and elegant manners. His gifts seemed sincere. I thought he would make the perfect father for Mary Clare. If I hadn't seen the newspaper article about him and his family…" She shook her head at the thought of what might have happened. She would have fallen into his web, and he would have won his conquest. She could thank God's faithful guidance for nudging her away from complete disaster. "I didn't see his true character until I resisted him. Then came his vengeance."

"You can't measure Sawyer by his father."

Fiona closed her eyes and leaned against the door. Not a sound came from within the room. Her heart told her that Louise was right, but her head cautioned her against putting her faith in a man. They always let her down.

Louise continued, "From what I've seen, Sawyer treats you with respect. He's been interested in you from the day we arrived here, but you never once said he pressed you."

"He didn't."

"So he cares about your feelings more than his own. He also attends church regularly and never visits a saloon."

Fiona opened her eyes. "How do you know so much about who goes to the saloons?"

Louise blushed. "When I'm walking around examining the local flora, I pay attention to where the men go after work."

"Why? Oh, I see." The answer was obvious and made perfect sense, given Louise's penchant for detailed notes. "That notebook of yours has more than plants and birds in it. You're also taking notes on prospective husbands."

Louise's blush deepened. "It's not wrong to notice things here and there. That's what a writer once urged me to do if I ever hope to write stories of my own."

"I had no idea you wanted to be a writer."

Louise shrugged. "A silly fancy is all."

Except it wasn't silly, and it had confirmed something very important about Sawyer. "You said he never goes to the saloons?"

"And he is trying to better himself, if what you told me is right. He bought the hotel."

"Yes, he did." But was that purchase possible only through family money? One way or another, she had to know if Sawyer had lied to her. "I need to check on something. Will you watch Mary Clare for an hour?"

She should be able to get an answer long before the ship's three o'clock departure time.

"I haven't changed my mind." Sawyer glared at his father.

If the man wasn't a customer, he would tell him to leave.

Father didn't accept this declaration any more than he'd accepted all the other ones. He removed his gloves, one finger at a time, and then set his hat on the registration desk.

"I'm not here to ask again that you return home."

"You aren't?" Sawyer watched his father warily.

The man's carefully groomed mustache and whiskers were reminiscent of the previous decade. Graying when Sawyer had last seen him, they were now snow-white. Even so, the man's skin didn't bear the lines of care that Mother's did. Father didn't worry. He forced circumstances until he got his way.

Father set his hat on the desk beside his gloves. "I returned to warn you."

Sawyer's defenses went on alert. Father did nothing out of concern or kindness. Whatever warning he was about to issue was bound to carry a hidden agenda, one that furthered Father's primary goal.

Father settled his black gaze on him. "Are you going to ask me to sit? We might take advantage of the furnishings, such as they are, in this tiny lobby."

"Since I'm working, I prefer to stand."

Father smirked. "There are no other customers."

The man had a way of grating on Sawyer's nerves with every sentence he spoke.

"The day is young," Sawyer said through clenched teeth.

"Very well. I simply thought that such news shouldn't be taken standing up."

Now Father had his attention.

The man somehow managed a look of concern. "I dislike bearing bad news."

"No, you don't."

"In matters of business, perhaps you are correct, but

when it comes to my family—" Father shook his head "—it pains me. But the hurt will be swift and soon heal."

"Get on with it or leave."

"Courage. That's what I always liked about you, Paul. You could stand up to anything and anyone. That's the sort of man I want running my company after I'm gone."

Sawyer shot him a glare. "I thought this wasn't about begging me to return."

"You're right. It's not. It's about your future, though." He cleared his throat and looked over Sawyer's shoulder as if he couldn't bear to witness Sawyer's reaction. "I left earlier to inquire about passage on the schooner that is heading for Chicago after it finishes loading lumber. While doing so, I happened to see a familiar face." He paused, doubtless waiting for Sawyer to react.

He did not.

Not having gotten a reaction didn't stop Father from finishing his tale. "Someone I met in New York City when I was there on business." Again he gave a great sigh, as if fearing the results of what he was about to divulge.

"You should have been an actor," Sawyer spit out.

Father's eyes bulged. Sawyer had offended him. In Father's view, actors rated no higher than laborers laying track.

Then he unexpectedly chuckled, though there was no warmth in it. "Funny you should mention acting. The acquaintance I'm speaking of was in nearly the same trade. A singer, she calls herself, though her talent is not great."

Sawyer's blood ran cold. He thought he had prepared himself for anything Father might throw his way, but he had never imagined he'd hear this. Only one woman in Singapore was a singer from New York City. He would not listen to any made-up slander about her. "Fiona's voice is exquisite, though I wouldn't expect you to recognize that. You never had an ear for music."

"Fiona. Ah, yes. I see you're already acquainted." Father shook his head as if deeply sorrowed. "I'd hoped what I heard wasn't true. Tell me you're not…involved with that woman."

Sawyer would say no such thing. "Whatever you plan to say about Fiona can stay with you. I don't want to hear it."

"Oh, you'll want to hear this. You need to hear it." Father wore that smug grin that drove Sawyer crazy. "I attended one of her concerts in New York. No doubt the theater owner, hoping to secure my patronage, pointed me out to her, because after the concert she approached me and, shall we say, suggested she could—"

"Stop!" Sawyer gripped the desk so he didn't punch his father. "There's nothing you can say that I will believe."

"Believe it. Her reputation is well-known. You can ask anyone from the city. They will have heard of her."

"Because she's a stunning soprano."

"Because she has been mistress to many a wealthy man."

"Lies." Sawyer didn't believe anything his father said. "Nothing you say can convince me otherwise."

"Don't listen to me, then. Read the newspapers. Her exploits of last July were well-documented in all the New York papers."

"I don't place any stock in newspaper reports. They print whatever will sell the most papers."

"Believe it or not." Father feigned nonchalance remarkably well. "I simply wanted to help you avoid a costly mistake. She got a great deal of money from business acquaintances of mine."

"I don't believe you."

"Where else do you think she got her fancy gowns and jewels? The middle daughter of eight from an Irish tenement doesn't have that sort of money."

Father knew an awful lot about Fiona. How? For that matter, why? Father only went to that level of investigation when he had a purpose in mind, but he couldn't possibly know that Sawyer felt strongly enough about her to offer courtship. He hadn't even written Mother about it. Was Father actually speaking the truth? Sawyer couldn't believe it, didn't want to believe it.

"She earned it with her singing." But he was less sure of that. Even if she was in the newspapers, she wasn't famous enough to earn the sort of money that could buy the lavish jewelry she wore. Sawyer knew from the few times he played piano for hire that a musician didn't get rich.

Father's laugh cut through him. "Believe that if you must, but it's not true. She's only after a man's money."

Money! The truth hit Sawyer between the eyes. Father had made a big mistake in his argument, proving it completely false. This time Sawyer had it right.

"No, she's not." Confidence boomed with each word. "She doesn't know I'm your son. She thinks I'm a poor lumberjack who can't afford a new shirt. If she's the fortune hunter you say she is, she would have nothing to do with me."

Father tapped an index finger on the desk. "She knows. Don't fool yourself. She knows."

A cold breeze raised goose bumps on Sawyer's

arms and shattered the confidence he'd just displayed. "How?" But he knew the answer. Father had told her.

"That doesn't matter. What you need to ask yourself is if you want to be tied to a woman who goes from man to man without settling down. You might think she'll behave once she's married, but that sort never does. It's in her blood, son, and nothing you do will reform her."

Sawyer heard a gasp. He looked toward the front door and saw Fiona, an expression of horror on her ashen face.

It was over in the worst possible way, but Fiona was not one to give people the satisfaction of knowing they'd gotten to her. So after the initial gasp, she gathered her wildly racing emotions and faced both men.

"I presume you were speaking of me." The comment was directed at Evanston, but she watched for Sawyer's reaction.

He flinched and looked down a moment. Color flooded his cheeks, but he looked just as determined as her not to back down.

"Miss O'Keefe," Evanston said, false politeness oozing from each word. "How fortuitous you arrived when you did."

"Fortunate for you." She hoped that's what *fortuitous* meant. "And for whatever you're trying to gain." She focused again on Sawyer. "Did he convince you that I am a wicked woman?"

Sawyer paused a moment before answering, "No."

Her spirits lifted. "Then you trust me."

This time Sawyer's hesitation took much longer. His gaze darted between her and his father. Her heart sank. He didn't know who to believe. In a fight against a parent, she would lose every time.

Sawyer cleared his throat. "Just tell me why you never mentioned what happened in New York."

The fact that he'd asked her that question meant Evanston had told him the lies already. "The way you told me about your father?"

Sawyer looked away, his jaw working. "I didn't think it was important."

Evanston had the nerve to cackle, as if they were following his plan exactly. "Good. Good."

"You're saying that your father is not important." She glared at Evanston, but he didn't drop the triumphant grin. "Your family is highly important."

"You didn't tell me that you grew up in the tenements."

How did he know that? Oh. Evanston probably searched that information out. She jutted her jaw. "And you didn't tell me that you grew up in a mansion."

There. The differences were out. She and Sawyer had always been at opposite ends of the spectrum, though not in the way Fiona had thought. In fact, quite opposite. Each had hidden the truth from the other, a fact that Evanston had used for his purposes. Fiona couldn't let the villain steal her future again. At least he didn't know about Mary Clare. Yet.

"It wasn't a mansion." But Sawyer looked guilty while claiming that. "Though it might seem like that to someone growing up in poverty."

She was getting nowhere, and Evanston was lapping up every moment. Had she walked right into his trap? She wished she'd arrived sooner, but it had taken too long to assure Mary Clare that she would return.

"I've been on my own for ten years," Sawyer added stiffly.

He had talked about enlisting for the war and the

ten years that followed, but not his childhood. Now she knew why. Sawyer wouldn't look her in the eye. Evanston, in contrast, chuckled with glee. Why didn't the older man leave? He'd already done the damage.

She glared at Evanston, holding his gaze until he blinked and murmured that he should go to his room.

Sawyer's jaw worked. "That would be good."

Fiona couldn't miss the tension between father and son, and yet Sawyer believed his father. Not her. The disappointment crushed her. Until that moment, she hadn't realized how much Sawyer meant to her. Yes, the thought of leaving him hurt, but to know he didn't believe her was somehow worse. His admiration and affection meant more to her than that of any other person.

Only after Evanston was gone did Sawyer speak. "How did you meet him?"

"Your father?"

Sawyer flinched. "Yes, my father, Winslow Evanston III, to be precise." Animosity colored each word.

Fiona's throat ached, but swallowing didn't ease the pain. "What did he tell you?"

Doubtless it hadn't been complimentary.

"I want to hear it from your lips."

The fact that Sawyer's expression hadn't eased one bit frayed her nerves. "He attended one of my concerts." She paused to watch his reaction.

"Go on."

"He introduced himself as an admirer and after the following day's performance, brought me flowers. The next day he brought perfume and then a silk scarf."

Sawyer winced with every revelation. It couldn't be easy to hear such things about one's father.

"I was accustomed to men offering gifts," she said slowly, making sure he heard, "and had learned how to

politely refuse them and the advances that followed."
She paused. "Your father laughed off my refusal."

Sawyer's jaw clenched. "Go on."

Even remembering what happened next hurt, but
Fiona would not burst into tears. Her sisters might, but
Fiona was stronger. Life on the stage had taught her
that much.

"I let him buy my supper one night, a mistake I wish I
could take back. He had acted the gentleman, and I'd let
my desire to marry cloud my perception. Once I agreed
to dine with him, he assumed he had broken down my
defenses. Now, up until this point, I didn't know much
about him. He'd introduced himself as Mr. Evans. Ironic,
don't you think?"

Sawyer's frown only intensified.

Fiona felt the bond between them slipping. What did
the Bible say? The truth will make you free? Well, she'd
had enough of hiding.

"The night he brought me a ruby necklace raised my
suspicions, but I foolishly accepted it."

"Is that how you got your jewelry? In payment for
favors?"

The accusation seared through her, but she would not
stop until the full truth was out. "Once I really thought
about it, I realized he had told me nothing about himself.
I asked around and learned Evans wasn't his real name.
I saw a newspaper story about him being in town and
learned he was married with grown children."

Sawyer's face twisted with distaste.

She did not stop. "I returned the necklace the next
day, but the damage was done. He expected something
in return for his favors. I refused. Unfortunately, reporters were near enough to overhear my rather heated
words. I thought I'd saved my reputation. Instead, the

following day the newspapers slaughtered my reputation. The day after that, I lost my singing engagement."

When she'd hinted before at the trauma that had forced her to leave New York, Sawyer had been sympathetic. Today, compassion battled doubt while she told the story. Just one chapter remained.

"That's why I came here in answer to Garrett Decker's advertisement."

"To save your reputation."

"To begin again." She ached to tell him the hope of her heart. He might scoff, but she couldn't leave without him knowing. "To have a family of my own."

Sawyer looked shocked. "Then, you accepted Carson Blakeney's attentions because…you needed to marry."

"Yes."

"You didn't love him."

"I didn't."

Sawyer set his jaw again. "That's why you gave your attentions to me too. Because you needed to marry."

Oh, how her heart was breaking. It hurt so badly that she could barely draw a breath. "No. Not entirely."

"Of course it was." He paced the lobby's threadbare rugs. "When Blakeney fell through, you needed to find someone else, so you answered the newspaper advertisement."

She gasped. "How do you know that?"

He pulled an envelope—her envelope—from his pocket. "Because I'm the one referred to in the advertisement, not Mr. Stockton or anyone else."

"You?" She tried to wrap her mind around this revelation. "But you don't want to marry."

"It was a mistake." He threw the envelope onto the registration desk. "Pearl and Roland were teasing me.

It wasn't supposed to be published, but it got in a stack of paper that Mr. Hennigan picked up from Pearl."

The truth slowly dawned. "Then you truly don't want to marry. It's all just a grand game you're playing with other people's emotions."

"There wasn't any way to take it back."

"You could have asked Mr. Hennigan to print a retraction. You could have posted something at the mercantile. Instead you let us—me—go on believing that there was a real suitor in search of a wife." What a fool she'd made of herself in front of Mr. Stockton. No wonder he'd thought her a maid. No wonder he hadn't sought to introduce himself. No wonder she'd received no reply. It was all a great joke.

"But you weren't interested in marrying me until you learned I'm heir to a fortune," he said, lashing back.

"That has nothing to do with my decision." Or did it? She had rejected Sawyer in favor of what she thought was a wealthier man. Too late she'd learned just how wrong that choice was.

He seemed not to hear her, instead pacing from door to registration desk and back again, over and over until it left her dizzy. "You needed a husband and a father for your niece. I was the best option left. What an idiot I was to think you might have appreciated me for who I am, not for the wealth I might have one day."

"First of all, I didn't know you were an heir. Second, I don't want your money, not one cent of it." There, she'd said it, and surprisingly it was true. She didn't want anything that came from Winslow Evanston.

"Good. You're not getting anything from me."

So that's what it came down to. For all of Sawyer's talk about making his own life here, he still held on to the family fortune like a lifeline. "Fine. You can have your money, your hotel, your grand future. Take it all. I don't want anything to do with it or with someone who lies about who he is."

Fury carried her out the door. It slammed that door behind her and strode down the boardwalk with purpose. Fury would have to carry Fiona and Mary Clare to a new life, for she had nothing left here.

Chapter Seventeen

Sawyer stared at the closed door. Fiona had walked out on *him*. He should be angry, but aching disappointment crowded in instead. Even though she hadn't given him time to counter her claims, he had no defense. He was guilty.

He had lied, had hidden his identity from the woman he intended to court. That was not a good foundation for any relationship, least of all one that could lead to marriage. His parents were a fine example of what not to do. Marriage must be based on openness and honesty, like Roland and Pearl. Nothing hidden from each other.

Yet he'd begun on the wrong foot and continued on that path. From the advertisement to his parentage and change of name, he'd forged a trail of secrecy.

The creaking of the staircase told him Father was coming down. The brief interval between Fiona's departure and Father's appearance meant he'd listened to every word.

Father approached the desk with a smug grin. "Well done, son."

As a boy, Sawyer had longed for his father's approval. Today it rang flat in his ears. "No, it wasn't. I let a good and honorable woman slip away."

"Good? Honorable?" Father snorted. "You don't believe her story—"

"I believe every word." Sawyer would not let his father manipulate him this time. The rumors of Father's indiscretions had now been proved. "I know about your mistresses and how you've broken Mother's heart."

Father's face darkened. "Now, boy, that's no way to talk to your father."

"I'm not a boy any longer. I'm a grown man who intends to make his own way in the world. I know what I've seen, and I want nothing to do with you or your business empire. Life isn't about conquest and fortune. It's about the people you love."

"Soft-hearted nonsense."

Sawyer stood firm. "The only way to live. I've made a lot of mistakes, but I'm not going to let dishonesty be one of them. For the last time, I will not return to Chicago, and I will never work for you. This is my home, and I'm going to do everything in my power to convince the most beautiful woman in the world to give me a second chance."

"You'd throw away a fortune for a woman like that?"

"I'm stepping away from a fortune for a noble, compassionate woman who cares more about others than her own comfort." That finally sank in. Fiona's attempts to marry weren't for selfish reasons but for her niece. He wouldn't blame her for turning him down, after all, he had nothing to offer, but he had to try. "Goodbye, Father. I suggest you take that ship to Chicago."

Father's lips pressed into a hard line. "That's your final word?"

"It is."

"If you give up your inheritance now, it's irrevocable."

"I understand."

"I won't change my mind, no matter how much you beg."

If Father thought that would prod Sawyer in a different direction, he was wrong. Sawyer was no longer the son who chafed under Father's "guidance" but went along with it anyway. He was a new man. He'd shed the old Paul and become Sawyer through and through.

Sawyer Evans didn't care about building a business empire. He cared about providing for his family, sure, but God was the ultimate provider, and Jesus said that God would provide all we needed. Sawyer would work hard and trust God for the rest. That included the family part. Somehow he needed to make amends to Fiona. Whether she forgave him was up to her, but he had to do his part. It began with bidding Father farewell.

"I don't beg." Sawyer stood tall but with ease and confidence. "I won't ask you for anything ever again."

Father stared a long moment, as if determining the truth behind Sawyer's statement. Apparently deciding Sawyer would not back down, he ascended the stairs. A short time later, he descended, carrying his bag, and walked out of the hotel without a glance in the direction of the registration desk. No doubt Father intended the snub to stir up guilt. Instead, it did the reverse.

Sawyer had never felt so free.

Fiona packed Mary Clare's few belongings into her large trunks along with the most serviceable gowns she owned. A remote northern island wouldn't give her any occasion to wear finery except at Sunday service. Even that, she suspected, would be less formal than Singapore's makeshift services in between stops from the circuit preacher. Mr. Adamson hadn't given her many details about life in Harmony, though he had agreed to her proposal.

"Take the jewelry," Fiona said to Louise.

Mary Clare had been playing with the necklaces and earrings for over an hour, pretending she was a grand duchess ordering around her servants, Louise and Fiona. Since Fiona had suggested the duchess command that her trunks be packed, all was proceeding well. Separating the jewels from Mary Clare might be more of a problem.

Louise looked dubious. "Are you certain? You might sell them. Or Mary Clare might inherit them."

"They're worthless glass."

Louise's eyes rounded. "Glass?"

"Glass." Fiona would have laughed if she wasn't still steaming over Sawyer's unspoken reprimand. Clearly Louise thought the same as Sawyer, that she had been given all her finery in exchange for favors. Fiona was tired of being judged. "I paid a night's wages for the whole lot. I think the previous owner got the better end of the deal." She picked up the fake emerald necklace and pointed out where a piece of glass was missing. "The glass stones fall out all the time. Usually I find them right away, but this one is gone. I never had a chance to get another made."

"It's lovely," Louise breathed, her cheeks uncommonly pink, "but where would I wear such finery around here?"

"To concerts." But the word caught in her throat.

Once Fiona left, there might not be any more concerts. Sawyer would be too busy running the hotel and working at the sawmill to play piano or violin. Only the possibility of making a profit would tempt him to waste time playing music. Like father, like son. Why hadn't she noticed that drive to succeed? Sawyer had skimmed past her idea of turning the hotel into a boarding school in favor of grandiose plans befitting a hotel in the heart of New York City, not in tiny Singapore.

"I'm not sure there will be any concerts." Louise echoed what Fiona had been thinking, except with a sigh of disappointment. "No one could take your place."

Her plea tugged at Fiona's heart, but not as much as the thought of never seeing Sawyer again. Only anger dulled that ache, and he was the cause of that ire. She'd thought he was different, that he didn't judge people based on appearances and rumor. How wrong she'd been. Instead of standing up for her, he'd believed that deceitful father of his. The very presence of Winslow Evanston had made up her mind. By now he'd probably begun spreading the same vile rumors as in New York. She must take Mary Clare away, so she didn't have to endure the taunts and shunning sure to follow.

"Please stay," Louise pleaded.

"I can't." Fiona glanced at Mary Clare, who was promenading beside the bed with her right arm extended as if to a nobleman. The glass rubies glittered in the sunlight streaming through the window. "You know why."

"Sawyer loves you. I know he does. At least try to mend your differences."

What could she mend? As much as she'd longed for Sawyer's affection, he was Winslow Evanston's son. The connection was there. It would always be there. Nothing could change that. She would take her broken heart north and make a new life for her niece.

"It's not possible," she said, picking up another night-gown to fold.

"Anything is possible for the Lord."

"Maybe for God, but not for me."

"But—"

"Enough, Louise. This is how it has to be." Though she'd told Louise about Evanston last night, she couldn't tell her that Sawyer was the man's son. That information was Sawyer's to disclose or not. "Mary Clare, give Louise the necklace. You and I need to go downstairs to eat some dinner."

"No! The grand duchess declares that she is not hungry."

Louise quietly cautioned Mary Clare, but Fiona sighed. Raising a child was not going to be easy. Memories of her younger siblings rushed in like flies through an open window. Fiona had failed with them. She could not fail with her niece. How could she do things differently? As a child, she hadn't wanted to watch her younger brothers and sisters. So she'd ignored them. She could not ignore her niece. Perhaps joining Mary Clare's world would work.

Fiona stood with as regal a pose as she could manage. "The grand duchess might not be hungry, but Queen Fiona is. Since she will not eat without the company of her favorite duchess, your attendance is requested and required."

"Oh. All right, then." Mary Clare jumped up to sit on the bed. She then began to undo the necklace.

Fiona stopped her. "Keep it. The duchess must have her jewels, after all."

Louise gave her a grateful look.

Mary Clare grinned, hopped off the bed and hurried to the door. "Are we going now, Queen Fiona?"

Fiona reached out a hand, which the little girl grasped. Warmth, compassion and love flooded through Fiona's heart. She was doing the right thing. It must be right.

Since Father refused to leave on the next ship, Sawyer hurried to the boardinghouse to warn Fiona. No doubt Father was up to something, and it probably had to do with Fiona. Sawyer was ashamed of his father's behavior. That he'd slandered Fiona made him furious. Sawyer had botched things with her too much for reconciliation, but he could at least caution her.

The Bible said to forgive. Receiving forgiveness depended on giving it. By that measure, Sawyer had to forgive Father if he expected to receive forgiveness from Fiona. That was a tough order. Sawyer would find a way to do it, but he couldn't forget.

"That's up to you, Lord," he murmured.

"What's up to the Lord?" Roland Decker settled in beside him, stride for stride. "Or maybe I should say what isn't?"

"Right." Sawyer hunched against the chill breeze. Dark clouds gathered on the horizon, signaling rain was on its way. "That doesn't make it any easier to forgive— or to apologize."

Roland nodded. "All I can tell you is that it has to come from the heart."

"That might not be enough." His thoughts wandered to Fiona. "I made a big mess of things."

"Well, for the really big apologies, a gift always helps. Now, I'm not speaking as the store manager, mind you. I'm speaking from experience. When Pearl was angry with me—for good reason—I bought her a new dress."

"That worked?" Sawyer had a tough time imagining Pearl excited over a dress. She was much too practical.

"Well, I had to have Sadie give it to her."

"Oh."

Sadie was Roland's niece. Pearl had rescued the little girl in the schoolhouse fire last November, so she had a tender heart for her. Who held a spot in Fiona's heart? No doubt her niece, but Sawyer didn't know the little girl. The stranded Harmony-bound ladies? Fiona displayed both compassion and frustration around them.

"I need to haul my new merchandise inside before those storm clouds drop their rain. I wish you well." Roland hurried to the dock behind the mercantile, where a stack of crates had been unloaded off one of the ships.

Sawyer tossed around Roland's advice but couldn't find a practical way to use it. Fiona loved pretty gowns, but he couldn't possibly afford one that met her standards. Moreover, he stood no chance of convincing Mary Clare to give it to her. They hadn't even met yet.

So forget dresses. The other traditional gift, flowers, wouldn't work either. Other than a few intrepid crocuses that had popped up around the Elders' house, there wasn't a flower to be found. He'd never seen Fiona read. She would enjoy sheet music, but she had a copy of everything Roland had in stock.

No, the heartfelt apology was the best he had.

The boardinghouse was only a short distance from the mercantile, but it felt like miles while Sawyer considered what to say. He'd never been good at speeches, something his father had pointed out countless times while growing up. *You'll never be anything if you can't persuade people*, Father had told him over and over. He'd enrolled Sawyer in special classes designed to teach speech-giving, but Sawyer was no Abraham Lincoln. In the heat of the moment, his mind went blank.

Too soon the boardinghouse's plain and simple porch loomed before him.

Simple. That was it. He'd keep it simple.

Sawyer scaled the steps two at a time and knocked firmly on the door. He heard nothing at first. Finally footsteps padded across the wooden floor. Very light footsteps, perhaps one of the more petite ladies, since the *Bayshore Clipper* wouldn't depart until midafternoon.

The door slowly opened, and he saw no one.

Take that back.

When Sawyer lowered his gaze, there stood before him one confident young girl of perhaps seven or eight years old. Her dark hair was long and straight, and could use some brushing. Fiona's ruby necklace was draped around her neck.

"Hello," the girl said.

"Hello. You must be Fiona's niece." Sawyer searched his memory for the girl's name. "Mary Clare."

"Actually, I am the Grand Duchess Mary Clare."

"Ah, forgive me, Grand Duchess. May I beg an audience with your aunt?"

The girl scrunched her nose while she considered his request. "You wanna see her?"

"Yes, please. Tell her it's Sawyer. Mr. Evans." He hoped Fiona had calmed down since the encounter at the hotel.

"All right." Mary Clare turned and tromped down the hallway and into the dining room, leaving the front door wide open.

Sawyer stepped inside and closed the door behind him.

Mrs. Calloway came flying out of the kitchen, wiping her hands on her apron as she too headed for the dining room. When she spotted Sawyer, she changed direction and jerked her head toward the parlor.

Sawyer followed her into the room. "What is it?"

Mrs. Calloway grasped both his shoulders. "Don't let her go. I'm tellin' you. Do whatever you got to do, but don't let her go."

"Fiona?" A chill swept over him. "Where is she going?"

"She's up and decided she has to join those crazy people in their colony—what's it called… Harmony or something like that—up north on an island, but I'm tellin' you she'll regret it. You hafta make her see sense."

Sawyer couldn't believe it. Fiona was not the type for a utopian colony. A big city? Yes. Homesteading a remote island? Never. "You must be mistaken."

"Not one bit. Honest truth as sure as I'm standin' here. And it's going to be a sad day for our church, I tell you. Miss Fiona's the only person in the whole area who's got half a voice—yourself excepting, of course."

Sawyer stifled a grin. "If she's only got half a voice, then I'm barely a quarter."

"There's no time for quibblin' about particulars." Mrs. Calloway pointed toward the hallway. "She's in the dining room. Get down on bended knee. Tell her what you've been wantin' to tell her since she set foot in town." The woman winked at him. "I know your little secret." She patted her ample chest. "But it's safely locked in here. Unless you don't do the right thing. Then there's no telling what'll pop out of my mouth."

Sawyer was tempted to tell her that the secrecy wasn't necessary, but she added, "I haven't told a soul. I always give a man a chance to do the right thing before I take charge."

Sawyer took that as a warning—an unnecessary one but one worth heeding. "Yes, ma'am."

Mary Clare appeared in the parlor doorway. "The queen don't want to see you." The girl then walked away.

"The queen?" Sawyer had no idea what the little girl meant.

"Miss Fiona." Mrs. Calloway chuckled. "I never heard so apt a title. She's the queen all right."

"Mary Clare calls her aunt the queen?"

"Oh, it's a little game they're playing." She chuckled, but an instant later grew somber. "Go after her. Make her see reason. She can't take that child away to that place. You have to stop her. Please."

It was the last that told Sawyer this was no ordinary situation. Fiona must indeed be planning to leave Singapore for Adamson's colony of Harmony if she was bringing Mary Clare with her. She wouldn't fit in there. Neither would the little girl. These sorts of colonies didn't encourage the sort of individuality that Fiona and Mary Clare exhibited. Fiona's talent would be squashed.

He stepped into the hallway in time to see Fiona ascending the stairway.

"Fiona!" He hurried to the foot of the stairs.

She turned briefly. "I have nothing to say to you."

"But I need to warn you. My father insists on staying. I tried to get him to leave on the schooner that came in overnight, but he refused."

"I see."

Was that all? No thanks. No reaction at all.

She resumed climbing the staircase.

He'd better move on to the apology. "I made a mistake. I shouldn't have hidden who I was from you."

She stopped again and this time turned to face him. "But it's all right to claim to be someone you're not to everyone else?"

Sawyer ignored that jab. He had to finish his point. "I'm not that man anymore. I haven't been for a long time. It started ten years ago when I rejected Father's plan and enlisted in the war. I foolishly hoped I'd be killed. After one battle, that changed. So did I. I vowed never to go back."

"You turned your back on your entire family."

"No. I write to Mother. She knows I'm here and that I changed my name." Which was how Father found him. "My younger brother and I were never close, but I just learned he is now married."

"Then he inherits."

Is that what concerned her? Bile rose in his throat. Surely Father couldn't be right. Surely Fiona wasn't a fortune hunter. There was only one way to find out.

"I suppose he does." Sawyer watched her expression. "What's certain is that I won't."

Fiona didn't react at all. She appeared frozen in disbelief except that fury still danced in her eyes.

He offered one final explanation. "Once I learned what type of man my father truly was, I couldn't have my name associated with his. That's why I changed it. That's why I won't go back."

She nodded slightly, her expression still rigid. "I see."

She then resumed climbing the staircase.

That was all? She understood but offered no forgiveness? Or had he truly asked?

"I deeply regret the hurt I've caused."

Again she paused.

He took a breath and steadied his voice, which was getting ragged with emotion. "I regret not being fully honest with you from the beginning and hope you will forgive me."

She didn't move.

He held his breath.

Then, her back rigid, she walked up the stairs and disappeared from view.

Chapter Eighteen

Fiona O'Keefe didn't cry. Then why were tears stream-ing down her face? Why these wretched heaving sobs? No man had ever affected her like this before. She had broken off many a relationship before it got to the awk-ward, demanding stage.

"Get control of yourself. He's just a man, one not to be trusted." Then why did the sobs return, forcing her to once again press her handkerchief to her face?

Louise slipped into the room without knocking and closed the door behind her. "We all make mistakes."

"Don't counsel me." Then, regretting the way she'd snapped at her innocent roommate, she added, "I'm sorry."

Louise sat beside her on the bed. "It's all right. I don't know what happened between you two, but I can tell by the look of devastation on his face that he loves you."

Such words only increased the pain. It had gotten so bad that Fiona could barely breathe. "I can't take a chance," she managed to say between gasps.

"Why not?"

The answer was obvious. "I can't let Mary Clare anywhere near Winslow Evanston."

"But what does that have to do with Sawyer? He would protect you and Mary Clare."

Fiona swallowed the ache in her heart. In her despair, she'd nearly unveiled Sawyer's secret. "Perhaps he would for now, but what does the future hold?"

"None of us know the future."

Fiona's resolve strengthened. "Look at what happened to you. A bad choice is worse than not marrying at all."

"Why would you think Sawyer is a bad choice? He's been nothing but kind and thoughtful."

Fiona shook her head. "It might seem that way, but what's beneath the surface? Like father; like son?"

"What do you mean?"

Fiona gasped. Sawyer's secret had slipped out. Perhaps Louise had already made the connection. If not, she would hear about it. She might as well hear it from a friend. "He's not who he claims to be."

"I don't understand."

"He's not a lumberjack." Fiona's throat ached from holding back the tears. "Oh, he might well have cut down a tree or two, but he's no illiterate drifter moving from one camp to the next."

"He is exceedingly well-read, but that's not a crime."

"Lying is."

Louise spoke barely above a whisper. "How did he lie to you?"

"Sawyer is the son of the man who ruined my reputation in New York, Winslow Evanston." There. She'd said it. But the speaking didn't relieve the pain. If anything, it made it worse, for deep down she knew that Sawyer was nothing like his father. Still, she couldn't take a chance.

"But they don't have the same last name."

"Sawyer changed his name to distance himself from his father."

"That's a good sign. He doesn't want to be associated with his father."

Fiona shook her head. "Changing a name doesn't change a man's nature."

Louise sat quietly for a moment. "Does it follow that a child is always like the parent?"

"They inherit traits."

"Then you are like your mother."

Fiona choked on the thought. "No! Not at all." Her mother acquiesced to her father's poor decisions instead of lifting her voice in opposition.

"Perhaps Sawyer isn't at all like his father."

"It's different." Though Fiona knew she was grasping at straws, she had to find something to relieve the anguish tearing her apart. "I came from nothing. He comes from wealth."

"Mmm." Louise didn't articulate her thoughts further.

"You believe I'm being unfair."

"Just a bit hasty."

"I have no choice. I need to protect Mary Clare."

"And you think living in Harmony will keep away anything that might hurt her. Do you really believe that?"

Fiona hated that Louise made sense, but she couldn't admit it. "What do you know?"

"I know that no place is so remote that evil can't find it. Our only hope is in God."

Fiona needed more than faith to protect her young charge. "I am responsible for her. That means doing all I can to keep her from hurt and pain." Fiona blotted the remaining moisture from her face with her handkerchief. "I couldn't live with myself if I had an opportunity to act and didn't do it. Mary Clare's needs come first now. Speaking of Mary Clare, where is she?"

"Serenading Mrs. Calloway and the ladies in the parlor. She's very accomplished and sure of herself for her age."

Fiona warmed at the praise for her niece. "That she is. Such an imagination!"

"Do you think the grand duchess would be content living in a colony on a remote island?"

"At least she will be alive."

"She would be alive here too."

"But I have no means to support her here. In Harmony, our needs will be provided for. It's a community where all work together and share the fruits of the labor."

Louise merely gave her a look of disbelief.

Spoken aloud it did sound unrealistic. But Singapore had its own issues. "The only business likely to hire in the foreseeable future is the hotel." That meant working for Sawyer. And through him, Winslow Evanston. Never.

"Mmm-hmm."

The inarticulate response made Fiona stare at her roommate. "That's all you have to say?"

"I'm saying it's not the worst job a lady can have."

"Of course. Working in the saloons would be much worse. They've asked me to sing there countless times."

"Yet, you didn't. Why?"

"Isn't it obvious? It would only confirm the lies and rumors that Winslow Evanston is probably spreading right now."

"Sawyer would uphold your reputation."

Fiona gritted her teeth so the tears didn't return. "Stop." It was too painful to explain.

"He truly does love you."

That's what hurt. He loved her. She loved him. But they could never be a family. Sawyer's father had sealed that.

Louise plucked at her sleeve. "I read the newspaper stories back in New York."

"Then you knew all along that I was the one they called Madam Songbird?"

Louise nodded somberly. "But I could also tell the stories weren't true. I have some experience with that."

Fiona held her breath. Louise seldom said anything about her past. "You?"

"My late husband vilified me publicly when I discovered he had developed a...relationship with a woman I'd considered a friend. He said my coldness pushed him into the other woman's arms."

"No one who knows you would believe it."

"He was a persuasive and well-liked man. They believed him."

"Oh, sweetie." Fiona clasped Louise's hand.

"It's all right. He joined the war effort as a cavalry officer, intending to gain influence in Washington but ended up getting shot." She stared blankly ahead. "It was both heartbreaking and a relief. It might be wrong to think that way, but since coming to Singapore, I've learned that I do have value."

"Of course you do."

"And so do you. Stay. Not for Sawyer or any other man. Stay here for yourself and Mary Clare. Show everyone who you truly are."

Fiona shook her head. Louise didn't understand. Louise had lost both trust and love for her husband. Fiona's trust in Sawyer was shaken, but she still loved him so much that just seeing him hurt. She couldn't possibly live in the same town and beg work from him to make ends meet. She couldn't face his father again, and the man was bound to visit often with his son here. Worst of all, she couldn't watch Sawyer court and marry another woman.

She rose. "My mind is made up. We sail at three o'clock."

The walk back to the hotel turned wet when the dark clouds unleashed a downpour. Sawyer barely felt the rain. Every word from the discussion with Fiona replayed in his mind. What had he done wrong to drive her away? Why couldn't she forgive him? Father's slurs against her were bad, but surely she could see that he was not at all like his father.

After drying off, he absently arranged and rearranged the registration book, the pen and the figurine of a girl in traditional Dutch garb and wooden shoes that the VanderLeuvens had brought from Holland.

"That statue reminds me of our happiest times." Mrs. VanderLeuven reminisced from the door to the dining room. "We were young and just bought the hotel. We hadn't a cent to our names and owed the bank more than we thought we'd ever be able to repay." She dabbed at her eyes. "Sometimes I wish for those days again."

The lesson wasn't lost on Sawyer. Having a strong financial foundation wasn't the key to a solid marriage. He'd begun to think that too, but he was only half of the equation. "Fiona wouldn't agree. She'll do anything not to return to poverty."

"Now, now, don't you go believin' everything a woman tells you." She clucked her tongue. "Sometimes a lady doesn't know her own heart."

That didn't help the situation at all. "Thank you, Mrs. VanderLeuven."

"Don't let her go."

Why did every older woman give him the same advice? Sawyer glanced at the grandfather clock. Five minutes before three o'clock. "It's too late. She will have boarded by now."

"Then you'll have to hurry."

Sawyer couldn't forget Fiona's silent retreat up the staircase. "I don't know how to convince her."

"Did you try giving her a ring and asking her to marry you?"

Sawyer gaped. He'd done a pile of persuading and completely missed the obvious.

"Youth is wasted." Mrs. VanderLeuven shook her head. "Plumb wasted."

Sawyer looked down at the registration book. "The hotel—"

"Will still be here. Go." She waved her arm until Sawyer got the hint. "Run if you have to. You don't want to miss her."

The lobby door swung open, ushering in a burst of wind and Sawyer's father.

The man had the audacity to grin. "She's gone. Good riddance, I say. No Evanston would tie himself to a poor immigrant."

Something inside Sawyer snapped. "Maybe no Evanston would, but an Evans would be honored. Fiona O'Keefe is the finest woman I've ever met, and I will do whatever it takes to win her hand." He tugged on his coat. "I hereby forfeit any claim to your fortune. You can put that in writing and send it to me. I'll sign it." He skirted his father. "If you don't, I'll have it drawn up myself."

"Son—"

"Oh, and one more thing." Sawyer pointed at his father. "You will respect Fiona as much as you respect Mother. I won't hear one word against her. Ever."

Sawyer dashed out of the hotel and clattered down the front steps. He didn't have a ring at hand, and there was no time to stop by the general store. He needed something else to pledge his commitment, but what did he have?

A stone—rare as those were—lodged in his shoe and forced him to stop. While pulling off his shoe, emptying it and replacing it, he looked back at the hotel. The hotel! Of course.

Shoe replaced, he ran down the boardwalk toward the dock. He could see the smokestacks of the sidewheel steamer. The improperly named *Bayshore Clipper* was puffing black smoke and appeared to be pulling away from the dock. Though gasping for breath, he increased his pace. The only woman he'd ever truly loved was leaving, and this was his only chance to stop her.

Each board in the boardwalk seemed a million miles from his destination. Other people strolling along became obstacles. He jumped off the boardwalk and slogged through the sand to avoid one couple. Amanda Decker stepped to one side, and he swerved around her, just brushing her market basket as he passed.

"Sorry," he apologized to her. "Sorry, but I have to hurry."

"Go." She too waved him on.

Did everyone in town know of his affection for Fiona and the fact that she was leaving? He didn't have time to think about it. The docks loomed ahead, and the *Bayshore Clipper* had already cast off its lines and was pulling away.

"Fiona!" The word barely squeaked past his gasps for air.

With hands on his knees, he both tried to catch his breath and scan the ship's railing. The six young ladies stood together, waving at those gathered on the wharf to see them off. Fiona should be with them, but he couldn't see her or Mary Clare. Had she changed her mind?

Then the ship moved farther from the shore, and a ray of sunlight streamed through a break in the clouds. Like a stage light, it caught Fiona's brilliant red hair. His heart leaped, and the next moment thudded to a stop. She stood on the bow, with Mary Clare at her side. Both studiously looked forward rather than at the shore.

They did not see him.

"Fiona!" he yelled, having regained sufficient strength.

She didn't budge.

He cupped his hands around his mouth and tried again.

Still she didn't hear him, or chose to ignore him.

The ship blew its horn again. It was leaving, taking Fiona away. He couldn't let that happen.

"No!" Sawyer danced along the dock. "Stop the ship!"

The vessel didn't change course.

He ran to the edge of the dock and waved his arms, trying to capture the attention of captain or crew.

Roland appeared at his elbow. "Take my boat." He pointed to a small rowboat pulled onto the shore beyond the end of the dock.

It would be next to impossible to launch the boat and row the distance to the ship in time to catch it, but Sawyer had to take that chance.

He took off at a run. Roland followed at a less torrid pace. When Sawyer reached the rowboat, he attempted to turn it over without success. It took both of them to flip it onto its keel. Sawyer grabbed one side, and Roland took the other. Together they slid it into the water. Sawyer climbed into it. Roland handed him oars.

"Thank you," Sawyer said as he dug them into the water.

The distance to the ship was great, but with each stroke he was closer to catching Fiona. He pulled with all his strength, and the rowboat skimmed past the logs crowded near the sawmill and then the mercantile. The westerly breeze from the passing squall created a light chop on the surface and slowed his progress. He dug deeper and pulled harder. His shoulders burned. His arms ached.

Still, the ship was too far away. The paddle wheels paused, signaling the ship was about to change direction from reverse to forward. Once it got momentum, Sawyer would never catch up to it.

He pulled on the oars with all his might. Though the day was cool and the water icy cold, sweat poured from Sawyer's brow. He had to catch that ship.

The paddle wheels churned, and the ship stopped backing and reached the moment of equilibrium when it was going neither backward nor forward. The current caught the bow and pulled it toward the middle of the river. Soon it would tug the nose downstream, and the ship would take off faster than any man could ever row.

This was his last chance.

He'd gotten the rowboat within twenty yards. Fiona could see him if she looked his way, but with the lowering sun in his eyes, he couldn't see her. He stood in the rowboat, ignoring the perilous rocking, and cupped his hands around his mouth again.

"I love you, Fiona O'Keefe, and I want to marry you!"

The ship's nose turned just enough that the broadside

of the ship blocked the glare of the sun. That's when he saw Fiona hurry to the railing. Had she heard him?

"Fiona O'Keefe, will you marry me?"

A cry came from the ship, but the churning and splashing of the paddle wheels drowned out any words. The ship came about, and now, pointed downstream, headed on its way.

Chapter Nineteen

Fiona strained to hear what Sawyer was shouting, but could not. Other passengers insisted he wanted to stop the ship. One even claimed she'd heard him call out Fiona's name. That alone raised such a storm of emotion that Fiona had to hold on to the damp railing for support. He shouted again, but she couldn't hear over the chatter of the passengers and the churning of the paddle wheels.

One thing was certain. Whatever the reason, it was important enough to risk his life. He'd rowed in front of the ship and stood up in the rowboat yelling something. Standing up in a rowboat!

She shrieked when the boat wobbled perilously. The last of the ice had just floated out a week ago. She gripped the railing, praying for him to stay dry. He flailed his arms and steadied the rowboat. The man might not have sense, but he had fine balance. Then the ship turned and headed down the river to Lake Michigan.

She could not let such effort go to waste, so she made her way toward the pilothouse, Mary Clare in tow.

"He proposed," an elderly woman told her friend as Fiona passed. "From a rowboat. Can you imagine?"

Proposed. Urgency prickled across Fiona's skin,

and she hurried her pace. Sawyer had proposed? Was it possible? In spite of her anger and coldness toward him, he'd still proposed? Her heart pounded, and she knew in that instant that she could never make a life in Harmony. The man she loved was in Singapore. Yes, his father and her niece complicated the situation, but people who loved each other worked things out. They moved forward in faith. Wasn't that what Louise had been trying to tell her?

"Stop, Aunt Fiona! I can't keep up," Mary Clare protested, panting hard.

Fiona slowed to her niece's pace, but the urgency still pounded at her temples. Sawyer wouldn't have gone to all that trouble and risk for something trivial. But when lives were at stake, his courage surpassed that of anyone she'd ever known. She'd seen that the night of the shipwreck.

She climbed the stairs to the pilothouse, brushing aside a crewman who tried to direct her back to the passenger deck.

"You can't go in there," the man insisted, his face red. "No children. No women."

Fiona ignored the latter and directed Mary Clare to wait for her outside.

Before she'd finished, the captain opened the door and invited them both to come into the small room filled with shiny brass instruments and a big wooden ship's wheel.

"What troubles you, ma'am?" the captain asked after the crewman closed the door behind them.

"Did you see the man in the rowboat?" Fiona went on to explain that Sawyer would only have done such a thing if it was urgent. "Could we possibly return?"

She hesitated to explain further, but one of the crew

chimed in that the man in the rowboat had asked some-one aboard the ship to marry him.

That made two witnesses. Fiona could barely breathe as she waited for the verdict.

Beneath his graying whiskers, the captain smiled. "Anything for love."

Love. Was it possible Sawyer truly loved her? Had love driven him to risk his life in the icy river? She would soon find out.

After nosing out into Lake Michigan, the captain turned the vessel to return to port. The mate grumbled about the extra fuel used, but the captain paid him no mind.

Mary Clare looked up at Fiona. "Are we going home?"

Fiona's heart tugged. What did the little girl con-sider home? New York? Fiona couldn't give her that, but maybe, just maybe, she could give her a home with parents who loved each other and wanted the best for the family. Truly, there was nothing more important than that.

When the ship rounded the curve, and Singapore ap-peared from behind the dune, Sawyer was still sitting in the rowboat in the middle of the wide bend. At nearly the same instant she spotted him, he began to row to shore. Deep, strong strokes propelled the craft across the shimmering water like one of those whirligig water bugs that danced around on the surface near shore. He headed for the bit of land past the docks, where he could drag the little boat ashore.

Fiona turned to the captain. "Thank you, sir. I real-ize it was a lot to ask."

The man pretended it was nothing, but it clearly was. She had cost them at least an hour on their schedule.

Fiona left the pilothouse, holding Mary Clare by the

hand, and wound her way down to the main deck and then forward as far as the crew would allow. She kept looking for Sawyer but didn't spot him until the ship pulled alongside the dock. He stood over by the general store talking to Roland and didn't appear in any hurry to greet the ship. Her nerves increased. It was worse than stepping on an unfamiliar stage for the first time. What if the woman and crewman had heard wrong? What if Sawyer hadn't been waving at her at all? What if he'd been trying to catch someone else's attention? Such as Dinah.

Fiona gnawed on her lower lip. She'd made this decision, had turned an entire ship around and now she must go through with it regardless of the outcome.

Ashore, a few of the curious stepped out of shops and homes to see what was going on. When the ship's crew extended the gangway and only she and Mary Clare disembarked, she would have a lot of explaining to do.

"You didn't answer me," Mary Clare pointed out.

"What?"

"Are we going home?"

"Oh. Yes, I suppose you could say that. We'll return to the boardinghouse."

"Good."

"Good?" That reaction surprised Fiona. "That's what you consider home?"

Mary Clare looked up at her. "Home is where you are."

Tears rose in Fiona's eyes. She looked away and blinked rapidly. Home might be a boardinghouse, but it didn't matter as long as she had Mary Clare. She knelt and hugged the little girl close.

"For me too." She gave her niece a rather teary smile. "We will make the boardinghouse home."

Mrs. Calloway would take her back. Fiona had no doubt of that. What she would do to support Mary Clare and herself was another matter. She might have to beg Sawyer for employment if what he'd shouted from his rowboat wasn't directed to her.

"Miss Fiona!" The breathless cry came from none other than Dinah, who'd appeared with Linore at her side. "I heard you're goin' back. I wanna stay here too."

Fiona steeled her expression. Maybe Sawyer *had* been waving at Dinah. If so, Fiona had made a tragic mistake.

"I thought you were going to Harmony."

"You know I don't wanna." Her gaze drifted to shore, and Fiona's spirits sank. Dinah *was* looking for Sawyer. "Please help me."

"I don't know what I can do," Fiona began.

Dinah interrupted. "You don't have to do nothing 'cept explain to Mr. Adamson if he asks why I'm leavin'."

"But where will you live? What will you do?"

Dinah's eyes sparkled. "I'm gettin' married."

Fiona caught her breath.

Then Dinah started waving madly. "There he is! There he is! See, Linore. I told you he loved me."

Fiona clenched her jaw. She could not watch Dinah marry Sawyer. She could not live in the same town with them. Perhaps she might go to Saugatuck or even Holland.

"Lenny!" Dinah shouted, leaning over the railing.

Lenny? Fiona didn't recognize that name. When she looked to shore, sure enough, one of the sawmill workers was waving up at Dinah.

Fiona let out her breath in a whoosh.

Dinah danced along the railing, trying to get closer to her beau. Linore didn't follow.

Fiona turned to the usually bubbly redhead. "Are you staying in Singapore too?"

"No. *I* honor my promises." But there was something wistful behind the defiance.

"I wish I had a place of my own. Then I could invite you to stay with me."

Linore shrugged, her emotions now shuttered. "Like I said. I honor my promises."

"Then why come up here with Dinah?"

"In case Mr. Adamson followed. I was supposed to distract him."

Oh, the games young ladies played. Seeing as Mr. Adamson had yet to appear, Fiona hoped Dinah's rebellion didn't create a scene.

"Dinah doesn't need me, though." Linore wore a tough expression, but there was a lot of hurt underneath it.

Fiona understood. "If you ever want to return, I'll do my best to help you."

Linore's defenses temporarily dropped before they went up again. "I can't see that I'd ever come back, but thank you anyway." Then she trudged off.

If only Fiona had the means to start that school. She didn't and likely never would. Even if Sawyer had proposed to her, he not only wasn't well-off, he was in debt.

"You're squeezing my hand too tight," Mary Clare informed her.

Fiona let go. "I'm sorry. You can be on your own, but don't leave my side. And hold my hand when we walk off the ship on the gangway." The narrow, shaky walkway didn't feel quite safe.

Mary Clare heaved a sigh. "I'm not a baby."

"No, you're not. But you are my responsibility. I promised your mama I'd take care of you."

"That's what Aunt Lilli said, but she doesn't think you'll be any good at it. I heard her tell Aunt Peg that she'd bake her an apple pie if I didn't get sent right back there."

That sounded like Lillibeth.

"Well, I'm not sending you right back there." She would deal with the problem of Winslow Evanston later. Maybe Louise was right. With the proper support and perspective, Mary Clare would learn to identify and ignore falsehoods.

"Good," the little girl said. "I like it here."

So did Fiona. Crazy as it seemed, she'd grown to love the lumber town with its sandy streets and ever-changing population. She stood and watched as the town came into full view. Singapore was about as far from New York City as a girl could get, but it had a warmth that Fiona hadn't found in the city.

Mary Clare tugged on her sleeve. "There's that man who was in the boat." She pointed to shore.

Sure enough, Sawyer was on the dock now, looking uncommonly somber.

Her nerves fluttered again. Had she made a big mistake? Was he only trying to warn the captain that there was a problem with the ship?

He scanned the ship, looking for something or someone. Please, let it be her.

"Oh, Sawyer." She sighed. "Paul."

Paul Evanston. Could she get used to that name? Would she have an opportunity to try?

A sob choked out, and tears burned in her eyes. Her hand went to her lips. She could not break down and cry in public. Fiona O'Keefe did not do such things.

"Why are you sad?" Mary Clare asked.

Fiona swallowed hard. "I'm not sad."

She looked away, not wanting to see if he looked for someone else. His father was still in town. The thought of facing Winslow Evanston again set her nerves on edge. Perhaps she should begin educating Mary Clare now.

"Some people say bad things about me."

Mary Clare looked up at her. "Like that man in the newspapers?"

Fiona blinked. "You can read already?"

"I know how to read names, and I saw yours." Mary Clare tilted her head. "I asked Aunt Lilli what the newspaper said, and she told me. She said that rich people think they can say anything they want, but I'm to remember that what matters is what God says about me."

Fiona was stunned. Her sister had said that? Lillibeth had more sense than she'd given her credit for. "What does God say about you?" she asked hesitantly.

Mary Clare didn't hesitate. "That I'm a princess."

Then that bit wasn't about Celtic royalty after all, it was all about the best royal family possible. Fiona hugged Mary Clare. "That's right. You are God's daughter. Since He's King, that makes you a princess."

Mary Clare nodded emphatically, certain of that truth.

Fiona let her niece's simple faith soak in. What was true for little Mary Clare was true for Fiona too. Status didn't come from fancy gowns or social standing, it came from her relationship with the one true King. A weight lifted from her shoulders, and a laugh bubbled to her lips. How simple! And yet how perfectly earth-shattering. Nothing else mattered.

"Miss?" One of the crew interrupted her thoughts.

She blinked back the tears of joy. "Yes?"

"We're ready for you and your daughter to disembark now."

Her daughter. And God's daughter. In that moment, she knew beyond all doubt that they would be all right. Storms would come, but the Lord calmed storms.

The crewman motioned them forward.

She took Mary Clare's hand.

The girl walked with certainty. So could Fiona, knowing God walked with them.

Sawyer paced the dock in front of Roland, who was tolerating his impatience like a mother tolerated a child's petulant cries. It was taking an interminably long time to moor the ship and extend the gangway. Moreover, he could no longer see Fiona or her niece. After Mary Clare had pointed him out to her aunt, both had stepped back from the railing.

"I need a ring," Sawyer growled as he passed Roland for the umpteenth time.

"I don't have a ring in stock, but she'll appreciate your idea more than any jewelry."

Sawyer wasn't so sure. "This is Fiona we're talking about. Haven't you noticed her jewelry?"

"I heard she gave it all away, along with most of her fancy gowns."

"What? Fiona would never give away her finery." Unless she didn't intend to return. He clenched his jaw.

"You'll have all the answers soon." Roland clapped him on the back. "Come to the store if you need anything."

Sawyer barely heard his friend. The ship had finished mooring and was now discharging someone. It must be Fiona. Sawyer closed his eyes. *Please God, let it be her.*

When he opened them again, Fiona was making her way down the gangway, one hand on the railing, and the other clutching Mary Clare as if terrified the little girl would fall overboard. The girl, on the other hand, looked perfectly calm. She waved at Sawyer and gave him a big, somewhat toothless smile.

Sawyer waved back. In the past he would have felt like a fool doing that. But today it felt right, natural. From what Roland had told him, Mary Clare had traveled from New York City in the escort of people she did not know. That took a lot of courage from a girl of seven, the same sort of courage her aunt had.

Fiona reached the dock and at last looked his way.

He took off his hat. At her frown he hastily put it back on. What was proper for such occasions? A man didn't propose to a woman every day. Moreover, he'd forced a whole ship to turn around just to bring her back. Hopefully she would accept his proposal.

After a deep breath, he hurried toward them.

"Fiona—Miss O'Keefe," he said, a bit out of breath. "Miss Mary Clare."

The little girl stuck out her hand. "Pleased to see you again."

He shook it. "You're very polite."

"Miss Gulliver—she's the one who took care of me on the train—said that good manners can take a person far. I didn't need anyone watching me, but Aunt Lilli insisted." Her sigh told him just what she thought of that.

"Your aunt was right. You should always travel with another person—an adult," he added at the sharp look from Fiona.

Mary Clare rolled her eyes. "I figured that's what you'd say. That's what all the adults say, as if they know better."

"We have learned a few things over the years," Fiona interjected.

"Not everything, or we wouldn't have had to come back." Mary Clare pointed to the gangway. "There's your trunks, Aunt Fiona. Does that mean we're staying?"

Instead of answering right away, Fiona looked at him. The lump in his throat melted. She cared for him. He could see it in her eyes…along with caution. She'd been hurt badly. By his father. He wouldn't let anyone hurt her again. That included his father.

Fiona looked down at Mary Clare. "Perhaps we will stay. At least until the next ship."

That statement stabbed through Sawyer, threatening to erase the hope he'd just built. "You could stay longer."

Fiona didn't give anything away in her expression. "Do I have a reason to stay?"

Mary Clare looked from her aunt to him and back again before heaving a sigh and wandering off to the pile of trunks.

Though his heart hammered on his rib cage, Sawyer focused on Fiona. "To run your school."

"But I don't have a school." She paused, then her eyes widened as the meaning behind his statement struck. "What are you saying, Paul Evanston?"

He cringed at the name. "That man is dead. He died a long time ago. I'm Sawyer Evans now and for the rest of my life."

The corners of her mouth twitched. "Like a stage name."

"No, a new man, like Saul becoming the apostle Paul or Simon becoming Peter. The old man is gone. I'm my own man, Fiona. I've broken all contact with my father.

After what he did to you…" He fisted his hands. "It was heartless and unthinkable."

"It could have been worse if I hadn't seen him for who he is."

Sawyer shuddered. "I'm glad you did. I'll do everything in my power to prevent him from reaching you or Mary Clare."

"Thank you." She did look grateful. "But you haven't answered me. What school?"

"The one in the west wing of the hotel."

"There's no school…" Again her eyes widened. "How is this possible?"

That was the stumbling block in his plan. "It will take time…and a lot of work, but I promise you that I will see it built." He'd thought it over while waiting for the ship to dock. "The west wing is most easily separated from the rest of the hotel. We can make a new entrance and block the hallway that leads between the main hotel and that wing so the ladies have complete privacy."

Her smile could have lit a city street. "But how is this possible? It sounded like you barely had enough to refurbish the main part of the hotel."

"I've thought about it, and there's only one way I can see to make it work."

She looked genuinely puzzled. "I can't afford to rent the space."

He wanted to reassure her, but he had to take this slowly so she didn't retreat. "No. Another arrangement. One that benefits both of us."

Now she looked wary. "And that is?"

If he hadn't seen the slight tremble of her chin, he would have thought her completely in control of her nerves. A fool would take advantage of it. A man in love wanted to calm those nerves as quickly as possible.

He dropped to one knee and took Fiona's hand in his. "Miss Fiona O'Keefe, I do not deserve a woman as talented, beautiful and intelligent as you, but if you would do me the honor of agreeing to be my wife, I will spend a lifetime trying to please you."

A wee gasp came from behind Fiona.

Sawyer spotted Mary Clare before she ducked behind Fiona's skirts.

"Well," Fiona said slowly.

A fold of her skirt jerked noticeably. "Do it," came the whispered advice.

"Mary Clare!" Fiona pulled her hand from Sawyer's grasp and extracted her niece from behind her. "This is between Sawyer and me. I don't need your prompting."

He gave the little girl an encouraging smile. "Maybe you do."

Fiona looked him in the eye. "Don't you think I can make up my own mind?"

"Of course, but this decision affects Mary Clare too. You said you intend to raise her."

Fiona jutted her chin. "I do."

Sawyer sat back on his heels. "Then this is a family decision."

Fiona's hackles eased. "I suppose you're right."

She looked to Mary Clare, but Sawyer wasn't done.

He bowed before the little girl. "I would love to have the grand duchess join my family, if her aunt agrees to marry me."

The corners of Fiona's mouth twitched upward a moment before she reined in her amusement. "How can I trust you to keep your promises?"

"Ouch! But I deserve that. I made a lot of mistakes, Fiona, but they were all because I didn't want to upset you." He rubbed his chin. "Except I ended up doing just that."

"Yes, you did."

She was giving him nothing. "Can you find it in your heart to forgive me?"

Her expression softened, and a ray of hope burst through the clouds over Sawyer's head. "I might need to ask your forgiveness too. I should never have put so much hope in marrying a wealthy man."

Sawyer blinked, unable to believe what he'd just heard. "Then…"

"I do like you, no, more than like. I love you, and not for any inheritance or money you might one day have."

"That's good, because there isn't any."

She nodded but surprisingly didn't look disappointed. "Then I accept your apology."

Relief flooded through him. "Does that mean you'll consider my proposal?"

An eyebrow quirked upward. "Is that what that was?"

Sawyer choked. He'd gotten on one knee to ask her. What more did she want? He'd give his all.

He took her hands. "Fiona O'Keefe, you're the only woman I've ever truly loved. I don't have much to offer you but a place to live and a dream. But the fact is, I love you. I've loved you from the moment I first set eyes on you last August. You stepped off that ship like a queen, your hair blazing in the sun, and I knew I'd never meet another woman like you. I fought the attraction a long time. You don't do much to encourage a man, after all."

She actually blushed and averted her gaze, and Sawyer's heart skipped a beat. He'd gotten to her. He'd actually gotten to her. Maybe, just maybe…

"I love you, Fiona, and that means I want to include in my life everyone you consider important. That means

Mary Clare, if she'll accept me. I've always wanted a family, and I can't think of a better way to begin. Well, Mary Clare, what do you say?"

The little girl looked up at her aunt, who was still delightfully pink-cheeked. Sawyer longed to hold Fiona, to kiss her, to assure her that he would do all he could to give her what she wanted and needed. But a gentleman waited, and he didn't want to do anything that even hinted at what his father and the other louts had done to her.

Mary Clare next directed her attention to him. "Is the hotel that big building over there?"

Sawyer looked in the direction of her outstretched arm and nodded.

"Then I say yes," Mary Clare declared. "My mama's in heaven, and my daddy ran off before I was born, so I need a new one of each."

Sawyer's heart about broke. This time when he looked in Fiona's eyes, he saw tears there. She didn't even try to hide them. Instead, she hugged Mary Clare close and nodded.

"Is that a yes?" Sawyer had to be certain.

Fiona smiled then, not the carefully crafted smile she used on stage but an almost shy smile that trembled ever so slightly. She was strong, but she was vulnerable too, and the combination was irresistible.

"Yes," she said softly. "I accept."

Sawyer could have dropped to his knees in relief. The next instant joy overpowered him, and he swept her into his arms in an embrace. Mary Clare slipped a thin arm around his waist, subtly reminding him to keep the kiss short.

The soft, sweet kiss wasn't nearly enough. He looked deep into Fiona's eyes. The resistance was gone. For the first time, she really looked at him. Judging from her expression, she liked what she saw.

"After a proper courtship," she added, a mischievous twinkle in her eye.

"Courtship?" Sawyer hadn't expected that, not given her attempts to marry before Mary Clare's arrival.

"Courtship. Three months."

Sawyer didn't want to wait. He wanted to begin this new part of his life at once. Fiona would be his sounding board on ideas for the hotel. They would work together building a life and a family.

She grinned. "Disappointed?"

He couldn't hide anything from her. "A little, but I'll honor your request." It was now his turn to grin. "If you change your mind and want to shorten the courtship, I'm all for it."

She laughed. "Don't think you'll be ordering me around, Mr. Evans."

"I'm no fool, Miss O'Keefe."

His reward was the sweetest smile he'd ever seen. Then, before she could add one more stipulation, he kissed her again.

Epilogue

Three months later

Louise arranged the veil that covered Fiona's hair and flowed to the bottom of her exquisite wedding gown. Shimmering white silk taffeta rustled when she moved. It was far too dear, but Sawyer had insisted. His mother had sent it from Chicago, and Amanda Decker made the alterations.

Fiona dabbed at her forehead. July was no time for a wedding. The heat was oppressive, especially on the upper floor of the boardinghouse. With the itinerant preacher's approval, they'd moved the wedding to the boardinghouse since there were too many guests to fit in the former bunkhouse, which had been turned into a church and temporary school last fall. Both locations were hot. She should have decreased the length of courtship, but Linore's insistence on keeping her promises kept ringing in her ears.

Three months gave Sawyer time to fix up the public rooms in the hotel. When he was turning a profit, they would begin work on the west wing school. That delay was her gift to him, and it was an easy one to give. There wasn't any money for her school—yet. In the meantime, she and Sawyer would work together to make the hotel a thriving business. Mary Clare would attend school, and with musical parents like Sawyer and Fiona, she would get every chance to explore her God-given talent.

"You're beautiful." Louise sighed. "I'm honored you chose me to attend you today."

"I wouldn't want anyone else." That was the truth. Louise had been her truest friend and had tried to talk sense into her when Fiona couldn't look past old hurts to see the honorable man standing in front of her. She took her friend's hands. "Without you, there wouldn't be a wedding. You convinced me to trust Sawyer."

"But you took the step. I'm not certain I would be that brave."

Fiona laughed. "You might be quiet and reserved, but there's a courageous woman inside you."

Louise had endured worse than Fiona had ever faced. In her friend's shoes, she doubted she could have been that strong.

A knock sounded on the door, and then Pearl Decker peeked into Fiona's room. "There's someone here who wants to talk to you."

Fiona froze. Had Sawyer's father returned to spoil her wedding day?

"Don't look so frightened," Pearl said with a laugh.

She opened the door to reveal a woman Fiona had never met. Gray hair topped a formidably built stature. The woman's clothing was expensive and exquisitely tailored if conservative in its muted coloring.

"Miss O'Keefe." The woman extended a gloved hand as Pearl shut the door behind her. "I'm Paul's mother. I hope you will call me Rachel."

Fiona took the woman's hand, which grasped hers

with warmth. "Please call me Fiona." She couldn't help but wonder if Winslow Evanston had joined his wife.

Rachel smiled. "You are as beautiful as Paul described."

"Thank you." Fiona wasn't sure what else to say. "I'm pleased to meet you."

"I had to meet the woman who captured my son's heart and shook me from my complacency. You see, I've allowed Winslow to intimidate me for far too long. Not anymore. But I'm not here to talk about me. This day is all about you and my son." She opened her bag and extracted an envelope. "All the details are in here. Read it later. But I will tell you now that sufficient money has been sent to Paul's bank to build that school of yours."

Fiona's jaw dropped, and she couldn't pull it back up. That must be an enormous sum. "You did this for us? How?" She couldn't fathom Winslow Evanston giving a penny to a women's school.

"By standing up for what is right. When I heard that you wanted to help young women in desperate circumstances, I had to make it happen. All I had to do was convince Winslow that he could begin paying for his wrongs by funding your school."

Mr. Evanston had given the money? Fiona's admiration for Sawyer's mother blossomed. The woman had discovered the power she held in her marriage and was using it to help others less fortunate.

"Thank you." Fiona glanced toward the closed door. "Is he here?"

"Mr. Evanston?" Rachel lifted her chin. "I thought it best not to bring him."

Fiona smiled at the idea of Winslow Evanston being directed by his newly empowered wife. "That was a good decision. Sawyer has forgiven his father, but he doesn't want to see him. Not yet."

"Sawyer." Rachel sighed. "I can't get used to that nickname. But he's happy, and that's what matters. You gave my son hope, my dear." She dabbed at her eyes with her handkerchief. "I feared he'd given up. Now look at him. A businessman in his own right and, more importantly, a man of faith and integrity."

"Yes, he is."

Music began pealing from the piano in the parlor. The smattering of wrong notes told her Mrs. Calloway was playing, not Sawyer.

"Oh, dear." Rachel gave Fiona a parting smile. "It's almost time. I need to take my place."

A twinge of sorrow hit Fiona. None of her family was here, no one but Mary Clare, who was doubtless being instructed on her duties by Pearl. The little girl would walk down the aisle with Garrett Decker's son, Isaac. Though they made all sorts of faces when told what they were supposed to do, they would manage just fine. Fiona had hoped her parents might make the journey west, but they demurred, even when Sawyer offered to pay the fare. That left only Mary Clare.

Louise gripped her arm. "It's time."

"Then let's go." Fiona had waited long enough to marry. Though she'd searched in all the wrong places for a husband, God had brought the right man into her life.

Louise led the way down the hallway to the staircase. Guests were assembled below to usher Fiona into her new life. Tonight she would no longer live in a boardinghouse. She would have a home and a family of her own.

As she descended the staircase, she looked at the joyful faces of the friends she had made here. Pearl and

Roland, Amanda and Garrett, the VanderLeuvens, men from the sawmill all cleaned up and in their Sunday best. All smiled up at her. It brought tears to her eyes.

Then, as she entered the parlor to Mrs. Calloway's off-tempo accompaniment, she saw Sawyer and everything else faded away. He stood at the end of the room, tall and so handsome that she could barely breathe. She'd never seen this suit before. The coat was elegant and expensive. The crisp white shirt and silk tie marked a gentleman. But it was the expression on his face that captured her attention. Adoration, excitement, love. All that and more.

When she took Sawyer's arm, her heart raced like a schoolgirl's. With joy she repeated the vows that bound them together as one in God's sight. Sawyer loved her, and she loved him. Best of all, Mary Clare adored him. Today, they were more than sweethearts. They became a family.

* * * * *

If you enjoyed MAIL ORDER SWEETHEART,
look for the other books in
the BOOM TOWN BRIDES *series:*

MAIL ORDER MIX-UP
MAIL ORDER MOMMY

Dear Reader,

Thank you for joining Fiona and Sawyer through the ups and downs of their journey. It was fun to take two characters with opposing backgrounds and hopes and find a common ground for them. Sometimes things are not as they appear!

That's true of Astor House, the local hotel, which according to some sources did exist in historic Singapore. I love the pretensions of naming a lodging establishment in a small lumber town after the first luxury hotel in New York City. Someone had a lot of optimism!

The village of Harmony is fictitious, however, the islands of Lake Michigan have been host to some breakaway sects that established their own "colonies." The first and most recognizable was established by James Jesse Strang's followers who broke from Brigham Young and settled on Beaver Island in the mid-1800s. Books, articles and a museum on Beaver Island detail that episode in history. In the early 1900s, the House of David established a colony on nearby High Island. When I visited that island as a child, there were still remnants of buildings left, and I imagined they belonged to that colony.

It's been fun incorporating snippets of history in the novels in this series. I hope you will join me for the fourth book. Questions or comments? Contact me through my website at www.christineelizabethjohnson.com.

Blessings,
Christine Johnson

"Did anything you tried last night get Ellie's attention?" Kate
asked Conner.

"She seemed to like to hear me sing." Heat swept over his
chest at how foolish he felt admitting it.

"Well, then, I suggest you sing to her."

"You're bossy. Did you know that?" It was his turn to
chuckle as pink blossomed in her cheeks.

She gave a little toss of her head. "I'm simply speaking
with authority. You did ask me to stay and help. I assumed you
wanted my medical assistance."

No mistaking the challenge in her voice.

"Your medical assistance, yes, of course." He humbled his
voice and did his best to look contrite.

"You sing to her and I'll try to get more sugar water into
her."

He cleared his throat. "'Sleep, my love, and peace attend
thee. All through the night; Guardian angels God will lend
thee, All through the night.'"

Ellie blinked and brought her gaze to him.

"Excellent," Kate whispered and leaned over Conner's arm
to ease the syringe between Ellie's lips. The baby swallowed
three times and then her eyes closed.

"Sleep is good, too," Kate murmured, leaning back. "I think she likes your voice."

He stopped himself from meeting Kate's eyes. Warmth filled them and he allowed himself a little glow of victory. "Thelma hated my singing." He hadn't meant to say that. Certainly not aloud.

Kate's eyes cooled considerably. "You're referring to Ellie's mother?"

"That's right." No need to say more.

"Do you mind me asking where she is?"

"'Fraid I can't answer that."

She waited.

"I don't know. I haven't seen her in over a year."

"I see."

Only it was obvious she didn't. But he wasn't going to explain. Not until he figured out what Thelma was up to.

Kate pushed to her feet.

"How long before we wake her to feed her again?" he asked.

"Fifteen minutes. You hold her and rest. I don't suppose you got much sleep last night."

There she went being bossy and authoritative again. Not that he truly minded. It was nice to know someone cared how tired he was and also knew how to deal with Ellie.

Don't miss
MONTANA COWBOY'S BABY by Linda Ford,
available July 2017 wherever
Love Inspired® Historical books and ebooks are sold.

www.LoveInspired.com

Turn your love of reading into rewards you'll love with

Harlequin My Rewards

**Join for FREE today at
www.HarlequinMyRewards.com**

Earn **FREE BOOKS** of your choice.

Experience **EXCLUSIVE OFFERS** and contests.

Enjoy **BOOK RECOMMENDATIONS**
selected just for you.

PLUS! Sign up now
and get **500** points
right away!

Earn
FREE
REWARDS
Join
Today!
HarlequinMyRewards.com

MYR16R